Beach Rental

Emerald Isle, NC Novel #1

Beach Rental
by
Grace Greene

Emerald Isle, NC Novel #1

Kersey Creek Books
P.O. Box 6054
Ashland, VA 23005

Cover Design by Grace Greene

Trade Paperback Re-release: July 2015
ISBN-13: 978-0-9907740-5-1
Digital Re-release: July 2015
ISBN-13: 978-0-9907740-6-8
Original Trade Paperback/Digital Release: July 2011

DEDICATION

This book is dedicated to the friends who left us too soon, but who lived each day fully until they could do no more, and especially to those we lost to pancreatic cancer. John, Mark, and Glenda, and so many others—we miss you.

Beach Rental is also dedicated to my aunt and uncle, Sallie and Ronnie Smiley, who introduced me and my family to Emerald Isle and provided information about the area for this book. Thanks!

ACKNOWLEDGEMENT

Special thanks to Kim Jacobs of Turquoise Morning Press who originally published Beach Rental and to Jacquie Daher, editor, for her help in making this a better book.

I acknowledge my mom who showed me the importance of reading, and my dad who showed his children it was okay to pursue interests without fear of failure, and my sister who is my willing reader.

I'd also like to thank my writer friend, Nancy Naigle, for her help as critique partner in crafting this book. We Believe.

My loving gratitude to my husband, my biggest fan and supporter, and I thank God for directing my steps.

Author's Note: Beach Rental takes place on the island of Bogue Banks and on the North Carolina mainland in the towns of Morehead City and Beaufort.

I've tried to be true to the geography and allure of the Crystal Coast and Bogue Banks. For the purposes of this story certain merchants and locations are fictional. For instance, the grocery store in Morehead City where Juli works is fictional and you won't find the Front Street Gallery in Beaufort, but there are a many lovely gift shops and galleries on Front Street. The grilled cheese sandwiches at the Cox Family Restaurant in Morehead City are absolutely real.

BEACH RENTAL

On the Crystal Coast of North Carolina, in the small town of Emerald Isle...

Juli Cooke, hard-working and getting nowhere fast, marries a dying man, Ben Bradshaw, for a financial settlement, not expecting he will set her on a journey of hope and love. The journey brings her to Luke Winters, a local art dealer, but Luke resents the woman who married his sick friend and warns her not to hurt Ben—and he's watching to make sure she doesn't.

Until Ben dies and the stakes change.

Framed by the timelessness of the Atlantic Ocean and the brilliant blue of the beach sky, Juli struggles against her past, the opposition of Ben's and Luke's families, and even the living reminder of her marriage—to build a future with hope and perhaps to find the love of her life—if she can survive the danger from her past.

BEACH RENTAL

Chapter One

The Hammond's house glittered. Crystal, gold and silver reflected in the numerous floor-to-ceiling mirrors. The men wore tuxedos and the ladies, draped and fitted in their gowns and jewels, rivaled the decorations in the lavish rooms. It was the fanciest home Juli Cooke had ever seen.

Juli wasn't glittery. She wove her way among the guests with a tray offering canapés. Her white shirt was already spotted with chocolate and red wine. The blotches were right smack in the middle where her black vest couldn't hide them. Her feet hurt, bound in cheap black pumps.

She was twenty-six and definitely not a decoration. She felt like a utility—faceless, graceless, and silent. She paused as a guest chose a mushroom-capped hors d'oeuvre from her tray.

What were the Hammonds celebrating? It didn't matter. It was the same for Juli regardless of the occasion—just another slice of unlived-in time spent trying to earn a buck because it was the bucks that kept her afloat, fed, and in her small apartment.

A hip brushed hers as Carla whispered, "What's up with you and Frankie?"

"Frankie and me? Nothing." Juli glanced around.

"Then you won't mind if I ask him out?"

"Sammy's watching. Move on. I'll catch you later." Juli broke away and walked toward a group of people. Neither she nor Carla needed trouble from Sammy. As a boss, he was a tyrant. It paid to be alert if she wanted to stay below the trouble radar.

Nearby, a woman's voice erupted in laughter and Juli turned to look. The woman was leaning toward a tall, thin man with her hand on his sleeve as she stared up into his face. Her body language was as revealing as his. Juli felt a little sorry for her. Even as the woman spoke to him, the man appeared to ignore her while he scanned the room.

He had a lean build, light brown hair and sharp features. The woman shrilled, "Luke, you are so…," then the level of her voice dropped. He, Luke, was the one behaving differently from the rest of the group and should've been the one who looked out of place but, no, he made the other partiers look superfluous.

Juli caught his stare. An unexpected pull, a subtle magnetism, drew her. A tingle raced up her spine. Had he sensed her eyes on him? His gaze passed over and through her and moved on.

That's right, I'm nobody. It hit her like a punch in the gut. *An invisible nobody going nowhere.*

A knot of guests moved away and suddenly, she was reflected in a large mirror directly ahead. Unlike her own, muted reflection, everyone else captured in the mirror was sharper and more colorful. Humming began in her ears, growing louder as the room closed in around her.

The warm air thickened with a fog of perfume and alcohol. A thousand unnamed scents threatened to choke her.

She tried to beat back the panic and failed.

In the midst of the laughter and glitz, Juli fled to the kitchen, but instead of exchanging the tray for a freshly filled one, she carried it straight out the door and into the night.

****

Luke Winters tuned out the hum of nearby conversations and looked beyond the flushed faces around him. Every man wore a black suit or tuxedo and they all seemed to have dark hair.

There was nothing particularly distinguishing about Ben— other than his exceptional good nature—and that was no help here.

He'd told Ben not to come. There was no need. Marcel Hammond threw this party every year for business partners, clients, and friends. Ben wanted to pretend everything was okay and he wanted everyone else to pretend with him. Ben was his cousin, his best friend, and longtime business partner. Luke couldn't pretend, he was a realist.

He gave his glass to a passing waiter and interrupted the woman who was speaking to him. "Please excuse me. I have to find someone. Very sorry." He smiled in apology and gently detached himself from the small group.

Winding his way among the knots of people, nodding, waving or stopping for a quick, polite exchange before moving on, he traversed the room looking for Ben.

In the dimly lit hallway leading to the bathroom, two men stood close together. One was dressed as a waiter. Their hands moved quickly as they traded something—each having acquired an object that went directly into the new owner's pocket.

The action stopped Luke. He frowned, wondering at the boldness, or the need. They sensed him and looked up. Luke didn't recognize either of them but the waiter stepped back, nodded and walked past him down the hall.

Was the guy smirking? The other man, a party guest, kept his eyes down and tugged at his suit jacket as he brushed past Luke.

Was it any of his business? No. He'd mention it to Marcel later, in case the incident was as unsavory as it seemed.

The bathroom door stood ajar. Luke pushed it open. No Ben. He returned to the main party room, again scanning the shifting bodies. A hand touched his arm.

"Luke? You look worried."

Maia. He rubbed his temples. "I don't see Ben anywhere."

"Don't hover over him. He'll let you know if he needs help. In fact, he'll ask for help a lot faster if you aren't suffocating him."

She sounded fierce and it brought a sad smile to his face.

"He's sick, Maia. Don't tell me you're not concerned."

"Of course, I am."

11

He stared across the room. Sick was an understatement. Ben was dying. Not today or tomorrow, but within a few months. Neither of them wanted to say those awful words aloud. Luke looked down at Maia and touched her arm.

She stood straighter, adding a fraction of an inch to her petite stature. "Get back to work, Luke. Go talk to Amanda Barlow again. You left her broken-hearted. Take her a glass of wine."

"Please, no." Luke tugged at his collar.

"Please, yes. She's interested in buying artwork to decorate her new home. Even forgetting your own business interests—if that's what you want to do—please consider the artists who'd like to make the sales and those of us who work for you."

She was right. Ben was an adult of sound mind. Luke was here this evening for business opportunities. He had responsibilities.

He took the hand she'd placed on his arm and squeezed it. "Understood."

"She's over by the chocolate fountain." Maia tugged his sleeve. "Don't forget to mention the Bingham hardwood reliefs. They'll look outstanding integrated with Charlotte's etchings in Amanda's window room. She'll love them."

"On my way." He straightened his jacket and brushed at the front. "What about you?"

"Well, I won't be going back to the chocolate fountain, that's for sure, or I'll need a whole new wardrobe." She laughed and her dimples deepened.

"Maia, in case I neglected to mention it earlier, you look lovely. And you're right, Ben's an adult. Go have some fun. In fact, didn't I see Ed Larson earlier?"

"Ed and I have been past tense for a long time. No worries, remember? Just take care of business." She turned away.

"Maia."

"What?"

"Sometimes we take you for granted."

Her cheeks pinked up. "No problem. Now, go talk to Amanda about those etchings."

****

Only a few guests strolled along the brick paths in the light of the Chinese lanterns because the air was cool and most of the ladies showed a great deal of bare skin. There were always guests who found the gardens irresistible, especially since the Hammonds didn't allow smoking in their home. At this moment, no one lingered nearby. Juli stood on the steps and gulped air.

The freshness of the coastal North Carolina evening washed over her. It cooled her hot face and stilled the buzzing in her head. As her breathing steadied, she could almost smell the sea salt crispness in the air even though they were a mile or more from the ocean.

She shivered as her taut muscles relaxed. She didn't understand the panic attacks. They'd become more frequent. Was this one over a stranger? It wasn't as if she wanted a man in her life.

Or anyone. She was good alone. It was better that way. Simpler. No confusion or disappointment about who could be trusted or depended upon.

She didn't want to go back inside yet. Hugging the empty tray to her chest, she stepped down to the brick path. A short distance away, an ivy-covered alcove sheltered a bench half-hidden in shadow. She hurried toward it, not seeing the outstretched pants leg until it was too late and she nearly landed on top of the person already seated there.

"Sorry," Juli gasped and stepped back.

"My fault. Too quiet. I'm sorry."

A man's voice. He sounded weak, but the darkness disguised his appearance. Moonlight filtering into the alcove touched him, increasing the pallor of his skin which seemed almost to glow in the dimness. Juli smelled no alcohol, but it didn't mean he wasn't drunk or drugged up.

"Are you ill?"

He answered softly. "No, I just need to rest."

"I understand. Sorry I disturbed you." She started to move away.

He leaned forward. The light picked out his profile. "Are you working here tonight?"

She looked at her tray. It marked her, labeled her. An emblem of her status. She wasn't worried about status. She'd given up the luxury of pride a long time ago.

"I'd better get back." She turned and the rubber tip of her heel caught in a gap between the bricks. It tore off. After some inelegant stumbling, she avoided falling, but that was the least of her worries. She grabbed the heel from the ground and removed her shoe. "No, no, no—" She tried to push the heel back on, but knew it was futile. It was a cheap shoe, not intended to be fixed, but discarded when its life was done.

"No spares? Maybe glue would help."

She didn't answer. She closed her eyes and worked to pull herself together. Her head ached. Her ponytail, worn low on the back of her head, was too tight. It hurt her scalp.

Everything was spinning out of control and she was too discouraged to care—almost.

The man spoke again. "Sorry, not funny. Are you alright? What will you do now?"

She sat on the bench beside him. Her eyes had adjusted to the dark and she could see him more clearly, but his eyes were still no more than black holes in his face, as dark as the night.

Her skirt rode up her thighs and she tugged at it. The skirt wasn't made for sitting. Wait staff don't sit.

Juli shook her head. "I'm going to get fired. I wouldn't care except I'll have to find a new evening job."

"This is extra work? Moonlighting?"

She liked the sound of his voice. Low and warm, it soothed the rougher edge from her mood. "I can't live on what I make at my day job."

"Why would you be fired? It's not your fault the shoe broke."

"I shouldn't have been out here." Embarrassed, she added, "Sorry. I'm whining."

"Me, too. I drove and shouldn't have." He rubbed the back of his neck. "I was sick recently. I'm better now, just overestimated how much better."

She heard the forlorn note in his voice and something moved in her heart, a little tilt that nudged the complexion of the evening and her attitude, some sense that *she* was the lucky one sitting here. She wasn't used to being the fortunate one and it moved her to friendliness.

"I caught a ride in with someone else and he won't be leaving for hours." She decided to write this job off and her spirits lifted. She suppressed a laugh, but it warmed her nevertheless, and the lightness coursed through her. "Honestly, getting fired is no big deal. I never liked this job anyway."

He spoke slowly. "Do you drive?"

Had she heard him right? "I have a license, if that's what you're asking." She'd owned a clunker until recently, but sold it for scrap when she couldn't afford repairs and insurance, too.

"Where do you live? Beaufort? Morehead City?"

She answered, but with hesitation. "Morehead City."

"I live in Emerald Isle. If you drive me home, I'll pay for the cab to your house, or back here to Beaufort, if that's what you prefer. Plus a bonus for your time."

"What?" She stared at him. Her eyes were adjusting to the dark and his features were becoming clearer.

He leaned forward, his shoulders hunched. "Drive me home. I live on the island. I'll pay for your cab to wherever you want to go."

He was thirty-something, maybe forty, she guessed.

"Are you joking? You're a stranger. I don't see an axe or duct tape, but—" Was she crazy? Sitting here chatting with a strange man in a dark, lonely garden? She sat straighter, pressing her upper arm against her side, feeling the reassuring pressure of the pink mace sprayer tucked into the interior pocket of her vest.

"My name is Ben Bradshaw. I've been ill and I overtaxed myself. I couldn't hurt a kitten. I'll give you the money for the cab now, if you'd feel more comfortable." He reached into an inside pocket in his formal jacket. "Here, you can even hold my cell phone."

She eyed the phone in his hand. "Why don't you call a cab for yourself?"

"Because my car will still be here."

"Listen, I'll go inside and let the hostess know you want to leave. Some of the guests are friends of yours, right? They'll be happy to drive you home."

"I want to leave quietly. Not have anyone fussing or saying I told you so. Or seeing I had to leave my car behind because I was too weak to drive it."

Juli looked at the bright round moon, at the couples walking nearby and at the cheap broken shoe in her lap.

Sometimes it was important to know when to call it a day.

She held out her hand for his phone. "My name's Juli Cooke. It's nice to meet you, Mr. Bradshaw. I need to get my backpack and tell my ride I'm leaving."

"It's Ben, please. I'll wait here." He brushed the back of his hand across his forehead.

"Don't get any ideas, right? This is just about a ride home. Nothing else."

He nodded. "Thank you."

Sammy Robards was in the kitchen. She saw him note her entry through the back door and watched anger flash across his face.

He stabbed his finger in her direction. "Is that what you're paid for? I've got guests in there. You're paid to serve them."

She held her shoes in one hand and the tray in the other. Without a word, she handed him the tray and kept moving. What was there to say?

Frankie was in the coatroom. He looked startled, caught hiding from work. He was only marginally reliable although people tended to like his gently tousled sandy hair and boyish looks.

"I don't need a ride home tonight. I'm leaving now. Got another ride." She knelt and scrounged in the back behind the hanging wraps for her backpack. It wasn't exactly where she'd left it, but her fingers finally touched the mesh side pocket and she pulled the pack out. When she stood, Frankie was giving her a look, no doubt amazed.

He followed her to the door. "What are you doing? Where are you going?"

She glanced back over her shoulder. "I'm going home."

"How are you getting there?"

"No worries. I've got it handled. I'll see you tomorrow or the next day."

The tall man who'd stared through her, Luke, the one who'd made her feel invisible, stood in the coatroom doorway. They nearly collided. Guests always wanted something, but if she was walking out on the server job, she certainly wasn't going to fill in for the coat check person and definitely not for this snobby guy who'd started her whole evening crashing downhill. She swerved around him and kept going, glad to exit the back door for the last time.

Ben was where she'd left him. She sat on the bench to pull her sneakers out of the backpack and shoved the broken shoe and its mate into it, along with her little white server cap.

"Ready?" Ben asked.

She had doubts, but she'd made her decision. "I am."

When they moved into the light, she saw how truly pale he was. She touched his arm, then pulled her hand back, resisting the impulse to offer support. "Are you okay?"

"I can manage. I don't want to draw attention." He leaned back against a white pillar while the valet brought up the car.

When Ben went to the passenger side door with an unsteady gait, the valet smirked and eyed Juli in her server outfit. Ben didn't seem to notice and Juli ignored it. A server leaving mid-party with an unsteady guest was bound to give a bad impression. That was life.

Ben asked, "You know the way to Emerald Isle?"

His car was decent, but nothing fancy. She could manage it, even in the dark. "I do."

"I'll give you directions to the house after we cross the bridge."

After that exchange, Ben went silent. The silence was heavy and awkward. Nagging tales about foolish women who get into cars with strangers nipped at her nerves. Yet, she couldn't imagine any threat from this man. Had her good sense abandoned her?

To fill the emptiness, she began to talk—more than usual. As they drove through Beaufort and crossed the bridge into Morehead City, she told quirky, probably rude stories about the foster families she'd grown up with, about her co-workers, about the lessons she'd learned for getting by in life. Juli chatted on, surprised at herself. It was unlike her to open up her history for inspection. Once or twice she suspected he'd fallen asleep, but when she looked at him, his eyes were fixed upon her and he seemed fascinated by her monologue. So she talked. She knew the words were lost in the void, spoken to a man she'd never see again.

That night she felt as clear-headed as she ever had. Juli suspected it wasn't necessarily a good thing. When life as you know it pauses, and you realize there's nothing else to do but to go on in the same unsatisfactory way you always have, it's a black moment. Driving through the night, over the bridge, and along the ramrod straight, mostly dark, Atlantic Avenue that stretched the length of the island, Juli sensed a change coming. She caught her breath and her fingers tightened on the steering wheel.

Soon after they crossed the town line into Emerald Isle, Ben said, "Turn here."

His house looked impressive, a duplex rising several stories. It seemed immense in the moonlight and on the far side, the beach side, the full force of the Atlantic Ocean crashed onto the shore, sounding violent and reassuring and timeless, all at once.

She experienced a first—a serendipitous flash of being in a place where she belonged.

Wishful thinking.

She parked his car in the open area below the house and walked with him to the base of the wooden stairs. The stairs scaled the exterior side of the house. They were steep, especially in the dark with the night wind whipping around from the ocean side, flinging sand and salt.

"You're welcome to come up while I call the cab service." For the first time, he seemed nervous. "I don't have their number programmed in my cell."

"No, thanks. I'll wait down here."

"I understand." He drew some bills from his wallet. "Here. I can't thank you enough for your help. I'll go up and make the call. If you get worried or it takes too long for the cab to arrive, let me know."

"Your keys and your phone." She handed them to him.

He started up the stairs and she couldn't help watching—he moved like an old man. Well, he'd gotten his wish and was home now, and she had picked up a nice bit of cash.

Juli perched on a low rock wall to wait. It was dark, but only about eight o'clock or so.

The street was quiet despite the many houses and most had their exterior lights on. Above her, a window scraped open. She looked up.

He called out, "Are you okay down there?"

"Fine." She waved. The house blocked most of the onshore breeze, but she was still chilly. She pulled her sweater from the backpack and settled in to wait. The tangy smell of the ocean and the sound of surf, artificially loud in the quiet of night, transported her a thousand miles away from practicality and reality.

The mood was lovely and lasted until the cab dropped her off at the entry to her second floor walkup on the backside of a renovated apartment house. Not bad. Worn and slightly dingy,

GRACE GREENE

but as neat as she could make it—it was her own place and she worked hard to support herself.

She was self-reliant and proud of it.

Juli tossed her backpack into the corner behind the sofa. When she removed the elastic band from her hair, she sighed and massaged her fingertips into her scalp. It felt as good as getting out of those pumps.

So much for Sammy and his catering crew. She'd stuck with that job as long as she had because it was convenient to grab a ride with Frankie, but everyone had their limit and she'd met hers this evening. Convenience and a paycheck didn't justify every job.

She needed to concentrate on finding work that offered some kind of future.

Chapter Two

Juli watched Ben Bradshaw walk into Singer's Market on Tuesday morning. Her cheeks grew warm and she tensed when he stopped to survey the line of cash registers.

She hadn't expected to see him again, not ever, and she didn't believe in coincidence. She raised her hand to get his attention.

He was thin, but had a hint of color in his cheeks and a sparkle in his warm, toffee-colored eyes. "Miss Cooke, I was hoping I could talk to you." He glanced around. "I guess this isn't a good time?"

She smoothed her blue work apron and straightened her name tag with its big white letters.

"It's Juli, remember? I'm on the clock. I can't leave my register."

A female customer walked by with a sulky, pointed look at the empty-handed man who was obviously *not* checking out and stopped to glare before moving on to the next cashier. Any minute now the manager would be striding across the polished tiles to ask if there was a problem.

Juli couldn't afford to lose this job. The odd jobs she took came and went, but this one was her anchor.

He asked, "How about lunch? My treat."

"Are you a stalker? How did you find me?" She half-smiled, not sure whether she should laugh or prepare to defend herself. She tucked a loose strand of hair behind her ear. Her hair was always slipping out of its pony tail no matter what type of fastener she used or how tightly she secured it.

"You mentioned working at Singer's Market the other night."

"I talk too much." From the corner of her eye, she saw Al Smith approaching.

"Is there a problem?" Smith tried to sound stern, but with caution.

Juli knew Smith didn't want to risk offending someone who might only be asking where the cheese crackers were stocked. Her reply was brusque. "No problem here, Mr. Smith."

She turned away, gesturing to an approaching customer as she spoke. "My lunch is at noon. I'll be at Cox's, a few blocks over."

Presumably he'd be there, but should she show up? When they'd met at the party he'd been a nice guy whose path she'd crossed on a dark night, a guy who needed a favor and would never be seen again. He seemed different from the other guys who wasted their time coming on to her, but what did he want?

When noon hit, she folded and stowed the apron in her locker on top of her book. No reading over lunch today.

Cox's Family Restaurant was a favorite of the locals. In Juli's opinion, they had the best, to-die-for, grilled cheese sandwiches, and today the almost-stranger sitting across from her was willing to pick up the tab. Never turn down a free meal, right? She'd learned that from her third foster family.

They each took a menu from the holder and pretended to read it. Or maybe Ben wasn't pretending, but she was. Uneasiness was there at the table with them from the first moment.

This was foolish. This wasn't worth the price of the sandwich and it wasn't too late to leave. She reached down to the purse on the seat beside her and grabbed the shoulder strap. *No, not too late at all.*

He asked, "Are you from Morehead City?"

"No. Listen, I—"

"North Carolina?"

"Yes, but—"

"Hi, Juli. Ready to order?" Brenda stood by the table in her jeans and t-shirt, holding her order pad and pen. She gave Ben an appraising grin before turning back to Juli. And winked.

Brenda had winked.

Juli twisted the edge of the menu, anxious, but Brenda didn't tease her further. She just wrote down their orders and left.

Ben said, "I've eaten here many times over the years and I guess you have, too, since she knows you by name."

"Food's good, it's convenient, and I can afford it." It annoyed her that he seemed so pleased they'd both eaten here before. Them and how many thousands of others? A family with two kids was seated nearby, a quartet of retirees, two Marine Patrol officers in their gray uniforms—an endless variety. She and her lunch companion weren't special.

Juli watched him struggle to find a conversation starter while she considered whether to stay.

Ben cleared his throat. "I was born and raised in the area, mostly in Beaufort. Do you have family around here?"

They were in a public place in the middle of the day and here was Brenda, already heading in their direction, carrying plates. Juli released her grip on the purse strap.

"Good, convenient, and quick, too." Ben smiled at Brenda. "Thanks."

"Enjoy. Yell if you need anything." She put the check on the table and moved on.

Juli opened the paper napkin and spread it across her lap. As she picked up her sandwich Ben said, "Excuse me." He bowed his head and spoke words that took her back to being six years old. "Father, we thank Thee..."

She missed the end of the blessing and, instead, was tossed backward in time to a long-forgotten moment. His "Amen" returned her to the present with a breathless rush. She took a quick look around the room, but the other diners seemed not to have noticed.

Ben asked again, "Do you have any family around here?"

She took a long drink of ice water and set the glass down carefully. "We're not past the weather stage."

"Pardon?"

"Discussing the weather. We aren't past that yet."

His smile faltered. "I didn't mean to offend."

She'd blabbed so much personal business on the Friday night drive she could hardly blame him for asking, but being asked was different from volunteering info.

They ate in silence. Ben sat across from her, biting into his grilled cheese sandwich, lips trying to snare a great glob of yellow cheese that had squeezed out. He had a good appetite. She took it as confirmation he was recovering from an illness. He'd said something along those lines when they met, hadn't he?

His eyes were beautiful, but somber. She judged him to be in his late thirties, about ten years older than she. He was too thin and had an academic look, like a professor or something.

Juli dealt with her own grilled cheese sandwich while considering whether to re-start the conversation. She'd come across harsher than intended, but he'd handled the rebuff well.

She said, "You seem better today than you did the other night."

He jumped at the opening. "I am better. You were a lifesaver."

"Someone else would've driven you home."

"You were the one who was there when I needed a hand. My Good Samaritan."

"I was there, it's true, but not coming to help. I was running away from a job. I stumbled over you. Literally." Sammy would never take her back as a server and that suited her fine. She was tired of arrogant men, including the jerk at the party who'd looked through her as if she wasn't there. She should shake it off. That sort of thing had never bothered her before. Pride wasn't something she concerned herself with, but then again, maybe it had always bothered her and lacked only a trigger to set it off.

"Are you okay?"

She shook her head. "Sorry. Cobwebs. I usually eat alone.

You don't owe me anything, not even thanks. It was a good deal for both of us."

He nodded. "You work for a caterer and at the grocery store, too?"

"Grocery store, yes. Caterer, no longer."

"Not married?"

"No. On my own. Always have been."

"No family?"

She spoke sharply. "Enough with the questions."

"Just making conversation. Does any of this strike you as providential?" He wiped crumbs from his fingers with a crumpled napkin. He looked up, appearing chagrined. "Sorry, I know you don't understand."

"I understand the word."

"No, I didn't mean that, nor that it was providential you grew up in foster homes." He shuffled the salt and pepper shakers around. "What I'm trying to say is... The words sounded good in my head when I was thinking it out."

"Why *are* you here?"

"Would you have supper with me tonight?"

She knew she was being stalled. "I have to work the evening shift, but even if I didn't, why would you buy me another meal?"

"I'll meet you wherever and whenever you say. Timing is important to me. Forgive me for seeming secretive or mysterious."

What kept her here, talking? Him being a gentleman despite her barbs?

Most people had two sets of manners. One set—the pretty, on display set—they reserved for neighbors, friends and maybe their co-workers. The attitude they handed out to the help reeked. Maybe Ben had only one set. He seemed authentic and his interest in her was intriguing.

"I'm off at four, but I have to be back at work by six."

"I'll be waiting for you outside of Singer's."

"Just meet me here at the restaurant."

****

This time Juli felt less awkward and more in charge. She'd decided to take the meal at face value. It was just a meal, after all. Not a commitment. No one could make her do anything she didn't want.

Ben said, "I used to be involved in several businesses, but I've been making changes."

She chewed her cheeseburger.

"I was in business with my cousin, that is. We're about the same age. We're good friends."

Juli gave a little grunt, but offered nothing more as she took a long sip of iced tea.

"I have a sister, but she lives in Ohio. We lost our parents several years ago."

This time, she did speak. "I'm sorry."

He left openings for her to question him or to offer information about herself, but she didn't—deliberately. Finally, he, too, fell silent until the end of the meal.

"Could we take a walk?" Ben asked.

"What do you want from me?"

"Please?" He looked around at the filled tables. The supper crowd was building.

This was her neighborhood. Her turf. She didn't feel vulnerable here and she was curious. One walk and then they'd be done. Afterward, she'd send him packing.

A few blocks down route 24 a patch of nature was nearly lost amid the businesses along the busy road. The remains of an asphalted drive began at the sidewalk and led them back between the lines of oaks. There was no undergrowth, only dirt and grass, so they were perfectly visible from the road, yet set apart from business and traffic at the same time.

At the end of the spit of land, the cliff dropped off and the water below lapped at the rocks tumbled at its base. Across the sound, Bogue Island stretched in both directions—the water between the two shores glittered in the late afternoon light.

"You come here often?"

She shrugged. "Sometimes on break, I bring a book and read here. It's peaceful." She gave him a steady look. "Peaceful, but not too private. Lots of traffic out that way."

His gaze followed her pointing finger. "We passed a huge For Sale sign by the road. Do you worry you'll lose your peaceful spot?"

"Yes. No. It's a nice place to hang out when I don't have enough time to go home on break, but it's not mine—it's temporary. Everything's temporary."

The call of the gulls and the slap of the water relaxed her, as it always did, taking her out of her real life. She wandered over to an ancient live oak. It was bent by a century or more of relentless onshore winds, yet it thrived.

"Everything?"

"Yes."

He stared out across the water. She waited. Any minute now they would have the awkward 'can we date discussion' and she was pretty sure she was going to shoot him down.

Pretty sure? Was she actually considering seeing him again? In a no-nonsense tone, she asked, "Are you married?"

Ben paused. When he answered, his voice was so soft she almost couldn't hear him.

"I was. A long time ago."

"What happened?"

He turned away, but she'd already seen the sorrow on his face. No, she wouldn't see him again. She had enough of her own baggage; she didn't need his, too.

Ben spoke, his voice back to normal. "I have an offer to make. I hope you'll consider it."

Juli opened her mouth and shut it again. Not a date? She crossed her arms.

"I hope you aren't about to suggest something illegal."

His eyes widened. "No, nothing like that. A job, one might say, but better paying."

"What?"

"A business arrangement. Companionship."

She was startled. She examined her sleeve as if discovering a flaw and plucked at it, buying herself a moment. Around them the breeze whispered as it stirred the leaves of the oak.

When she had her cool in control she said, "I think you're trying to buy something I'm not selling."

"No, I meant it as said. A friendly companionship."

"Under your roof, is that it? I told you I'm not for sale."

"But that's just it—"

"Listen, Ben, I think you're a nice guy. Strange, but nice. I'd like to go on thinking it. Let me give you some advice. If you want companionship, get a dog. If it's love you're after, you can't buy it, not the real thing."

Ben leaned back against a low-hanging tree branch under the canopy of the oak. "That's not necessarily true. Arranged marriages have been around for as long as marriage itself. Marriage was often based on political or economic necessity. In many places around the world, even now, marrying for love is a luxury. Some cultures only have arranged marriages."

"I know that. I'm not stupid. I read." She kicked at a stray scrap of paper that had blown across the asphalt and sparse grass and had come to rest near her sneaker.

Ben's sad look was gone. He seemed to be enjoying the conversation now, almost as if he'd rehearsed his lines and was pleased he'd delivered them well. Why was she willing to listen? Everything costs something, even free meals. Maybe this was the payment she owed.

"Love often followed. Not always. Life was uncertain then and now. That's what prenuptial agreements are for."

"Prenups? You mean like rich people get? Always seemed cynical to me they go into marriage expecting it to end."

Ben shrugged lazily. "Proves my point. People get married for all sorts of reasons. Sometimes it's love, but marriage for love doesn't come with guarantees either."

What could she say? Her own experience could be cited as proof nothing good came of love. Ben was staring out across the water. It was a beautiful view, but couldn't compare with what he saw every day from his own front porch. She'd glimpsed his view in the dark and even that was convincing. He had the relaxed contentment of someone enjoying where he was and knowing that what he'd go home to was even better.

Some people were born to luck. Some weren't. Juli knew she was in the latter group. Had been all her life.

She checked her watch. "It's five-thirty. I have to get back to Singer's by six o'clock."

He faced her. "What if I said you didn't have to go back?"

"I'd say I don't enjoy hunting for jobs."

"Consider my proposition."

"You never said what it was."

Ben looked into her eyes. "You're a smart girl. You know what I'm suggesting."

"I think you'd better spell it out."

"Marry me."

As nice as he seemed, and she kind of knew what he'd been hinting at, she was still hurt he would play with her feelings. She wasn't well-to-do or well-educated, but she worked hard.

Juli glared at him and started to walk back up the asphalt drive.

"Wait, please." He grabbed her arm, then quickly released it. "Please. What do you earn per month? I'll double it. No, I'll triple it."

"I'm sure you've got some fancy friends who can help you out. Go ask one of them to marry you."

He was silent. She saw he was sorting his words for one last effort.

"Please think about it, Juli. For as long as the marriage lasts, I'll pay you triple what you'd make each month, with a guaranteed minimum."

"Okay, I'll play this what-if game with you. Why would I quit my jobs when, sooner or later, I have to go back to pounding the pavement, looking for others?"

"Use your imagination." He sounded rude, harsh for the first time. "Is Singer's Market what you want for the rest of your life? I can't believe you'd settle for that if you had the opportunity for more."

"More? With you? What kind of opportunity is that?" *Deep breath, Juli.*

"You'll have money. Money buys education. A better job. Who knows what else could open up for you? Remember, I'll guarantee a minimum. Dream a little."

Bitterness rose in her mouth and twisted her face. How easily he spoke the words. How privileged. So easy for him, and those like him to say, dream, as if it were no more complicated than picking an apple from the fresh produce bin.

"Companionship? Why now? Why me? Why marriage?"

"Marriage? Because we'll be living together in the same house. Even in a platonic arrangement, I'd only feel comfortable as husband and wife. I don't need a housekeeper. I mean it when I say I want companionship. Someone to hang out with. I think you and I would get along well. I liked you from the moment we met. I admire your strength of spirit."

"My spirit? Please. Don't patronize me or make me out to be something I'm not."

"I'm not perfect, either, but I'm a good judge of character. Always have been."

He held her gaze until she broke it off. She did a slow boil inside. There was nothing polite to say. In fact, there was no point in saying anything more because her supper break was over.

"Consider this, too. Marriage combined with a prenuptial contract will provide more protection for you and your financial interest in the arrangement." He reached into his pocket. "You asked why now? I'll tell you when you accept the offer. Until then, it's personal." He pressed his business card into her hand. "Call me, but don't wait too long."

Arrogant. She hurried up the drive to the road, then strode, almost ran, down the sidewalk. After she crossed the road she tucked his card in her jeans' pocket, down deep where it couldn't slip out. After all, never turn down a free meal and never close your mind to an opportunity even if the proposition sounded outrageous at first hearing.

The heat that set her cheeks afire lessened with each step she took, each step that left Ben behind and brought her back to the automatic doors of the market and the cash register.

Living day by day and letting the future take care of itself hadn't prepared her well for life. She feared she'd created her own, personal dead-end. Late in the evening, she stood at register number five. Sheila was at the express lane and doing double-duty at the customer service counter. Billy was re-stocking the plastic bags. They outnumbered the customers at this hour and closing was a short time away.

Time is relative, she'd heard it said. As she progressed through her twenties, she'd noticed her co-workers getting younger, except the older women who'd suddenly found themselves in need of employment because a marriage dissolved or a spouse lost a job. The kids had plans for better, or at least for Spring Break in Cancun or a car or whatever. *That's who I used to be.* The older women and retirees were earning extra cash until their health gave out. She wasn't there yet. The question was who didn't fit in this picture?

"Juli?"

"Sorry, Sheila. Didn't see you."

"Go ahead and close down your register. Have you been thinking about the assistant manager position? If you say you want it, I know Smith will be thrilled."

"He mentioned it. I'm thinking about it." She slipped her hand into her pocket and fingered the sharp edges of Ben's business card. She was still young, but her feet hurt and her lower back ached from standing all day.

All of her good intentions about getting more education or specialized training had come to nothing. It was hard to get ahead when your energy and time were dedicated to keeping a roof over your head and the utilities on.

She'd taken his card out and read it at break. It had the name of an art gallery with a Beaufort address, along with his phone number. She'd seen his house at Emerald Isle when she'd driven him home that night. A house on the oceanfront. An art gallery. The only time she'd ever experienced success was in middle school. Eighth grade art. Mrs. Timberlake had had great hopes for her. Until she was sent to a new foster home and a new school.

She worked an assortment of nothing jobs that earned her barely enough to live on. She did no more than tread water and was losing against the inevitable tide. Even applying for the assistant manager position was a problem. It would draw attention to her application and she'd probably have to fill out more paperwork. She'd gotten away with it when they first hired her, but she'd be pushing her luck to try it again. Her other employers didn't care if she'd graduated from high school, but Singer's would, especially since she'd lied about it from the start.

She bit her lower lip and stared at Ben's card.

How sad it was to think she'd peaked in eighth grade.

Chapter Three

By the time Juli dialed the phone her restless fingers had worried the sharp corners of the business card down to soft, papery edges.

"Hi, this is Juli Cooke." She groaned. Dumb. He knew her last name. He'd proposed, for heaven's sake.

"Juli. I'm glad to hear from you."

How could she be doing this? He sounded so eager. Like a kid.

"Don't misunderstand. I'm not agreeing to anything." Juli watched as a woman passed by on the way to the restrooms. Not a co-worker. Juli turned back to face the wall phone. "I have questions, some concerns."

"What would you like to know?"

Someone else walked by. Juli watched him turn the corner and disappear into the warehouse area.

She cupped her hand around her lips and the mouthpiece. "Not now. I'm at work, but I'm off early today. About two p.m., if you're free?"

"I'll pick you up."

"Where will we go?"

A moment of silence, then he said, "No worries. I'll think on it. We'll go out for coffee or an early dinner. Whatever you like."

"Park in the side lot and I'll meet you out there a few minutes after two."

They said goodbye and disconnected. The phone hung on the wall, still available. Her fingers itched to grab it back, re-dial and call it off, but then she touched the card again, in her pocket, in her hand. It was a stupid business card, not a lifeline.

What was wrong with her?

A trashcan with a rocking top was near the opening of the short hallway. She should call him back and ditch the card. It was the only decision that made any sense.

He had a nice voice. Warm eyes.

He was a stranger, almost.

She slid the card into her shirt pocket, nearer her heart, and hurried back to the register.

The clock on the wall above the front plate glass windows ticked with the slow gravity of molasses. As she was switching off the OPEN light above her station, one last customer ran up with a cart. She gritted her teeth and smiled. It was a thin smile because she didn't want to invite conversation. She was conscious of Ben sitting outside in the car, waiting.

"Cash?" Good, that was quicker. She slipped the bills and coins out of the cash drawer with nimble fingers and counted it back into the woman's hand. A man approached the register.

She said firmly, "I'm sorry. This register is closed."

She turned away, tugging behind her back at the apron ties. "Juli?"

"Mr. Smith. Hi. What can I do for you?" Doggone it. If only she'd moved a second faster. Managers always had a sixth sense for when you were in a hurry to get out.

"Can you stay this afternoon?" He smoothed his tie.

"Sheila approved me leaving early."

After a surprised pause, he said, "Roger called in sick. We're short-handed."

One hundred out of one hundred times, when asked to work longer or extra, she'd said yes. She felt her chest rise and fall and she kept her lips pressed together to keep the 'sure, I can' from slipping out. Finally, she said, "I'm sorry, but I have an appointment."

"Can you re-schedule? Or maybe take an hour and come back?"

"I'm not sure." Deep breath. "That is, I don't know how long it will take."

"We really need you."

"Mr. Smith, I'm sorry. I don't want to commit and then find out I can't come back. I don't want to let anyone down." She saw in his eyes she already had. "Marty lives nearby and can probably come in. Did you try her?"

"Not yet." He waited, using the silence to pressure her, but she didn't give in. "Well, if you're certain you can't stay."

"I'm sorry." She folded her apron and shoved it under the counter with the bags. A sinking feeling nearly swamped her. It wasn't fair. She'd done her part. It wasn't her problem Roger had called in sick.

Singer's wasn't going to fail and no patrons would go without milk, eggs and toilet paper because she took a few hours off.

She let Smith walk away, her fingers gripping the chrome partition of her cashier station.

Juli kept her back turned, fighting the need to say she'd stay if they needed her, that she could change her plans. They expected it of her. It was retail, after all. Groceries.

No, it was only groceries.

She held her head up, straightened her shoulders and headed for the door. She couldn't throw off the guilt. It tore at her as if she was crossing some invisible barrier, but from the wrong direction.

Forget it, Ben. I've changed my mind. She could tell him that and go back inside. Al Smith would be grateful and maybe this job would lead to a better one, after all, diploma or not.

Cashier to management? Did she believe that would happen?

Ben's car idled near the parking lot exit. The engine ran smooth and steady. He slipped out of the car when he saw her approaching.

Cashier to management? Never. Even if it did happen, Mr. Smith worked long hours, and for what? Was it about a paycheck? If it was, then it was a poor bargain because the money wasn't any better deal than the hours.

Ben extended his hand. "I'm glad to see you again."

"Ben." She accepted his hand for a quick shake. "What do you have in mind?"

"I know the perfect place for us to discuss this."

"Where?"

"Trust me?"

She did. She was stupid, a dunce, to trust this guy. But she did. With reservations, of course. She wasn't entirely air-headed.

He drove them over the bridge to Atlantic Beach, then several miles west until they reached Emerald Isle and his house—the route she'd driven four days earlier. Her pulse rate picked up. Her hands fisted.

He must have seen her tension. "Don't jump to conclusions, please."

She hopped out of the car before he could come around and open the door. They walked under the house, to the steps that led up to the crossover, near to where it joined the front porch.

"I'll wait outside. I want you to see where you'd live. Look everywhere. There are three levels. You'll see my room on the second floor. You can have your choice of the others."

She cautioned him. "I haven't agreed to anything yet."

"I know. Take as long as you like. I'll be here on the porch."

Did this seem as strange to her as the rabbit hole had seemed to Alice? She looked at the door, wondering if she was walking into a trap—as Alice had. Alice's trap had turned into a bizarre adventure. Juli had nothing against a little adventure, but bizarre she could do without.

"I understand your concern. Take my keys. Lock the door behind you. There's no trick."

Was her face so easy to read? As easy as his?

She looked out at the beach and to the left and right. House followed house in both directions, but no one was nearby. A partition divided this porch from its twin, the other half of the duplex. Out beyond the dune barrier was a pristine white-sand beach. A boy chased a dog. A couple of people had fishing poles and their cast lines rode the swell of the waves. A family group was building a sand castle.

"Okay."

He nodded and smiled, anxious, but calm. He walked over to one of the white rockers, sat and stared out at the ocean.

She took him at his word. When she entered the house she locked the door behind her.

From the inside, looking out through the glass panel in the front door, she watched Ben.

He continued facing straight ahead, but he'd stopped rocking. She read tension in the set of his shoulders and in the stillness of his hands on the arm rests.

This was important to him. She didn't get it.

She was drawn to him. He wasn't like anyone she'd ever met. Substantial, but not putting on airs. He spoke his mind, but wasn't arrogant or aggressive.

Juli rested her forehead against the cool glass. She wanted to touch his shoulder and reassure him. Reassure him about what?

There was a vulnerability to him. It showed in his guileless, light brown eyes.

She unlocked the door and stepped back outside. His head turned and his face expressed dismay in the sad eyes and the downturned corners of his mouth.

"That was quick," he said.

"I don't need to tour your house. I can see it's nice." Juli walked to the rail and leaned back against it. "You need to make me understand why you want to do this."

Ben nodded. "I heard what you said the night you drove me home."

Her face flashed hot. "I said a lot of things I shouldn't have."

"No," he shook his head. "I heard in your words that you're alone and unsettled in your life. I enjoyed the stories. They said a lot about you—about how you make the best of whatever situation in which you find yourself and how, if you don't like the current situation, you make a new one."

He'd gotten that from her stories? He was a dreamer, hearing what he wanted to hear.

He scratched his head. "It made me think about my own life. I've lived a good one and I've been blessed in many ways. Recently, something changed. Things are different now. I'm sort of like a fish out of water, flipping around on the ground, hoping to make the best of it, but with no idea how. Until I met you."

"What changed?"

He focused on his fingers. "I'm dying."

People didn't talk like that, not in her life. She rejected the sound of it. "We're all dying."

He looked up at her. "Some things, some subjects, can't be avoided."

"What's wrong with you?"

"Cancer. It's a quiet cancer and by the time it was found, it was too far gone for standard treatment. Or rather, treatment that might cure it. It's in my pancreas."

She wet her lips. Her words had been stolen. 'I'm sorry' covered things like stepping on someone's foot or breaking up with a boyfriend. Her hands were on her cheeks. She put them back down and grabbed the rail behind her.

Ben said, "I have the faith I need to deal with the truth, but in the meantime, I don't want to spend my remaining time alone."

"You know people. You have friends, even family. You aren't alone."

"They're grieving. I'm alive, but they are already... I can't blame them. I know how I'd feel if the roles were switched and I was the one who was dealing with losing a loved one, but with them around all the time, upset, I can't find any normalcy. I want to feel ordinary for a while yet. An ordinary man with a regular life."

"How long?"

"No telling. If I took treatment, it would probably extend my time, but it would also have side effects. If I can't be cured, then I want to enjoy myself while I can."

She waited for the answer.

"More than two months, less than nine. It's hard to say how long it'll be before I'm not feeling up to an active life. I don't need a nurse. I'll hire nurses when it's time."

She tried to see into the future. A wife—in name only, of course. And soon after, a widow? Ben was obviously real, but the rest of the picture couldn't take shape. She shook her head *no*. Not necessarily refusing, but in disbelief at this proposal.

He rushed into his next words. "My attorney will have an agreement drawn up by tomorrow. I'd like you to take a look at it. Take it to an attorney of your choosing. The agreement will be simple and straightforward. Please don't refuse before you've read it."

Could she watch him sicken and die? Was it kinder and more honorable to walk away and leave him on his own? He could find someone else. Who else? Would there be another woman as crazy as she was? One who would consider this?

"You can find someone else."

"Maybe. Maybe not. But I won't know because I won't try." He shook his head with a wry chuckle. "You're it. I don't say that to make you feel guilty. I say it so you'll know you're special. I never thought of this as a possibility until I met you. I apologize for the rush, but each day is important to me because it's one less day I have."

"It's time for me to leave." She handed him the keys.

"Would you like to go for a coffee or something?" He fingered the keys, staring down at his shoes.

"Just take me back to Singer's."

"But you're not refusing?"

"I'll think about it."

"Thank you."

She gave him credit for not forcing the conversation on the

drive back. She stared out the window, watching the rows of colorful homes with glimpses of dunes and ocean between them, past the beach stores and the marinas, then they crossed the bridge and were back in Morehead City.

Ben pulled into the parking lot they'd left not much more than an hour earlier.

"I'll call you." She tried to keep her voice even, not wanting him to try to read an answer in her inflection.

His lips moved. He wanted to speak, but didn't. She exited his car and watched him drive away. She could walk home from here.

Her work apron was in the store. She'd shoved it under the counter. She should've taken it with her. It could use a washing.

She paused outside the glass doors. If she went inside they'd ask her to stay. She could use the hours, but wasn't in the mood. The prospect of returning to the register caught her breath short. Made her feel trapped.

Any luster this job once had was gone and it was Ben's fault.

Chapter Four

Juli held Ben's hand self-consciously. She'd certainly done tougher, more embarrassing jobs in her life. Her part in this was simple and with the ocean breeze gently brushing her hair and toying with her skirt, the working conditions were exquisite.

She looked at the guests, at the pastor, and told herself this was merely another kind of temporary work. Juli focused on the silky coolness of the damp sand beneath her bare feet.

She'd take it one day at a time.

Ben's friend, Maia, had given her a posy of daisies and baby's breath to hold. Tiny green stems and leaves peeked from within the frothy white.

Juli was glad to have Maia at her side even if she was more of a stranger than Ben. At least, Maia was friendly. Luke Winters wasn't. He was Ben's cousin and closest friend. He was also the tall, aloof man at the party the night she'd met Ben. She'd recognized his arrogant face immediately.

Luke stood near Ben scowling like a bad omen personified. She'd been invisible to him at the party, but now, she was squarely in his sights. Ben's hand was steady in her clasp and reassured her. If Ben was aware of the negative waves of emotions coming their way he chose not to acknowledge them.

Juli ignored Luke. She never deliberately tried to give offense, but neither would she beg for anyone's approval.

The pastor's voice brought her back to the task at hand.

"Do you take this man to be your lawfully wedded husband? For richer or poorer, in sickness and in health, forsaking all others, for as long as you both shall live?"

"Yes." A gust of wind snatched the word away from her

lips. She spoke again, more forcefully, defiantly, "Yes."

"Do you take this woman to be your lawfully wedded wife? For richer or poorer, in sickness and in health, forsaking all others, for as long as you both shall live?"

"I do." He said it strongly not letting the wind or the roar of the ocean overpower his affirmation, as if denying reality the chance to diminish his happiness.

A short distance down the beach, with waves churning around their knees and thighs, two darkly tanned men worked together casting a large red net fastened to a frame. They hefted the straight ends together out of the water and it billowed, catching the wind before they bent, dropping it back down into the rushing waves. She admired the grace of their actions in unison.

She squeezed Ben's hand. Together was a new concept for her. Ben returned the squeeze and met her eyes. Today his skin was flushed. From the sun or from the nuptials? His face showed happiness with a hint of apprehension in the set of his lips.

The warmth of his touch pulled her from her thoughts. She gasped as Ben slipped the gold wedding band, then an engagement ring onto her finger. The engagement ring was unexpected.

The diamond glittered with captured light and the gold had a shiny, new sheen.

Juli heard, "I now pronounce..." and anxiety rushed through her, but there was no invitation to the groom to kiss his bride.

This was a tremendous leap for both of them, but what was the risk? The prenup was the safety net and time was on her side. She knew empathy wasn't her strong point, but she could be kind to a dying man.

"Allow me to be the first to congratulate you, Mr. and Mrs. Benjamin Daniel Bradshaw."

The pastor extended his hand and they shook in turn.

Maia said, "Ben and Juli, stay where you are. Stand close

together and smile." She was grinning broadly and holding a camera in front of her face.

They obeyed as she snapped a few photos. Then the pastor took one of Ben and Juli with Maia and Luke on either side—the entire bridal party.

Ben's sister, Adela, did not attend. Luke represented the official family displeasure. He offered congratulations with a dour expression.

"Juli. Best wishes." He barely brushed her outstretched hand with his own.

She stared into his eyes, refusing to release him gracefully, angry that in his world she was invisible, or if visible, then unwelcome. He broke away, but not before the amber lights in his eyes flashed, warning her of his suppressed anger.

Luke took Ben's hand and wrapped one arm around his shoulders, pulling him in for a quick hug without a word said. She had the distinct impression many words had already been shared privately and Ben had moved forward regardless of his family's feelings on the matter.

There was no reception following the ceremony. They moved together, a small group of conflicted well-wishers, across the soft mounds of warm sand and up the rough, weathered steps to the wooden dunes crossover leading to Ben's home.

Their home.

Three stories of duplex, named *Sea Green Glory,* rose on pilings above an open parking area directly below. The homes on the oceanfront had names. Most were weekly rentals that ran from weekend to weekend. There were only a few hotels in Emerald Isle. Most were further down the island in the Atlantic Beach area and near the bridge to Morehead City.

The crossover ended at the porch on the main living level. Luke, Maia and the pastor headed for the stairs to go below to the parking area, but paused to look back.

Maia's round cheeks dimpled in a kind smile. Overshadowed by Luke's stern demeanor, she looked especially petite and sweet. She waggled her fingers in a goodbye wave. Luke touched Maia's arm and they left.

Ben turned to face his bride. "Are you regretting our agreement?"

Was she? A reasonable woman, certainly a woman with money and family, would never have agreed to his proposal. But a woman who was on her own, who'd grown up in a succession of foster homes and who understood cash, not dreams, fueled life—that woman might accept it, and had done so.

What had Ben purchased? He deserved better than a hardboiled cynic. Juli smoothed the sharp edges from her manner and adopted a softer attitude.

"Regret? No. It feels strange. Unreal."

"No wonder. We moved quickly."

"*You* moved quickly. I now understand what being 'swept off my feet' feels like." They'd met a week ago. How had a man as mild-mannered as Ben managed to find a fiancé, get the prenup drawn up, and arrange a wedding on the beach, however small, within four days?

"I have a surprise for you." He escorted her to a chair beside the round white patio table. "Sit here. I'll be right back."

There were faint noises coming from the far side of the wooden partition as, only a few feet away, the renters on the other side of the duplex packed up. They'd leave first thing in the morning. That half would be re-occupied when the new renters arrived later in the afternoon.

Ben lived in his half, the western side, year-round.

The waves rolled in, gulls squawked and scavenged from the few beach-goers, and she, Julianne Cooke Bradshaw, sat on her new porch and wondered how long her marriage would last.

Within minutes, white-coated strangers appeared with linen and fine china. They whisked around the table efficiently placing crystal goblets and gleaming silverware on the tablecloth. It reminded her of the Shirley Temple movie, *The Little Princess*, when the two girls awoke in their cold, dark garret to find hot food and warm, luxurious garments had been left while they slept.

Something was happening in her chest. A warm fist squeezed her heart and hot tears blurred her vision. She closed her eyes. She wouldn't cry. She would not.

His fingers encircled her wrists and, gently, he pulled her hands away from her face.

"Juli?"

She looked down at Ben, her husband, kneeling at her feet. She didn't love him, and might never, but in the few days she'd known him, she strongly suspected he was a man worthy of love.

"Is this wise?" she asked.

"It's a little late to ask now, isn't it?" Ben said, but he was smiling.

The words spilled out. "I don't know what you expect of me. I mean, I thought I knew, but now I'm not sure." She drew in a rough breath to halt the babbling.

"I want only what I told you when I proposed this arrangement. Companionship. No more, no less. Nothing you don't want to give."

"Companionship? I'm not, I mean... I have no social skills. Not much education. No glitter. You'll be bored or disappointed."

Ben kissed the backs of her hands. "I want you to be yourself."

"But I don't love you. You don't love me."

"I don't want you to love me. That would be cruel. Remember what I told you? I don't want to be alone. I'm grateful you agreed to help me."

Who was this man? *A little late to wonder, Juli.* The sight of his hands caressing hers didn't disturb her, although a detached part of her brain noted these were the hands of a man she barely knew. That small, internal voice was silenced by compassion. She disliked it. It made her feel vulnerable.

"Ben, we are so different. What do we share? Nothing."

"I have faith, Juli. This will work."

"I wish I could say the same."

Ben kissed her hands. "I have faith enough for both of us, for now."

She slipped from the chair down to the porch floor where he knelt. "I will do my best not to let you down." For the first time, she felt genuine vows had been exchanged. They were married.

It was a strange kind of marriage, true, but a union nonetheless.

****

Juli noted Ben's pale complexion and the tired look in his eyes. He was exhausted from the events of the day. She knew they both suffered from the strain of *what next?* He had his companion, she had a new bank account, and neither knew what to talk about. She played along when he pretended the awkwardness was normal and expected, but the pretense itself was fatiguing.

He rose from the sofa. "If you prefer to read there are books in the bookcase. I'm sorry about calling it an early night, but I have a surprise for you tomorrow morning. We'll go out for breakfast. I want to take you someplace special."

She tensed as he paused near her.

"Thank you, Juli. Sleep well." With a soft sigh, he went upstairs.

There were three bedrooms on the second floor. Ben had offered Juli the choice of the two unoccupied rooms. She'd chosen the one with the private bath. It also had sliding doors opening onto a shared balcony and the view of the Atlantic was amazing. The topmost floor was half a story, one bedroom and bath. Odds and ends were stored there, but Ben was willing to turn it back into a bedroom if she wanted it. She'd told him not to bother. She'd brought some personal belongings over the previous day. Not much because she traveled light.

Their financial arrangement gave her a lump sum up front and a weekly stipend. If she stayed for the duration and didn't party too hearty or fool around, she'd get another chunk at the end of the contract period. Juli knew little about cancer, only what Ben had explained, including the prognosis of six months, more or less. She didn't know where the pancreas was or what it did, but she didn't want to admit it to Ben because she didn't want him to think she was ignorant.

In the end, she'd be moving on again, as she always had, only this time she'd have a healthy bank account.

Juli stood alone on her wedding night in the living room of a strange house. She still wore her wedding dress, borrowed and blue. Maia had gotten it from someone somewhere as a loaner because Juli didn't own a frilly dress.

She toured the main floor. The furnishings were simple and uncluttered. Ben had shown her around, of course, but that was polite-looking. Juli opened the cupboards and checked out the contents of the fridge. Beyond the kitchen was a room facing the road, away from the ocean. Ben's study.

Back in the living room, she channel-surfed, restless and apprehensive again. If this was the high point what would the next weeks be like?

The air, close and warm, crowded her. Internal claustrophobia, like she'd experienced at the Hammonds' party, moved in again. It wasn't true claustrophobia, but more like a panic attack. The increased heart rate, the thrumming sound in her ears and the shallow breathing drove her outside.

The wind whipped her skirt. The earlier teasing breeze was gone. Moonlit clouds scudded across the night sky, unnaturally white foam rode the crashing waves, and all around was darkness with the ranks of rentals guarding the coast, a bulwark against the Atlantic night. She intended to go out to the porch, perhaps to sit in one of the white-painted rockers. Instead, she walked along the crossover, shivering as the brisk night touched her skin. The smell of salt and wet sand overrode all others. She descended the steps, stopping only when the delicate, trailing edges of the waves washed over her toes.

The natural cathedral that had graced their wedding now

gloried in an array of stars. She tingled from her toes to her hair. She'd never experience this feeling before—miniscule beneath the heavens, yet part of an infinite, encompassing embrace.

The ocean ran up the beach and tickled her feet. She stretched her arms wide, not only for the universe, but for tomorrow and tomorrow and tomorrow, right here on earth.

There'd be no cash register to log into in the morning, no waitressing in the evening and no shelf-stocking on the night shift. She didn't need to be a utility ever again, at least not for a long time. The prenup guaranteed her a comfortable future if she didn't screw it up.

The girl who had no dreams, now had opportunity with a capital O—and an obligation to do right by her husband, the man whose loneliness and approaching death made hope possible.

Chapter Five

In the morning, Juli overslept. She hadn't slept this late since—maybe never. She rushed out of bed and into the shower. Was she keeping Ben waiting? She pulled on her jeans and was still buttoning her shirt as she unlocked her bedroom door—at just about the same moment as his door opened on the other side of the hall.

They emerged from their separate rooms like congenial acquaintances who, by chance, exit their hotel rooms at the same time.

"Did you sleep well?" Ben asked.

She nodded. "Yes, very."

"Ready for breakfast? I have somewhere special in mind."

Conversation was sparse. Awkwardness was abundant. Ben drove them across the bridge into Morehead City, then across the bridge to Beaufort.

The wind-buffeted water was choppy far below. As they passed over each bridge, Juli stared at the whitecaps as if she'd never seen such things before because it was a reprieve from conversation. When Ben cleared his throat she looked at him, but didn't push it when he failed to speak. He parked in a public lot and they walked quietly down the street past several stores.

They brunched at a restaurant overlooking the waterfront. When the food arrived and they started eating, Ben caught her eye.

She took a sip of water. "Yes?"

"When you said there was no one you wanted to invite to the marriage ceremony, I thought maybe you didn't want your family and friends to know, but now I'm wondering."

"I told you about my childhood. I grew up in foster

49

homes."

"Not even any extended family?"

"What's this with you and food? Or is it being in a restaurant that gets you curious?" She tried to keep her tone light but warn him off at the same time.

"Have you stayed in touch with any of them? The foster families?"

"No. They did what they did for their own reasons. I tried to keep my part of the bargain by not being a problem child. It was a business relationship."

Ben sat in silence for a moment, then leaned forward to say, "I know there's payment to cover some of the care, but a business arrangement? There are people who take in foster children because they want to help. There are. I know there are."

She shrugged. "I'm sure you're right and sometimes the chemistry perks, but it wasn't like that for me. They weren't cruel, they didn't mistreat me, but I wasn't any more interested in getting close to them than they were in getting close to me."

"Because your mother abandoned you? When you were five, you said? And that first foster family practically did the same two years later?"

"This is ridiculous. I'm used to being on my own. Maybe it will change someday, but I'm better alone. I always have been." She heard the careless stupidity of the words as she spoke them. She searched Ben's face. Did he think she was talking about the two of them and their arrangement?

The waitress placed the check on the table beside Ben's plate. Juli was glad of the distraction. He scanned the numbers, and then slipped some bills from his wallet. He left the money lying there on the tablecloth.

Juli stared at the cash. Someone could snatch it as soon as they turned their backs to leave—before the waitress could return for it. Ben should at least put the small stack under the edge of a plate. She waited and watched him. He showed no concern.

She decided to copy his attitude. Juli folded her napkin and laid it on the table next to her plate. Ben stood behind her to pull out her chair, an unexpected act, but it was her own response that surprised her. She felt special, warm and tingly, and the smile that grew in her heart appeared on her face. Ben took her hand as she rose. The other diners smiled at them and admiring eyes watched them as they passed by on their way to the exit. Everyone loves lovers, right? Juli enjoyed it, grateful no one knew the truth.

Ben led them from the restaurant and down the sidewalk. The traffic was light because it was barely May, but it wouldn't be long before tourism was in full swing. They jaywalked across the road and, as Ben moved ahead, she followed along, grabbing peeks through display windows until they stopped at the Front Street Gallery. She recognized the name from Ben's card.

The gallery building was the first in a long row of shops and restaurants, situated between the block of shops and a house that was probably no longer a residence. It was set a few feet further back from the sidewalk than the other businesses and not attached to the row. It gave the building distinction, sort of set apart from the rest.

Concrete steps with a painted iron railing let up to a large wooden door, also painted black and with a large plate glass window insert. Through the display windows, colors of every hue caught the attention of passersby with the message of *come in and see more.*

She'd never been in a real art gallery. Never went in to those kinds of stores because she knew she'd be spotted as someone who didn't belong.

"Have you ever been in here?"

"No, I enjoyed art when I was kid, but never did anything about it."

The walls were hung with paintings and prints, some in groupings, some spaced politely along the walls. There were several tables holding crafty knick-knacks and small artwork, all looked locally made.

Maia rushed over. "Good morning, Ben. Welcome, Juli. Can I show you around?" She moved between them and took their arms, but she addressed Juli. "We are very much a local gallery and we make it a point to support and represent local artists and craftsmen. We have colorful, crafty items for tourists who are looking for souvenirs and fine art for those who want to take a reminder of the coast with them to hang on their walls. A lot of our customers are locals who want to bring the color of the beach life they love into their homes."

Ben said, "Bring the beach inside—that's what I'd like to do. Our house is plain. I never noticed before, but it needs color. Juli, I'd like you to choose some items."

"You mean buy a painting?"

"Yes, and whatever else you like."

She'd always lived for the day because today had been as much as she could manage. Choosing artwork to decorate Ben's house seemed frivolous. His house looked great as it was.

"I have to think about this."

"Take your time and look around." He faced Maia. "Is Luke in?"

"He's in the office."

Ben touched Juli's arm. "I'll be back shortly."

He left her standing there. Juli watched him walk to the back of the shop and knock on the closed door with only a pause before entering, to speak with Luke.

****

Luke had entered the gallery by the back door that morning—his usual entrance and exit.

Maia was already at the counter out front and the sign on the door was turned to OPEN. He waved as she looked up and went directly into his office.

Sunday noon. Before he'd even left home, he'd thought about ditching the business casual and taking the boat out, but since Ben had bowed out of most of their business interests, the workload was burying him. So much for the joys of small business ownership. He pulled the invoice folder for the

Charleston gallery from the inbox.

He heard a knock on the door and looked up as Ben entered.

"Busy?"

"Always. Come in anyway and have a seat."

"Juli and I had brunch at the grill and then walked over. I wanted her to see the gallery. She's going to pick out a few things for the house."

Luke nodded, at a loss for words. He looked away. "She's here?"

He lowered his voice. "I left her with Maia. I hope they'll hit it off. From what Juli's said, I don't think she has many friends and no family at all. She's always worked too hard, no time for play. It's going to be different now."

Different for all of us, Luke amended, silently.

Ben touched the folder on the desk and spun it around. "Charleston? How's business down there?"

"Hal's a good manager, but he doesn't have what it takes to make bigger decisions. He had an opportunity for a nice show by a local artist, but passed on it because it would've meant a quick turnaround—quicker than he could handle."

"What about Jerri? From the Dunes Gallery? She was looking for a position with more responsibility. Hal isn't big on ego."

Luke leaned back in his chair and it squeaked. He felt more peaceful than he had in a while. He could almost pretend it was old times again. "Dunes got smart and offered her more." He glanced down. His running shoes were peeking out from under the desk like an invitation, a reminder. "There are other prospects. But it takes time and more time. I'm short on that."

His easy mood evaporated. He reached up and pressed his hands against the sides of his head, then worked his fingers against his temples. *Shake it off, Luke.*

"I know I left you hanging."

"No, you didn't. I procrastinated." He slid the folder back and flipped the top shut. "I'm glad Maia wasn't interested in leaving the sales floor. No one has her skill with the customers. I couldn't manage without her there. The rest I'll figure out."

"We already talked about this, but…"

Luke knew Ben wasn't referring to their current topic, the staffing problem. He shook his head, no. He didn't want to go there again. "Drop it."

Ben said, "I'm happy."

"Good. I'm glad."

"I mean it. I feel like I have a fresh start."

"Look, Ben, it's simple biology. You're not the first guy to fall for a pretty woman who's a few years younger. I just wish—"

"Wish what?"

"You could've taken her on a few dates. Gotten to know her—to know you could trust her. I get that you don't approve of people just moving in together, but marriage can be inconvenient in a real life kind of way when the whole thing goes south." Or, he thought, if she turns out to be a thief. He hadn't told Ben what he'd seen at the party in the coatroom. And now, while he might grouse about Ben's actions, it was too late to lay that kind of speculation on the table. He rapped his knuckles on the desk.

Pastor Herrin should've talked sense to Ben, not given his blessing. But who was closer to Ben than Luke? No one. And even he had failed to convince Ben to settle for something other than marriage. Ben had moved forward so uncharacteristically fast he'd caught them all by surprise. In the end, what did you say to a dying friend, a cousin who was more like a brother, who was determined to have his way?

You showed up at the wedding and kept the peace by keeping your mouth shut.

"Come on out and speak to her."

"I saw her yesterday at the wedding."

Ben sat in silence.

"I *spoke* to her yesterday." Exasperated, he threw in, "Alright, but Ben, don't push this too far—you might be mesmerized by a pair of dark blue eyes and good legs, but she's not my type. I prefer a woman who doesn't marry a stranger for money. A little integrity and self-respect would be a good start. You married her, she's nothing to me." Nothing but the woman who was going to break his cousin's heart. He froze at the hurt on Ben's face wishing he could call back the angry words.

Ben rose and rearranged his expression into a smile. "I understand, Luke. I know you better than you know yourself and you don't mean half of what you just said. You wait and see. I've always been a better judge of people than you. Am I right?"

Luke nodded. It sounded weird to say this about a guy, but Ben saw with his heart, not his head.

"For now, be kind. That's all I ask."

They stared at each other for a few, long seconds. Luke shrugged. He'd never had Ben's capacity for patience. His faith. Was Ben really asking so much of him?

"Okay. Lead the way."

Chapter Six

Juli couldn't stop sneaking a glance at the office door every few seconds. The fact of Ben and Luke sitting behind a closed door discussing who-knew-what shouldn't concern her, but it did.

She and Ben had a business arrangement. Personal issues with inconvenient relatives should make no difference.

"Juli?"

She jumped, clapping a hand to her chest. "Oh. Sorry. Guess my mind was elsewhere."

Maia laughed. "I didn't mean to scare you. Take a look around and I'll check on the customer who just came in."

She hadn't even heard the bell. Maia and the customer moved over to the counter. Juli strolled around checking out the pottery and the wood carvings. A four-foot-tall, carved white egret made her pause. The sleek feathering cut into the wood begged to be touched.

The bell rang again as the customer left.

"He's a beauty, isn't he?" Maia had returned to stand beside her. "A local artist, Paul Hemmings, carves wildlife from native woods."

"Do you think Ben would like him?" Juli looked more closely. "There's no price tag."

Maia giggled and put her arm around Juli's shoulders and gave her a quick squeeze. Juli was surprised by the impetuous embrace.

"Girl," Maia said, "listen to me. Ben didn't mention any price limits, did he? Just go with what you like. Plus, he gets a nice discount."

"Okay, I like it."

"I'll wrap it up."

Ben and Luke walked out of the office together. Ben had his hands in his pockets. Luke's arms were crossed. They were about the same height. Ben's coloring was warmer and softer.

"What did you choose?" Ben took the wrapped egret from Maia. "I recognize this. Excellent choice, Juli. I've admired this piece many times. Can't think why I didn't get it myself a long time ago." He leaned toward her and touched her arm.

Did he want to kiss her cheek? She thought so and she wouldn't have minded, but didn't encourage him. It didn't feel natural. Instead, she returned his look with eyes she hoped were glowing. If Ben wanted Luke to see he was happy with his decision, she'd be delighted to help.

When they returned to Ben's house, there was a car in the area beneath the house where the pilings created parking spaces. A car top carrier was still strapped to the roof, but items were sitting on the asphalt behind the car as if awaiting their turn to make the trip up the side stairs.

"The neighbors are here." Ben checked his watch. "They're a couple of hours early."

"The neighbors?"

"I meant the renters. Our neighbors for the week."

"They're early?" She'd found Ben's remark odd. Did he care about their arrival time?

"Check-in with the rental management company is usually four p.m., that's all I meant."

Juli had lived most of her life in apartments. Privacy and quiet were nice, but a little noise wouldn't bother her. In fact, neighbors might even be a handy distraction, something to talk about while she and Ben got their relationship sorted out.

Ben's footsteps dragged as they climbed the stairs up to the door. Juli carried the egret.

He napped. Ben tired easily, but otherwise he seemed good. Juli had trouble reconciling what he'd told her about his condition with how well he looked. She pulled the wrappings from the egret and placed the tall, carved bird beside the fireplace. Not satisfied, she tried it next to the front windows. She couldn't decide so she left the egret near the table where Ben had started a jigsaw puzzle.

She picked up the box lid and examined the picture. He'd chosen a puzzle of ocean and sand. The only focal point was a tiny buoy almost lost in the water. No wonder most of it was still undone.

The sofa was white rattan and the cushions were covered in a beachy, turquoise pattern, but with a couple of pillows properly arranged, it was comfy. Juli tucked her legs up beneath her and fidgeted with the pillows again. She tried to read, but the words failed to keep her attention.

After several pages, she gave up. Second day of marriage. It would take time to settle in. To feel at home.

By the time she felt at home, it would be over and she'd be gone. In the meantime, what would she do?

Bored people found distractions to amuse themselves and often made bad choices, wealthy or poor. One look at the magazines on the rack at the grocery store could tell you that.

Many times, stuck at the cash register during a lull, Juli had imagined what she could do with the free time, if she had extra money. Boredom, and the ability to do something with it, had seemed like a luxury.

She laid her head back against the sofa and closed her eyes. What had she dreamed of while waiting for customers? Hobbies? And something else—a GED.

It looked like she was going to have lots of free time now, for a while, anyway. It was up to her figure out how to fill it and stay out of trouble.

****

"I'd like to take a walk on the beach if you'll come along," she told Ben after they returned from supper at a local restaurant.

"Sure, let's walk into the sunset."

Emerald Isle lay east to west versus the usual eastern coastline that ran north-south.

A woman who looked like excellent grandma material was seated in a rocker on the renter's side of the porch. She had pouffy, graying hair and was swathed in yards of pink terrycloth.

They removed their sandals at the end of the crossover. "Can we leave our shoes here? I mean, other people use this walkway. Will the shoes be safe?"

"It's fine. Only the renters will be using our crosswalk." Ben continued, "The renters will assume we're also renters if you don't say otherwise. Not trying to hide anything—or I am, but if the toilet stops up or a light bulb needs changing they are less willing to leave a voicemail with the management company if they know they can knock on the owner's door. Don't put personal touches on the porch. Looks too permanent. Gives us away."

They struggled through the thick drifts of dry sand pushed up around the base of the steep stairs. When they reached firmer sand, she hooked her arm in his. He looked pleased.

"I thought you owned only the half you live in. You own both sides?"

"I used to rent out both sides and stayed here only a few weeks during the year. I moved here permanently last year. For most of the business interests I have, I've either sold or stepped out of active management."

"Businesses? Like what?"

A child ran along the edge of the water, dodging the reach of the waves. A woman with a white furry dog passed them, the dog straining the leash and setting the pace.

"Like the gallery. I was hands-on until recently. It has always been my favorite, my first love, business-wise. I turned my interest over to Luke. Over the years, we've partnered in a number of efforts."

The breeze blowing onshore gentled as the sun sank lower. The salt and seawater blended with the air and smelled of something elemental, perhaps of life itself. It touched a core within her. It steadied her.

"You and Luke—you two were, are, very close. I guess you've noticed he's not thrilled about me."

"Not you. It's me he's worried about. He's having trouble letting go."

"You mean, like letting you live your own life?"

"No, I mean accepting I'm leaving his—that I'm dying."

Her stomach clenched. The steadiness she'd felt now seemed suspect. "You seem so well. Tired some, but who doesn't get tired?"

"I have to deal in reality, Juli. You and I are enjoying each other's company—I am and I hope it's true for you—but we met nine days ago. You aren't emotionally invested. We don't have history. Remember you asked why I didn't have a friend move in for companionship and I said it would be cruel? Well, that's what I meant." He paused a few seconds before adding, "I'm not afraid of death. I know where I'm going when I die."

Reality. It wanted to hang over her head like a smog-filled cloud and she detested the awkwardness of the topic.

She ran a few steps ahead of him, then spun around to look him in the face. "In this world, none of us have more than the moment we're in. You're here. I'm here. Tomorrow can take care of itself."

He held out his hand. "Juli, come stand here beside me, please? I want you to see this."

She returned to stand beside him. He pointed ahead, to the west. "Look."

He touched her hand lightly and she clasped his in return. The sunset had been growing as they strolled up the beach and was now aflame, burning high as if the houses lining the western end of the beach had ignited. Dark wisps of clouds, like smoke, streamed up in the midst of the conflagration, and a high whitish-yellow glow backlit all of it. It looked like onrushing Armageddon.

She moved closer to him. Her cheek touched his shoulder and, after a brief hesitation, he put his arm around her back. When the sunset lost its strong color, they strolled back along the beach in the growing dark.

As they crossed the rough walkway back over the dunes, Ben said, "Luke asked us to join him for dinner later this week or next."

Sharing dinner with Luke wasn't likely to aid good digestion.

Juli looked up at the clouds and then back down at the few scattered shells on the crossover.

She kicked at them with her toe, wishing she could kick this decision somewhere down the road.

"Juli?"

"Fine. If you'd like to go, we will."

She reached out and took his hand back into her own. No one could ever say she didn't keep her side of a bargain.

Chapter Seven

In the morning, Juli was surprised to find Ben downstairs ahead of her. He was seated in the rattan swivel rocker. Thick cushions softened the seat and back. The chair swayed back and forth as he read. When she stepped down onto the landing, a stair tread creaked and he looked up.

"Good morning," he said.

"Hi." He was holding his Bible. The brown leather Book appeared here and there around the house. This was the first time she'd actually seen him holding it.

Out beyond the window, a cloud moved away from the sun and the early morning rays brightened and touched Ben, gilding the angles of his face and lighting his hair. It gave him an almost insubstantial air. Translucent. The unseen cloud slid back into place, taking the eerie image with it. Juli released the breath she'd been holding.

She said, "You look a little pale this morning."

"I woke early and couldn't get back to sleep." He closed his Bible and laid it on his lap.

"There's a package for you on the counter."

"Really?" She picked up the small box. "A cell phone? But I have one."

"You mentioned your plan didn't allow for many minutes."

"Sort of. It's prepaid."

"I put you on my plan. Unlimited minutes. I added texting, too. Everyone seems to be doing that now." He laughed. "Everyone, but me. Seriously, I hope you like the phone. If you don't, we'll go by the store and switch it. It's already charged."

She felt strange holding the box and didn't open it.

Texting? Everybody but her, too. She didn't have anyone to text. "Thanks. I'm sure it'll be fine. I'll look at it later."

He didn't answer. If he was disappointed that she didn't do some kind of happy dance, well, he needed to get over it 'cause she wasn't a happy dance kind of gal.

She clapped her hands together. "I'll get breakfast cooking. Do you have any preferences?"

"Nothing for me this morning."

"What? Well, we'll get it on your plate and then, if you still don't want it, no problem."

Ben pressed his lips together, but nodded.

She turned the radio on while she broke the eggs and cut up the chives. She was humming along with Jo Dee Messina singing, *"I'm alright,"* when Ben interrupted.

"You like to cook."

He had moved closer and was sitting on the stool at the counter.

"I don't have much practice. I don't know if I *like* to cook, but I like to cook in *this* kitchen. You have a nice kitchen." She tossed some cheese into the eggs.

He looked at the cabinets, then the ceiling, as if an answer was hanging there. He looked disturbed. Had she been heavy-handed? She took a step back from her insistence he should eat.

"I don't want to bully you into eating. Are you feeling sick this morning?"

"Not sick, just not hungry, but I've changed my mind. Those eggs look good. Maybe a small portion with a slice of toast."

"Toast coming up. With jam."

"Toast with strawberry jam."

"You got it."

She put the food on the plates and the plates on the table.

Ben gave her a funny look. "Is that a small portion?"

"Eat what you want. Don't worry about eating it all." She cut into her omelet. "Ben, there's something I want to ask you."

He perked up. "Go ahead."

"Last night you talked about going out to eat with Luke?"

"Yes. Is it a problem?"

"Where will we go? I hope it's casual."

"Casual's good."

"Glad to hear it because my wardrobe is limited."

Ben pointed to the large wooden key hanging on the wall by the side door. It had hooks with keys to the house, car and storage shed. "You have the checkbook to your new account. Take the car anytime you like. Buy new—whatever you want. Don't all women like to shop?"

She didn't answer. Shopping wasn't something she'd done recreationally.

Ben misunderstood her silence. "Was that sexist? I'm sorry."

"No, it's not that. I'm not much of a shopper."

"There are clothing stores on the island and in Morehead City, of course. Take Maia along if you want company. She'll be happy to go with you. In fact, I'll program the gallery number into your new phone. My number, too."

****

Foster family number one was kind, but had children of their own. She never belonged. It wasn't a bad spot to be in as a child, just awkward. Most everyone assumed she was being adopted but on their street and at school, the other kids in the family—the real children—made sure everyone knew Juli was just a foster kid. When foster dad number one's job required a move cross-country, the state found Juli a new home.

Foster family two hoped a child would save their marriage. After a few months, Juli was back with the state.

Family number three, an older husband and wife, taught her some valuable lessons such as never turn down a free meal, never miss an opportunity, and everything has a price.

But none of them taught her how to shop for a dinner dress or how to accessorize.

Juli felt as out of place in the fancier dress shops as she would've on a college campus.

Unless, of course, she was there working the cafeteria serving line.

She called Maia and said she'd bring the borrowed dress back to her.

"Nonsense," Maia said. "Keep it, but come over anyway and we'll do lunch."

When she arrived, Maia was tied up with a customer and other customers were roaming the store. Maia broke away momentarily.

"I'm so sorry. I'm here alone. My co-worker called in sick and Luke is out."

"Another time, then."

"Thanks for understanding."

Juli went to a few women's clothing stores. The clerks were better dressed than she was. Their smiles barely moved their lips and invariably they pointed her toward the clearance rack.

Suited her fine. Everything was pricey and most of it she wouldn't be caught dead in. Old lady clothes. She settled for a few clearance items so she'd have something dressier to wear, yet could still congratulate herself on getting a good deal.

On the way home, she stopped at a drugstore for toiletries. In the school supplies aisle, an inexpensive sketchbook and drawing pencils caught her eye.

A hobby would be good. After all, she'd been accustomed to working two and three jobs at a time. She even purchased a couple of paperbacks, the kind she liked that took her away to other places. From there, she dropped by the public library and picked up a pamphlet with information about getting a GED. Back in the car, she shoved the pamphlet into one of the books to make it less conspicuous.

This time, leaving Morehead City and driving across the bridge, back to Bogue Banks and to Emerald Isle, the familiar drive was welcoming.

Juli climbed the exterior stairs up to the side door and entered the house quietly in case Ben was napping. He wasn't.

Voices came from his study. The door was partway open and Luke was saying, "—idea what she's up to. Have you—?"

Ben interrupted. "I understand your concern, and Adela's, too, but you don't understand and I hope you're never in a position where you can."

Luke exited the room and saw her standing by the door. He paused for a heartbeat, then brushed past, opened the side door and was gone.

Was it ruder to say mean things about someone behind their back? Or to ignore the person like it didn't matter even when you knew they'd overheard? She relaxed her fists.

She didn't want Ben to know she'd heard. She opened the side door gently and then closed it again more loudly. "Ben, are you here?"

"Hello!" he called out.

"I saw Luke leaving."

He came out of the study. "He worries about me. About us. Worries we rushed into marriage."

"What did you tell him?"

"That we did." He laughed. "I told him I'm happy. I know it's only been a few days. Are you comfortable so far?" Ben began emptying the bags.

"I'm fine."

"Oh, hey, what's this?"

"A sketchbook and pencils. An eraser. Nothing much."

"I had no idea you were an artist."

"I'm not. I haven't drawn in years, but there's amazing scenery around here." She shrugged. "I might enjoy it again."

"You should consider a camera, too. Do you have one?"

"A camera? No."

"If you decide you want one, don't buy it without me. I know exactly what you need."

He wasn't really a husband or a companion, but more like a friend—a good friend with deep pockets.

Juli said, "Unload the refrigerator items. I've got a couple more bags to fetch. We need these groceries so I can cook. I don't have much cooking experience, but it isn't right to eat at restaurants every day." When he moved toward the side door, she waved him back. "No, I'll get the rest. Save your energy for our walk."

"I have something to tell you," Ben said. "I'll be going to church on Sunday."

She paused in the open doorway and waited. He'd come out of nowhere with the statement so she figured he was nervous about it.

"Yesterday, I didn't go because I wanted us to have the day together, but I do attend regularly. It wasn't something we discussed before and, while I'd like you to go with me, it's your choice."

"I don't have anything against going to church, but it's never been a part of my life."

Hope lit Ben's face, but this was a business arrangement. "I'll think about it."

He nodded. She was relieved her answer was enough for him. It was true she had no experience with religion and church, but it was also true she had no bias either way. She might try it out, but not right at first.

Juli threw him a bright smile. "I'll be right back with the last bags." She paused again.

"And tonight we have a date. You and I are going to figure out how to text."

****

Luke stewed all the way home oblivious to the bright blue sky of the Emerald Isle afternoon. The colorfully painted homes and low green shrubby growth contrasted with the well-manicured lawns. It was a scene he was familiar with having lived here most of his thirty-eight years, but he rarely failed to appreciate the gift anew—the gift of being able to live in this place and to have successful business enterprises with which to support himself and his employees.

Today, he gripped the steering wheel tight with one hand and the gear shift with the other. Not that there was need to shift on this empty road.

He was at war with himself, torn between removing himself from the equation altogether or trying to protect his cousin. Ben had sat at his desk with a grin on his face, a silly grin, a foolish one. Ben had always had a good heart, but he'd never been soft in the head—until now.

He acted like a teenage boy with his first crush.

It was a crush. Nothing more. It would burn itself out.

Luke turned onto his street. When he'd first heard about Ben's condition he'd been especially glad he lived nearby. Ben would need him and he wanted to be there for him.

A nearby buzz, then his cell started ringing. *The Flight of the Valkyries*. Adela's song.

Adela knew what was best, always, for everyone.

He couldn't speak to her—not in this mood. Wouldn't even touch the phone until it stopped ringing.

He pulled into the driveway and sat in the car.

Luke wanted to be happy for Ben, but what were the odds Ben and the girl just happened to be at the party, one a guest and one working, and they had met and Ben found her so attractive and engaging that in one evening he knew he wanted to marry her?

It was insane. It was too crazy by far to be by chance.

For Ben's sake, he wanted to believe, but seeing her aggravated him almost beyond bearing. Like the way she'd stood with one hand on her hip—a posture with attitude—when he left Ben's study. It hadn't looked like anger. More likely it was guilt.

She'd heard him. So what? He had genuine concerns and all of them were solely about what was best for Ben. It was his duty to do what he could for Ben's sake.

But it if were true and this was an honest relationship, then he had to be happy for Ben.

No, he'd seen her in the Hammond's coatroom with the young man who'd looked like trouble from the get-go. His manner was careless and underhanded, beginning with the scene in the dark hallway at the party.

Could it have been innocent? Maybe. But too many 'could've been innocent' events smelled like something bad. Then Juli had rushed into the room, spoke with the young man and began digging around in the wraps. Luke had stepped forward to ask them what they were doing when Juli left abruptly, nearly slamming into him with a backpack.

The owners of the missing items had reported their losses to the Hammonds and Marcel had engaged the police. Luke didn't know anything was missing until a few days later. He'd been all set to tell Marcel what he'd seen until he remembered Ben mentioning Juli, the girl he'd left the party with.

Ben not only mentioned her, he couldn't stop talking about her.

Luke remembered her, too. She was pretty, but when you lived at the beach pretty girls were everywhere.

He walked up the front steps and unlocked the door. He tossed his jacket onto the back of a chair and went into the kitchen for a drink. The housekeeper, Esther, had gotten the mail and left it on the counter.

Esther had also prepared lunch and left it in the fridge. She had some interesting ideas about what constituted a meal, but it was always tasty. Today he had chicken salad on whole wheat with bean sprouts.

He put the plate on the table and was struck by the empty seats. Just him. Always. Unless he entertained.

Ben saw the same.

Ben got comfort from his church family and faith, but when he came home, the chair on the other side of the table was empty. Luke had found comfort in church once upon a time. He looked through Ben's eyes and could almost see Juli sitting across from him at the table. It was an appealing vision. Not because it was Juli, of course, but for the companionship.

She was probably accustomed to using her looks to get her places. She looked young, but not soft. Wary.

Perhaps it was the quality of wariness that brought out the

protector in Ben. He had a strong need to fix people.

Maia had encouraged Ben. Maia believed everything Ben did or said was wonderful.

That was Maia.

Adela was different. The instant Ben told her he was planning to marry—*who?* A girl who'd been working a party—*when had they met?* Five days before—*and the marriage was going to take place when?* In three days—no wonder Adela had freaked. Even Ben stopped taking her calls.

He half-suspected Ben had arranged a hasty marriage to forestall Adela. For every good-natured bone in Ben's body, Adela was, well, the opposite. She wasn't mean, but her temper drove her way beyond good judgment.

Luke rinsed his plate and fork under the kitchen faucet and left them in the sink for Esther.

In the end, what it came down to was his duty to his cousin and friend. Even to Adela. It would be best for all concerned if he, Luke, confronted Juli privately and let her know he was watching.

Chapter Eight

When renters used their side of the front porch it was easy to hear them through the tall wooden divider. Today, all was quiet.

Juli had her sketchbook, pencils, sharpener and eraser laid out like surgical instruments on the white plastic patio table. While these instruments weren't as sharp, they were scary. She reminded herself it wasn't about success or failure.

This wasn't a commitment.

She started with the medium pencil and played around sketching shapes and shading them. Juli was bent over the sketchbook in her lap and didn't hear the renter coming up the crossover until she was at the house. Juli looked up. The woman stopped, first tugging at the hem of her knit tank top, then brushing sand from her arms.

"Hi, there. Name's Emily. Husband's James. I'm sure you've seen him coming and going."

"Nice to meet you, Emily. I'm Juli. My husband's name is Ben." She laid the sketchbook on the table and stood up.

Emily leaned against the railing. "Just you and your hubby? No kids?"

"Just us." She remembered Ben's warning not to let on they weren't renters.

"I hope my crew aren't bothering you."

"Not at all. We hardly hear anyone."

She laughed. "Lucky you. I could use some quiet. Are you an artist? What a great place to come and capture nature. I won't bother you. Creative people need their space, I know."

Children's voices rose, distantly from inside the house, perhaps in teasing or in anger. Hard to tell.

Emily said, "Better go. See you around."

"Bye." She waved.

Juli watched Emily vanish from view as she entered her side of the porch. She'd done it well, she thought. She'd maintained the image of being a renter without actually having to lie. The renter had taken her for a creative type.

She had to laugh. Two weeks ago this woman, or someone like her, could have been checking out at Juli's register, griping about the price of food, the lack of brands she wanted, the poor quality of the help, whatever. If Juli said the wrong thing, the woman might have complained to the store manager—all because she was in a mood, or mad at her husband or kids, and gotten Juli written up.

Here she saw Juli as a fellow vacationer who could afford one of these houses on the oceanfront for a week, and one stupid sketch pad and pencil made her a creative type who must have her *space* respected.

Footsteps sounded on the wooden steps coming up from the parking area below the house. That stairway led up to the crossover where it met the front porch. She leaned over the railing to see who was visiting and her good mood evaporated.

She and Luke were going to clash. She could feel it in her bones.

"Ben here?" He joined her on the porch.

Not even a hello? She bristled. "He's at his doctor's appointment."

"By himself?" After a long stare, Luke turned toward the beach and put his hands on the porch railing. His three-quarter profile was classic with a strong forehead and chin, and high cheekbones. Handsome. In a hard way.

The innate artist in her admired his bone structure and polished appearance. The worker in her scorned his long-fingered, uncalloused hands. His gray dress slacks and shiny shoes looked out of place in this world of sand and sea oats.

She asked, "What's your problem?"

He shrugged as if shaking off something unwelcome.

"Don't pretend. Spit it out."

"I wasn't going to pretend. I don't mind speaking the truth. Can you say the same?"

"What does that mean?"

He faced her, his demeanor proclaiming cool as he leaned back against the railing and let his hands hang from his pockets. He even slouched elegantly, but he couldn't hide the tension that started in his clenched jaws and seemed to run the length of his body.

He glanced past her to the sketchbook. She flipped the book over to a blank page.

"My concern is Ben. He met you two weeks ago and here you are. I don't know how you managed it, but I won't let you take advantage of him. He's vulnerable."

"He's a grown man and can make his own decisions."

"A grown man who found out barely a month ago he's terminally ill."

Ben hadn't actually told her when he'd found out. Had he married her on the rebound?

Instead of a bad love affair, he was rebounding from dreadful news? Yes.

"I can tell you I have no ulterior motives and this is a business arrangement—of Ben's design, not mine—but you won't believe me. It's me you have a problem with." She waited, but he didn't speak. "I'm not one of you. I'm a waitress. A cashier. A night-stocker. I never even graduated high school. But guess what? Ben likes me and wants to spend his last months with me."

"You think it's about pedigree? Well, I've got news for you. We aren't blue bloods either. But we're also not thieves."

Heat rushed up her chest, her neck, and flooded her face. "You need to explain that." She clenched her fists.

"Do I?" He pushed away from the railing and moved closer. "Maybe I should explain to the police instead. Items were taken from the coatroom. I saw you with your friend going through the jackets and coats."

She remembered Frankie being in the coatroom when she was about to leave. Other than that she had no idea what he was talking about. Had the act of getting her backpack looked suspicious to him? What an arrogant jerk.

"I don't owe you explanations. This arrangement is between Ben and me. When Ben is gone, you'll never see me again. In fact, you don't have to see me now. You can turn around and go. Leave me alone."

"Remember what I said. I won't let you hurt Ben—not without consequences."

Luke left. She went to the divider and squinted through a crack in the boards. No one there to overhear, thank goodness.

Did Frankie steal something from the Hammond's party? He'd looked uncomfortable when she entered the coatroom. Not just uncomfortable, sneaky. She didn't know if he'd stolen anything, but wouldn't be surprised if he had.

Ben came home. He smiled, but his eyes were sad.

"You look tired," Juli said.

"I am. I'm going up to take a nap."

"What did the doctor say?" Did she want to know? No, but she should ask.

He hung his keys on the wooden hanger by the door. "No change. He's happy with how I'm doing, considering. He says you're good medicine for me."

She responded with a polite laugh. Her presence wasn't some fast-acting miracle cure. Ben was hearing what he wanted to hear.

Should she mention Luke? It might seem odd to Ben if she didn't and Luke did.

"Luke dropped by while you were gone. He didn't stay."

"Oh?"

"Yeah." She'd told him so that was done. "I think I'll run some errands while you're resting?"

"Have fun."

Two weeks since she'd been proposed to, and a week married, Juli borrowed the car and drove back to Morehead

City. She didn't trust this deal with Ben. Whether too good to be true, or too weird to work, she didn't trust the arrangement to go as well as he thought it would.

In fact, given Luke's animosity and knowing the sentiment was likely shared by the rest of the family, Juli agreed the marriage and prenup had been the best way to ensure the contract terms would be honored—as Ben had suggested.

Regardless, when Ben was gone she'd need her own place again. Her apartment wasn't fancy, but it was affordable. It was locked up tight, too, all of the locks, including the ones she'd added to the door on the ground floor out of her own pocket.

The stairs were steep, narrow and dark, but she liked the second floor because it was harder to break into. Not impossible, just less convenient. She had nothing worth stealing, but her stuff still meant something to her. She'd only taken a few things to Ben's house, mostly clothing and personal items, half-expecting to bounce right back here instead of actually saying 'I do' with Ben.

"Hey, Jules."

Frankie had crept up quietly. It annoyed her. All the locks in the world didn't work if you were careless about using them.

"Hey, yourself."

Frankie lived on the first floor, front left unit.

"Where've you been?"

"With a friend. A sick friend. I'll be away for a while longer."

"Sam was rabid over how you left. I tried to smooth it over, but it didn't work. Maybe give him a little time." Frankie fidgeted, hands in pockets, hands on hips, leaning into the door frame, shifting his feet.

"I don't plan to work for Sammy again."

"I went by Singer's looking for you."

She grabbed her backpack from the corner and set it on the counter. "What did they say?"

"That you'd quit."

"I asked to take leave. They refused."

"Asked for leave so you could take care of a sick friend? Must be a really good friend?"

He leaned against the counter and toyed with one of the backpack straps.

Juli shrugged and dropped a bag of clothing next to the backpack.

Frankie moved in closer. "Seems kind of out of nowhere. You never mentioned a good friend like that. Must be one with money, huh?"

She wanted to say, 'not your business,' but knew it would only feed his curiosity, so she deflected with, "Did you steal anything during the Hammond's party?"

Frankie slapped the countertop. "Nice. Very nice. Why would you say that?"

"Just something I heard." She grabbed a paper bag from under the sink and popped it open. She threw in a sweat jacket and an old pair of sneakers. Morning jogs on the beach sounded like the height of luxury.

"From the police?"

"What?"

"You all but accused me of stealing."

"Oh. Well, you said you didn't." She grabbed the milk from the fridge. It was out of date so she poured it down the sink drain.

"Who asked? The police?"

"No."

"Who, then?"

"No one special. Someone mentioned something got stolen and I remembered how you acted when I came into the coatroom. If you didn't, you didn't. Forget it." She set the bag by stairs.

"I'll help you carry your stuff down." He reached for the backpack.

"No, thanks, I'm not leaving yet. I'd like to be alone. I have some things to take care of."

He cracked his knuckles. "Sure. No problem. I'll carry a

load down on my way out."

"No, thanks. I can handle it."

Frankie was dissatisfied and pouted. "What? Now, I'm a thief? I'm not good enough to touch your bags?" He nudged his shoe against one of the bags on the floor.

"Not what I said, Frankie." She wouldn't miss him. On the other hand he would likely still be here when she returned. No need to make enemies. "I appreciate the offer, Frankie, but no thanks. I'll keep in touch."

****

Ben was holding a piece of paper when she entered the room. In a low, serious voice, he asked, "Is there something you want to tell me?"

Guilt flared. What was it? Frankie? Keeping her apartment? Her stomach twisted. Was their deal over already?

"What do you mean?"

Ben waved the GED pamphlet. "Is this yours?"

The flush sweeping her body felt like it could've rivaled the apocalyptic sunset.

"It is yours, isn't it?" He laid the pamphlet on the counter next to the books she'd purchased. He rushed to her and touched her arms. "You aren't going to faint are you? Do you need to sit down? I was teasing. I'm sorry; I didn't mean to upset you."

She breathed deeply. "It's embarrassing."

He pulled her down onto the sofa. "Why are you embarrassed? I don't know how it happened that you didn't get a high school diploma, but I can help."

"No."

"I want to help you. Do you need to take classes? How does it work?"

"I can take classes or study on my own and then I take a test."

"The pamphlet says you can study online."

"I haven't really used computers. I don't have one and I'm not..."

"Come with me." He grabbed her hand, excited. "This

way."

Like an eager kid, he led her to his study and insisted she sit at his desk.

"Watch," he said.

That was the first of the lessons. It became part of their routine.

Ben enjoyed giving—giving to people in general, but especially giving to her.

Briefly, she was annoyed. Juli didn't want to be anyone's project, but then she realized it wasn't about her wants. This was what Ben needed to do for Ben. Good deeds. Something to leave behind.

If he needed a beneficiary of his good works or someone to be his project, then she could receive it gracefully. The benefit to her was unmistakable and satisfying to him.

****

During their first two weeks of marriage they became more comfortable with each other.

She marveled Ben had picked them as a good match so quickly and she hoped it would last. She wasn't drawn to him physically, but neither was she repelled. They touched and held hands. One hand over another, helping to guide a mouse, could feel intimate, and it did—friend intimate. A close friend.

Once or twice she gave Ben an opening to discuss his illness more fully, but he turned away as if not recognizing her interest. She was torn about pressing the issue. She was afraid he'd invite her to go with him to the doctor's office. Riding with him, even sitting in the waiting room while he met with his doctor, was okay, but as his wife, they might expect her to go with him to the examination room—way beyond the level of intimacy she expected to share in a platonic relationship.

But it was only the second week.

Almost every evening they walked toward the sunset, usually hand in hand. People nodded and smiled at them. Juli liked that and the feel of his hand in hers, or his arm around her shoulders, gave her a strange sort of satisfaction.

Most nights, Ben went to bed early and her restlessness returned. Juli would stand at the porch rail like a figurehead on the prow of a ship, but restless, watching the night. She was in her twenties. There was life out there in the world. Now that she had the luxury of rest and free time, she was lonely, especially in the quiet of the evening.

In Emerald Isle proper there was little night life to speak of, certainly none anywhere near this strip of sand where she and Ben lived. When the sun went down, and the families came in from their beach activities, all was peaceful. She was alone and adrift, or would've been adrift, except she was anchored here, moored for the time being at *Sea Green Glory*. She consoled herself that her feelings were natural given the circumstances, but she acknowledged they were also ungrateful.

It was important to remember this was business, a contractual arrangement, despite the wedding ceremony. Almost all of the benefits in this bargain fell to her. In good faith, she could do better by Ben.

In fact, she cared about Ben, but within limits. And the limit was friendship.

Juli vowed to withhold deep emotions from their relationship. She would do her best to make this a worthwhile deal for both of them, but to allow too deep an attachment to grow for a man who was soon to die, would be foolish.

Chapter Nine

Juli put off dinner at Luke's as long as she could. Finally, Ben insisted.

"I want you to get to know each other better."

She resolved to make the best of it. "Where are we going?"

"He invited us to his home."

"We were going to a restaurant."

"He changed his mind."

She kept her back turned, pretending to look out of the window, so he wouldn't see her face.

"What should I wear?"

Ben seemed to seriously consider her question. "You look wonderful in everything."

She huffed. "Please."

"Leave your hair long. I like it. If you don't mind, that is."

Juli remembered his kind words while dressing to go. She was foolish to be so apprehensive. It was only dinner.

She reached up and touched her hair, self-conscious, but smiling. Maia had convinced her to get it trimmed and add highlights. It still hung below her shoulders, but was much more flattering.

Juli wore a lightweight skirt with a scarf-like pattern and a solid red knit top, her clearance items. She checked herself in the mirror and was happy with the purchases. She tossed her head, pleased with how her new haircut fell back into place, cascading neatly over her shoulders. Juli agreed with Ben—she liked her new look.

Luke lived on the sound side of the island.

Ben drove. He asked, "Are you nervous?"

Juli stopped her fingers mid-tap and stretched them out on

the arm rest. "Yes."

"It'll be fine. Luke is a great guy. We've been close all of our lives."

The late afternoon light picked out the silver in Ben's hair. She hadn't noticed it before.

"You're both bachelors?" She laughed. "Or were, I guess before you and I got married."

"I'll tell you about my wife Deb sometime. We were college sweethearts and our marriage was over almost before it began. I had a hard time of it when she died."

"She died? I'm sorry, I assumed divorce."

"That's often what it is. People live longer; marriages last shorter."

"It happens."

"Luke divorced a long time ago. It was difficult at the time, but he's moved on. No one likes divorce. It's hard on everyone." He was quiet for a moment. "Given time and purpose, people are resilient. It's faith that gets us through the bad times."

Juli felt a flip remark coming on and she curbed it. Instead, she asked, "What about Luke? Faith didn't work for him?"

Ben sighed. "Luke fell away. When he needed faith in God and his church community the most, he turned his back." He shook his head. "But it's still in him, that seed of faith, and one day he'll understand it." Ben groaned. "*And*, I'm ashamed to say this is Luke's business. I shouldn't be talking about him like this."

"No worries. I won't say anything."

The wide concrete drive curved around attractive landscaping. The house was tan-colored brick with red trim. It was low and wide, seeming to sprawl across the top of a rise of land. The ground sloped down to Bogue Sound on the backside and Juli suspected the house was much larger than it appeared from the front.

They parked in the circular drive near the front door and near a wine-colored Toyota. Ben stared at the car.

"Whose car is it? Luke's?"

"No, it's probably a rental. My guess is Adela's here." Ben didn't move to get out.

"Adela? Your sister? From Ohio, right?"

"My older sister. Only sister, I mean."

"You look concerned, Ben."

"She can be difficult." He turned to face Juli. "But it's because she cares so much. It's hard for her that I'm…ill."

"Ben, I promise I'll be nice. No matter what."

"She'll love you once she gets to know you."

If Luke was anything to go by, and Adela was even more 'caring,' then Juli doubted Adela would ever like her. Juli did, however, expect courtesy and she knew how to hold her tongue and temper when she had to, no matter how provoked. Hadn't she done that in every job she'd ever held?

"Luke probably thought it would be easier for us all to get to know each other in a private setting rather than a restaurant."

She didn't hear conviction in Ben's voice.

They stood on the front porch and she brushed a speck of something from Ben's shirt sleeve. He knocked lightly on the door. It swung open as if someone had been standing just on the other side.

Adela had short brown hair. Her body was thick through the middle, but she was dressed smartly, casually. Juli was certain the garments came with a price tag that would've made her faint dead away.

Adela extended her hand. "You must be Juli."

Shaking Adela's hand was like gripping a block of jagged ice. Juli nodded, but the cordial smile on her face stiffened. Adela pretended to be nice and Juli hoped there was some truth behind it because she wanted this to work, but she saw no friendliness in Adela's eyes or posture.

Adela hugged Ben and looked teary.

"Hey, sis, I'm good, okay? Let's enjoy our evening."

She dropped her arms, releasing him, and he moved to Juli's side. He placed his hand on Juli's back. "I want to show you Luke's view. It's the best thing about this house."

Big sister's eyes turned hard. "Go ahead. I'll help Luke."

The aromas coming from the kitchen almost made up for the chilly reception, but Juli didn't relish sharing a meal in this company.

They stopped in the kitchen doorway. Luke was sprinkling something on a roast and returning it to the oven.

"It smells wonderful," Ben said.

Luke closed the oven door and stood, removing his oven mitt. He smiled at Ben. Juli was ready to give him a bright smile, but he conspicuously avoided looking at her. He said, "London Broil. Esther's recipe with her secret marinade. She got it started. I'm merely the finisher."

"I'm going to give Juli a tour. Call us if you need help."

Ben guided her to a railing that overlooked part of a room below, with two-story floor-to-ceiling windows. The green of the back lawn sloping down to the water, was tipped with gold from the late day sun. The water picked up the light and seemed to pass it along from wavelet to wavelet, shimmering. Down slope to the left, was a dock and boathouse.

In the room immediately below them, the furnishings were all burnished leather and deeply grained wood.

"It's beautiful," she told Ben. And it was, but it also looked lonely. Maybe he entertained a lot. For all she knew, he had lots of girlfriends.

They walked out to the screened porch and beyond it to the deck. It was peaceful—almost like a time out—a chance to prepare herself for what was to come.

"Ben?" She put her arm through his, their elbows on the rail as they leaned forward together. She detected tension. But these were people who loved Ben, no matter what they thought of her. She should be nervous, not him. And she was. Definitely.

"Yes?" He clasped her hand in his.

"We're good together, aren't we? You don't regret…"

"Don't worry, Juli. It'll be fine." He reached up and touched her hair. He ran his fingers down its length, smoothing the tresses over her shoulder until his hand reached her back. He leaned toward her and placed a tender kiss on her cheek.

Their first kiss. A friend's kiss, except for the insistent pressure on her back.

Instinctively, she moved closer and his arm tightened.

Adela cleared her throat. Juli turned, startled, to see her behind them.

"Dinner's ready. Come to the table."

Adela gazed at her with her lips pursed into a tortured-looking fake smile. Without a word, they followed Ben's sister back inside the house.

Ben held her chair as she sat. Juli smoothed her skirt before taking the cloth napkin from beside the plate. She situated the napkin in her lap and straightened the forks beside her plate, but there was a limit to the mechanics she could use to hide her fear before finally, she had to look up and risk the unfriendly faces.

Trapped at the table and feeling inappropriate—she wanted to climb out of her skin and be anywhere but here. She should've purchased the expensive silk blouse she'd fingered at the boutique, instead of this knit top. The skirt she'd bought was too cheaply made. No wonder it had been on clearance.

She tried to pretend she was as good as them, but it was difficult with Adela seated directly opposite her at the table.

Adela helped herself to the London Broil, then passed the dish.

"Luke is more like a brother to us than a cousin. We're all family here, Juli. Simple people. Did Ben tell you we grew up in the same neighborhood as Luke? When we lost our parents— we were already adults at the time—but when we lost our parents, we still had Aunt Susannah and Uncle Matt, Luke's parents. Have you met them? No, I suppose not."

She paused in buttering her roll and nodded toward Luke and then Ben. "We're proud of our family's accomplishments. Did you know both of them were honor graduates at Duke? That was before they pursued advanced degrees and went on to open a number of businesses."

Ben said, "Adela. Please. Enough. Let's enjoy our meal."

"We *are* enjoying this delicious meal and I know Juli will agree you are very special."

Juli nodded, but her smile felt as false as Adela's good manners.

"They are both very successful businessmen." Adela paused again. With her knife held dramatically aloft, she said, "Where did you go to school, Juli?"

Juli was tempted to lie, but she couldn't because Luke and Ben knew the truth. She looked at Ben beside her, then at Luke across the table. She could tell Luke was angry by the set of his mouth. She took a cleansing breath and said, "Nowhere special."

"Oh. Well, I understand you work in a market? Interesting work. And for a caterer?"

Juli watched Ben. He looked tired—as if he'd checked out. Luke watched him, too, and when Ben's shoulders sagged, Luke interrupted.

"Juli is an artist, Adela. Isn't that so, Ben?"

Ben perked up. "She is."

Adela opened her mouth to reply and Ben said kindly, but firmly, "Enough. If you want to get to know her better, invite her to lunch." He leaned toward Juli with an apologetic laugh. "I guess I'm not the only Bradshaw who interrogates over a good meal."

Juli laughed with him, but it was forced. Their amusement was surface only, just enough to cover the damage and let them escape with some dignity. She noticed Luke seemed more relaxed now, but she couldn't begin to read his face and didn't care to try. This wasn't even about her. This was a battle for possession of Ben, and Adela had the finesse of an out-of-control sledgehammer.

"Ben, I have a headache. Do you mind?"

Adela spoke, "There's still dessert."

Luke said, "I can wrap it up for you to take home."

They left with a few quick goodbyes. It was such a short

distance home neither of them spoke, digesting both meal and the dinner conversation in silence. The silence continued up the stairs. Ben preceded her into the house, but Juli walked past him and straight out the front door onto the porch and into the night.

Air. She needed air.

Juli was partway down the crossover, half-running by the light of the moon, before she heard Ben calling her name. The ocean sounded louder at night was less noise to compete. She continued for a few steps more, pretending she hadn't heard him over the crashing surf.

She put her hand on the rail. The wood was damp with sea spray and grainy with sand. She held the rail to steady herself and waited for Ben.

"Juli, what's wrong? Why are you out here?"

She shook her head, the jumbled thoughts and emotions stayed topsy-turvy and senseless.

"We missed our sunset walk."

Ben frowned and leaned closer. "What? Our walk?"

She raised her voice, "Our walk, Ben. We missed our walk."

He put his arms around her. He pulled her close. She rested her face against his shoulder and shivered. How could she explain they should never have gone to Luke's? That Ben should've stopped Adela? Once it was gone, you couldn't get it back—whether it was lost innocence, special moments, or peace of mind.

"I don't understand. I'm sorry we missed our walk, but there'll be more." He relaxed his hug and put his hand beneath her chin and lifted her face. "Come with me."

He pulled her to the end of the crossover and led her down the steps. When they reached the deep, dry sand her shoes bogged down and she stumbled. He stopped to kick off his shoes and she did the same. Juli was barely steady again when he tugged her hand and led her forward, near to where the tide was going out and the sand was wet and firm.

He kept hold of her hand, but slid his other arm around her

back, near her waist, and pulled her close.

"What—?"

"Shhh. Be still. Close your eyes and listen."

He shut his eyes, head up and listening. After a moment of uncertainty, she did the same.

Ben whispered, "Do you hear it?"

"What?" She felt the beat of his heart against her chest, echoing her own.

"The ocean. Do you hear its pulse?"

Juli closed her eyes again. "Yes," she breathed. "I do."

He moved, ever so slightly, one leg sliding outward and forward, then the other. She followed his lead and they began to move slowly to the timing of the waves. Juli folded her body into his and they moved in unison, round and round in slow and graceful rhythm.

It would never be performed in a ballroom—this dance belonged to the ocean, the sand and the moon, temporarily lent to a starlit couple in need of a little magic.

Chapter Ten

Ben slept late the next morning. Juli was out early hoping to greet the sunrise and to watch the smooth, controlled flight of pelicans skimming the waves in search of breakfast. The pelicans were, indeed, feeding, but no sun broke through the cloud cover. As darker, lower clouds pushed onshore, she turned back. She was almost to their crossover when she saw Frankie leaning against the steps.

Despite herself, her stride faltered. What was he doing here? How did he find her? She'd never been afraid of Frankie, but his unexpected appearance promised nothing good.

No good at all.

Frankie's wrinkled khaki shorts hung low on his hips. His loose-fitting, untucked polo shirt was stretched out of shape giving him a slovenly look. As she approached, he pushed away from the post he'd been leaning against. Juli tried to smooth the suspicion from her face.

"Surprise, surprise," she said.

"Ouch. I was sure you'd be impressed I found you."

"It's eight a.m. A little early to drop by."

"You've been gone a month. Like, vanished. I was worried. I had a friend check the license plate."

Ben's car, of course. "And now you're here, unannounced."

"Would your friend have minded if I'd called and asked for you? Or how about if I'd just shown up and knocked on the door? Not knowing what you've got going here, well, I didn't want to screw it up."

"The only thing going on here is a friend doing a favor for a friend. That's all."

"Cool. Glad to hear it. You never had the face for larceny. It shows everything you're thinking. So, are you going to invite me in?"

"What?"

"Invite me in. I'm housebroken. Your friend won't mind if you have another friend, right?"

Frankie was definitely not getting an invite into the *Glory*. Better to be blunt.

"Go home, Frankie. This has nothing to do with you."

"That's harsh, Jules. You sure this is how you want it? These people aren't your friends."

Frankie wasn't visiting because they were buddies. Frankie was fishing to see what he might catch. Juli took the next logical step on the rude road.

"You and I are neighbors who do favors for each other once in a while. No more than that. If you want to discuss it, we can talk when I come back to the apartment."

She moved closer to him. "Am I wrong? If you were here because you're worried about me, then it might be different, but that's not it, not at all. You think I have some kind of scam going on here and you want a piece of it. You couldn't be more wrong, Frankie. Plain wrong. Go away and let me help my friend."

"Sure." He tugged at his shirt and swaggered a few steps. "Whatever you say." He stopped and turned back. "Might be a time where you need me as a friend again." He spit on the sand. "I wasn't alone in that coatroom, Jules. You were there, too. Remember that."

Frankie sauntered up the beach away from Juli and the *Glory*. Had he come from up the beach?

He wouldn't have gone to the house first. He wouldn't risk messing up whatever dishonest game he thought she was perpetrating—not as long as he had a ghost of a hope of profiting, too. A few houses further up, he turned right and used someone else's crossover to leave the beach.

Uneasy in her heart, she turned toward the house. Luke

stood on the porch, looking her way.

What was he doing here? Had Ben gotten sick? Had he called Luke because she wasn't there to help him?

Juli ran the length of the crossover. "What's up? Is he sick?"

Luke was icy. "Ben left some medication over at the house last night. I brought it by. Was that the man from the party? The one you were with inside the coatroom?"

"Coatroom. What's the deal with the coatroom? I was there long enough to get my backpack. That's it. End of story. Is Ben up?"

She didn't wait for his answer, but brushed past on her way to the door. He grabbed her arm and stopped her dead.

He spoke in a low voice, "Don't bring him around here. Tell your boyfriend to stay away. You owe Ben that. If you think I don't mean it, test me. I'll give you up to the police in a heartbeat and you can explain it to them. Ben will be disappointed, but I'll do it if I have to."

He was holding her arm and his face was in her face. The anger in her body surged into the arm not being held, and perhaps some of the hurt from the evening before was still simmering inside. She swung with all her might. Her open palm hit his face with as much force as she could put into it. He released her arm like a hot potato, shock on his fine, high cheekbones, one of which was now bright red.

Juli's voice shook. "Don't talk to me like that, don't threaten me and never manhandle me. I suppose I should thank you for a lovely dinner yesterday. Consider yourself thanked."

She pushed him aside as she swept past and into the house.

No one was in the living room. "Ben?" She saw the prescription bottle on the counter and picked it up. It was pain medication. "Ben?" She was halfway up the stairs before he answered.

"I'm up here." He descended to the landing. "What's up?"

Sweet relief. "Luke brought your medication. You left it at his house."

"I know. He was upstairs. Is he still around?"

"I think he's gone now." He'd *better* be gone.

"Do you mind if we have a quiet day? Just stay in?"

"Good idea. It looks a little rainy, anyway."

Juli cooked breakfast and was pleasantly surprised at her growing skill. Ben said he wasn't hungry, yet again, but after a few listless bites, he ate. First, she thought, he ate to please her and then because he enjoyed the food.

Ben settled at the table by the front window with his cup of coffee. Jigsaw puzzle pieces were scattered across the tabletop. He picked them up, piece by piece, but did nothing except to put them down again. Juli wasn't in the mood to work a puzzle either. She needed to work off the negative energy from the early morning.

She pulled out the sketchbook and pencils from a drawer in the entertainment center.

"Don't say no," she said.

"Oh—" he groaned.

"You don't have to do anything but sit. You wouldn't want to stifle an artist, would you?"

He leaned forward with his elbows on the table and stared out the window. Juli sat across from him and after a few false starts she buckled down and kept going. She lost track of time.

"Can I see?"

Pencil stopped, suspended over the sketchbook. "See?"

"Yes, *see*." He laughed. "You look surprised. What did you expect?"

He rose and walked to where she was sitting. Juli held the sketchbook close to her, but not touching because she didn't want to smear the graphite.

"No, it's not ready."

"Hand it over, lady."

"Yikes." She tore the page from the spiral binding and gave it to him.

Ben held the edges of the paper delicately to avoid marring the surface, as if the graphite markings and shadings were more than they were. Juli appreciated the care he was showing, but was also embarrassed by it. The seconds ticked by as he studied the rough portrait. She was about to yank it back when he shook his head sadly.

"Is my nose really this big? And this ear—"

She jumped up and moved toward him, but his sudden grin stopped her. He pulled the drawing away, safely out of reach.

"I'm teasing. It's wonderful. Makes me look…maybe intelligent, possibly verging on good looking?" He grinned broadly. "Can I have it?"

"Oh, please. Give me a break. I've got a long way to go and a lot of practicing to do before I draw something worth keeping, if I ever do produce something worthwhile. There's no need to say those things, not for *my* ego."

His soft brown eyes were suddenly earnest. "I *am* serious. Is it brilliant? Probably not, not yet, but you have a style that shows through. You'll get better, true, but there's often beauty in the untutored hand—a flair that can be lost if you learn to follow convention too closely."

"Flair? Style? Please." She waived her hand dismissing his foolishness, yet inside she had a little glow. She didn't totally get what he was saying, and wasn't convinced he wasn't mocking her, but that hadn't seemed to be his style. She decided to take his words at face value, but with reserve, so she wouldn't look like an idiot if he *was* having fun at her expense. "You can keep it if you promise not to show it to anyone else."

Ben walked over to where Juli sat. He took her hand and turned it over, palm side upward, displaying the dark smudges picked up from the paper while drawing.

"The mark of an artist," he said.

He turned her hand again and lifted it to his lips and lightly kissed it. He released her and stepped away. She sat, stunned into silence, as he carried the drawing to his office and returned empty-handed.

"Safely tucked away," he said. "In case you change your mind."

She'd been thinking of doing exactly that before he kissed her hand. Instead, she said, "I'll be able to do a better one for you soon, I hope."

****

On the first day of June, Juli found a card waiting for her on the breakfast table. An anniversary card. A first anniversary card.

Humph. For the first month? It hadn't occurred to her to get a card for Ben. It was only a month, after all. Despite their growing friendship, this was a business arrangement, wasn't it?

Someone knocked on the side door. Juli put the card down and went to answer it.

The delivery man had an armful of red roses.

"Ben," she muttered under her breath.

"Pardon, ma'am?"

She signed for the delivery. "Thanks."

"Must be a special day."

"Must be."

She shut the door with her hip and set the vase of flowers on the table. Ben was standing at the foot of the stairs.

"I hope you like roses."

"Ben." She waved her arms as if to say 'why?'

"Do you?"

"Do I what?"

"Like roses."

"I like roses, but this is extravagant and—"

"It's a surprise."

"I wish you'd said something about gifts. I didn't even get you a card."

"I don't need a card. I wanted you to be surprised. I want to see you smile."

How could she not? She gave him the smile he wanted and then, impulsively, blew him a kiss.

****

It was foolish to think Frankie would go away and stay gone. Like a hyena roaming the African bush, Frankie scented an opportunity and his greed was so strong it was beyond his ability to deny it free reign. As Ben and Juli enjoyed their sunset walk, she gripped his hand fiercely.

He looked at her. "Is something wrong?"

"No, sorry. Stronger than I knew." She refused to look toward the crossover where Frankie was standing lest Ben notice and become curious. Her attention might also encourage Frankie to think he had more power than he did. He might do something reckless or stupid.

They were more vulnerable now. Frankie knew who Ben was—could recognize him.

She'd become protective of Ben, at least where Frankie was concerned.

It was time for her to take matters into her own hands, to face down Frankie and put quits to this. For the life of her, she couldn't imagine what leverage she'd use against him, but she'd think of something.

Frankie would be most easily found at the apartment house and, while there, she could give notice. She'd still need somewhere to live when the marriage ended, but there were other, better places, with new neighbors.

She drove into Morehead City the next morning while Ben was napping. Juli sat in the car outside of the apartment house, parked in the deep shade of a low branching tree, camouflaged, necessary or not. It was quiet on the street. No one was in sight and traffic was light.

Juli hoped to surprise him. Frankie didn't work mornings. He wasn't a morning kind of guy. His sunrise beach appearance was an aberration. He preferred evening work and, like Juli, picked up work where he could get it. In the foyer, the musty smell of the old house was familiar.

She liked it. It said history to her. A past with progression. Continuity? Still standing despite the blows life handed out.

Frankie's apartment was on the ground floor and shared the front door entrance with two other apartments. His was a studio apartment with a kitchenette.

Juli was nervous, surprised to find her hands damp and a low-level trembling throughout her body. She needed to get this over with. She knocked, then again, more loudly. When he didn't answer, she was disappointed and relieved, both at the same time. No matter how hard she tried to pump up her courage, she knew Frankie wouldn't be intimidated by her.

So, no Frankie, but at least her hands were steady again. She went down the hall and knocked on Mrs. White's door. It was usually a wait. Juli leaned back against the wall while she got into the right state of mind. Mrs. White was a nice lady, no question, but Juli wasn't comfortable around her roomies.

After a few minutes, a high voice called out, "Who is it?"

Juli stood with her face in front of the peephole. "Juli Cooke. From upstairs."

The wood paneled door swung open. "Well, hello, dear. Come in." She preceded Juli into the living room and motioned to the sofa. "Sit, dear, and I'll get us some tea."

Mrs. White's monster cat reclined on the back of the sofa. He would have looked no different on a rock ledge protecting his territory. Juli approached the sofa and he meowed. She went to the chair instead. As soon as her bottom hit the seat, Buster came in, drooling and slavering, butting the chair with his head. He liked to have his ears scratched.

Juli tried to push him away, saying in a low voice, "No, Buster, no." She broke off, embarrassed, as Mrs. White returned.

"Oh, you bad boy. Shoo, now." She handed Juli the glass of tea. "He's been such a naughty boy and I told him to stay in the bedroom. He's blind now. Old like me. Makes him cranky and needy."

"Poor Buster. I didn't know." She was relieved when Buster's limp, but still swinging tail vanished around the corner.

Mrs. White leaned her cane against the arm of the sofa and lowered herself onto the seat cushion.

"It comes to us all, if we live long enough, but I'm not complaining. I'm better off than most."

"How's your arthritis?"

She held up her hands. The reddened knuckles were enlarged and the fingers were crooked.

"About the same. You know, I try all sorts of things—anything that makes any kind of sense to try, but no help."

Monster cat slinked down the back of the couch and moved onto Mrs. White's lap. She dug her fingers into his fur and he purred like a freight train. He fixed his green eyes on Juli. Was it a dare? A taunt?

He's a cat, Juli.

"How is it going with your friend? How is he? Is he better now?"

Buster had maneuvered back into the living room and settled himself on top of Mrs. White's feet.

"Well, actually, that's what I wanted to talk to you about." She took a sip of tea. "He's about the same and I expect to stay away much longer."

Mrs. White laid one finger alongside her cheek and asked, "What else, dear?"

Juli tilted her head to the side, wondering. She hadn't planned to tell her about the marriage.

"Like what?"

The old woman's eyes twinkled. She reached over and grabbed a book from the end table. Her lap shifted with the movement and monster cat yowled.

"Oh, hush."

She opened the book and pulled out a slip of paper. Juli stared. A newspaper clipping.

Mrs. White extended her hand and Juli walked the few steps over to receive it.

"It was in the paper?"

"You're a married lady now. No photo, though. You should've had a photo and a longer write-up, dear." She leaned forward, catching monster cat in a vise between lap and bosom. "No need to hide it. Not from me."

"Hide what?"

"Well, the usual reason for a hasty marriage."

"Oh. No, it's nothing like that." She was aghast. "I was helping my friend and we—well, we decided it would be more convenient to marry."

How silly did that sound? Likely, Mrs. White agreed because she looked happily unconvinced.

"Well, if you say so, dear. You'll want to give up your apartment. I shall be sorry to lose you, both as a neighbor and a tenant."

"I'd like to keep it another month to give me time to clear it and clean it."

"You're a thoughtful girl. I'll miss you. Frankie said you'd be moving, although he didn't mention a wedding."

"He told you I'd be moving?"

"He wanted a look at the apartment. I said to him, 'now, you know I can't climb those stairs.' And he said, 'no need, Mrs. W.'—that's what he calls me—'no need, loan me the keys for a few minutes and I'll take a look myself.'"

"He's seen my apartment many times."

"Well, and that's what I told him. I wouldn't let someone go in there without your permission and unattended even if he is a friend of yours. Not the way to run a house."

"I appreciate you telling him no. I'm surprised he asked."

"That's because you're young, dear. People ask all sorts of strange things." She picked up monster cat and dropped him to the floor. He hit Buster on the way down and rolled to a stop. No one seemed perturbed, least of all Buster. She shook her feet and the dog dislodged himself.

"I don't know how I ended up with this menagerie. Sometimes things fall into your life and without you expecting it, they stick."

"May I keep the clipping?"

"Certainly, dear. Thirty days, is it?"

"Yes, ma'am."

"I'll mark it on my calendar. I'll call you if someone wants to see it, if you wouldn't mind meeting them here to show it for me?"

"I'm happy to. Let me know when you get some interest."

"Perhaps you could even bring your young man by to meet this old woman?"

"I'll see what I can do." She hugged Mrs. White and left. She didn't try Frankie's door again, but went straight out the front and around to her entrance at the back. She paused outside the door to read the clipping. It was small, only about an inch of text. It gave their names and the date of their marriage. *Cooke-Bradshaw Nuptials*. A ceremony on the beach, it said. The header was almost bigger than the article. She tucked it carefully into her wallet.

Who else had seen it? Maybe some of her old co-workers at Singers? Co-workers from other jobs, too, if they read newspapers, and if they remembered her name. No one would care.

Why did Frankie want to get into her apartment? Curiosity? Information?

In the pit of her stomach, she knew he wasn't done. He'd be back.

Today's effort to discourage him had been futile, but what could she do?

Her old apartment smelled stale. With no one around to open a window or sweep the floor, her two rooms appeared forgotten, almost lost in time. It looked unwanted and it was. The chipped vinyl and scarred Formica counter were leftovers from the past, all but forgotten. Like she wanted her past to be— forgotten. The vehemence of the feeling surprised her.

She looked through the cupboards and the drawers. The apartment was rented furnished. A few boxes—or trash bags— would take care of her belongings. She grabbed some shirts, then dropped them onto the bed. She'd come back with those bags and give all this to Goodwill or some other charity.

Leaving this time felt like goodbye.

As soon as she returned to the *Glory*, she knew. She smelled the cheap scent Frankie sometimes wore. He'd been in the house and he might as well have left his calling card on the kitchen table. A faint trail of sand marred the carpet near the front door. She stood immobile. Shocked.

"Ben?" She spoke softly, then more loudly, she called out, "Ben?"

No answer. She hadn't expected one. Ben had been napping when she left, but Luke was supposed to have picked Ben up soon after. They shouldn't be back yet.

Juli searched through the house, eyes sharp for signs of where Frankie had wandered and what he'd been up to. Papers might've been shuffled on Ben's desk. Maybe. Upstairs in the bedrooms things might be slightly out of place, but it was impossible to be sure. It could've been heightened imagination. At least, he'd tried to be discreet. Clearly, he intended no one should know he'd been here.

Suppose Ben had come home and surprised him? Or had still been home asleep when Frankie broke in?

Juli couldn't identify anything as missing. Perhaps some things had been moved in the closets? Perhaps. Maybe. Maybe not.

She checked the front and side doors for signs of tampering and found none. How had Frankie gotten inside? She checked the windows and they seemed secure. Frankie had either jimmied the locks or Ben had been careless with locking the doors. Frankie wasn't above taking advantage of an unexpected opportunity.

What should she tell Ben? She had to tell him something. Valuable items she didn't know about, or important papers, could be missing.

Had Frankie seen the contract?

She rehearsed the story: 'Ben, there was sand on the carpet when I came home. I can't be sure, but I think someone was inside.' She'd get him to check his study, just to be safe.

It sounded totally reasonable—a reasonable lie. Well, not entirely a lie, but close enough.

She was doing it for Ben's sake. She wouldn't do anything

to put Ben or his home in danger.

The scene played out as planned. Ben found nothing missing. He didn't say it aloud, but she could tell he believed she'd imagined the whole thing.

"Perhaps the side door didn't latch properly?" He placed his hands on Juli's shoulders. "The wind might've blown it open and then blown it shut again."

"Maybe," she said, but she knew the truth and this wasn't it.

"We'll be more careful. Okay?"

"As long as nothing's missing, you're probably right." She'd done what she could to warn him short of getting into the whole Frankie mess. "Could we have some slide bolts installed on the doors? I'd feel more secure."

Ben studied her face. He brushed her cheek lightly with his fingers. "I don't want you to be worried about anything. I'll take care of it first thing tomorrow."

She laid her head against his chest. His arms crept up around her and held her close.

When they separated, Ben frowned. "You look so serious. You aren't afraid, are you?"

"No, I'm fine." She was more than fine—she was moved by his kindness.

Ben hadn't argued that the doorknob locks and deadbolts were enough security. Without a second thought, he agreed to add those old-fashioned slide bolts—solely for her peace of mind.

She kissed him lightly on the cheek and went to begin cooking supper.

Later, standing at the porch rail and watching the evening pass into night, Juli reviewed the facts and was still certain Frankie had been the uninvited visitor. Ironic that he'd come snooping while she was at his place looking to confront him. He was taking a risk. He must believe, in a big way, he could profit from what she was doing. If he had intended the intrusion as a message or warning, he would've left obvious signs of his visit. The faint scent of cologne and the bits of sand from his shoes showed how careless he'd become.

Slide bolts couldn't be jimmied with a credit card or opened with burglar tools. It was good old-fashioned manual hardware that provided extra assurance, at least while she was at home.

****

The next day Ben and Juli ran errands together. Coming out of Food Lion, they crossed the parking lot and Ben opened the trunk to deposit the bags.

"What's this?" he asked. "Yours?" He held up her old backpack.

"It's mine. I forgot about it." She hadn't needed it or missed it. When they returned home, she carried it up to her room and tossed the pack into the bottom of her closet.

Chapter Eleven

The Harris family was replaced by the Smiths who were replaced by the Stabonacci's.

Those first weeks of marriage were measured by the ebb and flow of vacationing families. Mom and pop and kids, and whatever relatives had come along, packed up, loaded their cars—taking a quantity of sand with them in their clothing and toys—and departed each Sunday morning. The cleaning service swept through on Sunday midday. Platoons of men and women came in, cleaned and went on to the next rental. Late Sunday afternoon the next wave of guests arrived. Neighboring houses had a similar schedule, but for some of them, the change-out day was Saturday.

The world continued revolving around her while she was caught up in a sort of lull. The sun rose, the sun set, and in-between it shined gloriously. The sun, the tides, and the waves were the ticks of a living clock.

Ben commented on her restlessness. One day in mid-June, he pointed to an ad in the local paper and said, "Here you go, Juli. This is what you need."

"Art instruction?"

"I should've thought of her sooner."

"Her? Who?"

"Anna Barbour. Some of her work is displayed at the gallery. She's very talented, a professional, and someone you can rely on. Set it up on a week-to-week basis. See if you like it."

Alarm hijacked her composure. It was okay to scribble and scratch on her own, but hiring an artist to give her lessons? This felt like a 'show up or shut up' moment.

Ben crossed the room. He punched the numbers into the cordless phone and held it out to her. "Press Talk, Juli. Go ahead and give it a shot."

****

Juli pulled up in front of Anna Barbour's sound side home, double-checking the address, looking for any reason that would allow her to leave while telling herself she'd tried—any excuse that would let her off the hook.

When they'd spoken on the phone, Anna's voice was natural and friendly. Yes, she was interested in picking up another student, and no, it wasn't inconvenient at all—come on over whenever.

Nothing stood in Juli's way except herself.

She picked up her purse and exited the car. A flagstone walk lined with jonquils led to the front porch. She held her breath and pressed the doorbell.

Anna was tall and thin. Her hair was a graying blonde pulled back into a knot at the back of her head. There was something very basic about Anna, as if she could walk out the back door, pull on her dock shoes, grab her fishing pole and head out to the dock. Juli could see the dock through the large plate glass windows facing Bogue Sound. Lawn chairs, empty and inviting, sat at the far end overlooking the water.

"Come on in, Juli. I'm delighted to meet Ben's wife. You've got yourself a sweetheart of a husband there, but I guess you already know that."

Juli followed her in. "Yes, he's great. He talked me into contacting you."

"I'm glad he did." She stopped and gave Juli a long look. "Maia told me about you."

Juli didn't know what to say. "All good, I hope."

"Every word of it was marvelous. Maia said you were sweet and Luke said you were very attractive, so it's nice you've got them in your corner."

"In my corner?"

"It's none of my business, but I've known Adela for many

years. Be patient with her."

Anna showed her the small paintings she produced for local galleries and also sold at hotels on the mainland. "Mostly acrylic. Some oil. The larger sketches on the walls are in a variety of medium—pencil, Conté crayon, and pen and ink." She turned to Juli. "What medium have you worked with?"

It was a long, narrow room, and mostly windows, especially in the long exterior wall. It looked like an enclosed a back porch, but it was a big room, wide and long, to be used year round.

Easels, dinged and paint-spattered, were situated the length of the room, along the windows. What had been the backside of the house was unbroken but for the kitchen door and a kitchen window, and was hung from floor to ceiling with years of artwork.

"Is this all yours? I mean, did you do all of these?"

"This and more. Some are gifts from my students."

Juli was hypnotized by the eclectic arrangement. No rhyme or rhythm. Any piece could be moved at any moment to accommodate another work of art. A living gallery, it was inelegant and— "organic. It's organic."

"What?"

"This wall of art." Juli touched the empty nail holes. "It's growing and changing."

Anna laughed and nodded. "Yes. That's the essence of creativity, isn't it? I couldn't have said it better. Now, how about a glass of tea or cup of coffee?"

"I don't have any experience, not really."

"Of course you do. You couldn't go into rapture over my art wall if you didn't feel it in yourself. You can't tell me that feeling has never found expression."

"Back in school I practically lived in the art classroom. Mostly pencil. Some acrylic. But it was so long ago I don't think it counts."

Anna gazed somewhere over Juli's shoulder deep in thought, before she spoke. "We'll start with pencil."

She picked up several sheets of paper. "Take a look. I conduct several classes a week. I have a beginner class on Wednesday afternoons. The first page lists the classes. The rest are recommended supplies for each type of medium we study."

"A class? With other students?"

"Or you can start with private lessons."

Juli knew Anna could see her relief. Her cheeks grew hot. "Down the road a group might be okay."

"I'm glad Ben found you. That you found each other."

Juli was caught by surprise. Anna seemed so nice. So open. What did she know about the arrangement with Ben?

Anna continued, "I know I'm overstepping, but if I'm gonna step in big, I might as well go all the way." She leaned toward Juli. "Honey, I've known the Bradshaw family forever and Luke for about as long. I don't doubt your whirlwind courtship and marriage knocked 'em silly at first, but they know as well as I do that Ben—that special angel of a man—hasn't really been alive in many years. He never got over his first love, Miss Deborah Driver. They fell in love as kids. Everyone knew they'd end up together."

"How did his wife die? He didn't seem to want to talk about it."

"It was fate. Or chance. Who knows? Deborah went to the mall at the same time a delusional man off his meds started shooting a gun at everyone he could see. She died there on the sidewalk, along with her unborn child."

Anna continued, "Ben seemed to take it well. Too well. Everyone put it down to his faith which, make no mistake, helped him through it, but I don't think he ever grieved properly. It grew up like a wall around him. Oh, he was open to the church and found comfort there, but when it came to his personal life and finding love, the joy of living died within him."

They let the silence settle around them for a moment.

"When you're ready for the group, you'll know. You'll discover there are all sorts of ways to learn."

****

The next time Juli saw Frankie, she was coming out for an early morning walk. Frankie was half-hidden in the dark area around the base of the steps. She considered confronting him.

She looked at her hands remembering how they'd trembled when she knocked on his door. Only a few weeks earlier, right? How quickly she'd lost her survivor's edge. Her new role was intended to fit a softer Juli. Julianne, maybe. The girl she'd never been.

Juli stepped quietly back into the house.

She would have to ask Luke for help.

Maia and Juli had plans for lunch. When she got to the gallery, Maia was busy with a customer who looked like a serious buyer, so Juli signaled Maia to ignore her and strolled about, looking at the paintings on the walls. She found Anna's small, vivid, inspiring sunrises and flaming sunsets. Framed in black, they were grouped like panes in a nine-light window.

Juli browsed along the wall until she reached Luke's office, then stopped short of the open doorway. No noise, not even a rustle. Her heart thumped faster and her breathing quickened.

How could she consider asking Luke for anything? Especially something like this. She stepped back, away from the door.

Asking him for help would only confirm his bad opinion of her. She wasn't afraid of Frankie for herself. She wanted to protect Ben.

Everyone was temporary in this life she was living now. Once Ben was gone, she'd move on and never see these people again. She stepped forward.

"Mind if I speak with you?"

He looked up. His expression hardly changed, but a barrier whooshed into place between them. It amused and annoyed her. What did he have to fear?

"What do you want?"

She tried to appear cool and composed, but her pulse

thrummed in her neck. "I hope you'll help me."

Luke stood, motion tightly contained. "Come in."

Juli pushed the door almost closed behind her, but not totally. She didn't want full privacy, not with Luke. There was a chair near the front of his desk. When she sat, he sat.

She ignored pointless formality and spoke bluntly. "Remember the guy in the coatroom at the Hammond's house?"

"Yes."

"He thinks my arrangement with Ben can benefit him in some way. He's shown up around Ben's house a couple of times."

"Nice friend you have there. Perhaps he's found his past associations with you to be profitable."

Juli pushed back her resentment. "I can't help it if he's worthless. I've told him to stay away, but he won't. I don't want to worry Ben."

"Meaning you don't want to tell Ben."

"I recall you saying something similar. About not wanting to cause him unhappiness?"

"My motives are different." His stare never broke from hers. Challenge lit amber sparks in his eyes. "What does he want?"

"I don't know. He keeps insinuating I'm up to some scheme and he wants a piece of it."

Juli stood abruptly. "Go ahead and say it. You think I have a scheme going on, too."

"I know Ben came up with the idea of you two getting together. What I think is that he didn't understand what he was buying."

"Buying? That's not fair. It's an arrangement that benefits both of us. I'm not *bought*, and we didn't *get together*—we got *married*."

"A business arrangement," he insisted. "I can hardly blame you for taking advantage of his... offer, but at the same time, I'll do what I can to prevent you from hurting him, or taking him for more than he's agreed to give."

Juli waved her hands. "Never mind. I can see this was a mistake."

"Wait."

He moved from behind the desk and came to her, stopping inches away. She dug in her mental heels and didn't give ground.

"I'm waiting," she said. The words tasted bitter in her mouth.

"I'm being honest with you. I'd appreciate some honesty back."

"That sounds great. Why don't we start by you telling me why you think I'm a cheat and a fraud?"

He took a step back, crossed his arms, then uncrossed them and settled his hands on his hips.

"Amanda Barlow left a ring in her coat at the party. When she returned home she remembered the jeweler's box she'd put in her coat pocket earlier in the day. It was no longer there."

"How unlikely is that?"

"Pardon?"

Juli laughed in disdain. "A woman puts a jeweler's case with a valuable ring into her coat pocket and then forgets about it until she gets home from a party and happens to notice it's no longer in her pocket? For you, it's a foregone conclusion that the hired help stole it. Why am I not surprised? Sounds more like an insurance scam than a theft."

"I saw your friend going through the coats."

"What does that mean? He was probably straightening them. You know what? I don't like being put into the position of defending Frankie, but nothing you've told me is any kind of evidence. And then there's me. You also accused me of being a thief. What was that about? Guilt by association?"

"I saw you in there with him, also going through the coats."

Juli had moved behind the chair and her fingers were nearly numb from clutching the back so tightly. To be condemned and treated like a thief on so little, on no more than assumption, made her so angry she felt lightheaded.

"I was getting my backpack so I could drive Ben home."

They waited out a long moment of silence. Stalemate. Juli didn't know what he was waiting for, but the next move was his.

Luke turned to face the window behind his desk. His shirt strained across his back as he crossed his arms again. He turned slowly around to face her. "What is it you think I can do to help?"

"Tell Frankie you saw him."

"But you said—"

She cut him off. "I know what I said. Tell him you saw him messing with the coats and that a ring was stolen. Tell him if he doesn't stay away from Ben and Ben's house, you'll tell the police."

He frowned and shook his head. "How could that help? Won't he say if I had proof I'd have already called the police?"

"Maybe, but Frankie has history with the cops. If he thinks you, a respectable citizen, are going to put them back on his butt, he'll probably decide it's not worth the risk."

"But he isn't concerned about you turning him in?"

Juli didn't mistake his implication. "Hardworking and respectable aren't the same things. They won't listen to me. What would I say? Somebody told me they saw something? Frankie's not clever, but he's not stupid either." Juli was flat out of patience. "Look, I want him to go away until Ben is…until we no longer have to worry about Ben. After that, I'll deal with him, probably by ignoring him. By then, it won't matter."

"Are you afraid Ben will cancel the deal you made?"

She wanted to spit. "Let me know what you decide." Juli paused in the doorway with her hand on the knob. "If you think talking to Frankie will help, and you're willing to try, let me know. I'll call you when he comes around."

"Give me his address. Maybe I'll drop by."

His words dashed her like cold water. But this was what she wanted, wasn't it? Juli went to his desk, grabbed a pen and scribbled the address of the apartment house on a sticky note. Luke left it lying there on his desk, conspicuously not touching it.

She wanted to discourage Frankie, but not for Luke to delve more closely into her life.

Luke, going to where Frankie lived, to where she had so recently lived, made her uncomfortable.

Frankie could say anything, true or not. Luke would be a receptive audience. If that was the price Juli had to pay for his help, then so be it.

Frankie liked to fly low, below the radar, to avoid police attention. A few words from someone like Luke would keep him away.

Juli left his office without goodbye or thanks. Maia was nearby tidying a shelf. The customer had gone. Had Maia overheard them? Her plea for Luke's help? His insulting remarks? It was obvious she'd heard enough to make her uncomfortable because Maia's smile was without its dimples and her eyes looked dull.

"I've got to run, Maia. I hope you don't mind."

"Okay." Maia averted her eyes. "Rain check?"

"Sure." She walked past.

Maia called out, "Juli?"

Juli stopped. "Yes?"

"I'll call you later this week?"

"Sure." Juli left the gallery. Out the door and halfway down the steps, she turned back and saw Maia entering Luke's office.

It saddened her, but Maia was as temporary in her life as the rest of them.

Chapter Twelve

"So, it's clear you understand perspective." Anna drew in the air, her fingers tracing imaginary lines meeting at a point. In this case, the point was the end of the dock as it stretched out into the sound. Juli had drawn her lines on sketch paper.

Anna put her thumbs together as if framing the real-life scene before them. "Where you have the dock beginning, where it crosses the shoreline, uses overlap to reinforce the perception of perspective, of having three dimensions."

Today, the classroom was Anna's backyard. About twenty feet from where the water met the shore, they'd spread an old cotton blanket on the ground and put the chairs on top of it. The blanket discouraged the insects in the grass from biting their ankles. The grass beneath it made the blanket look fluffy.

"I remember those lessons from middle school. We used rulers, though."

"Well, it's no good making the lines too perfect, unless maybe you're drawing a machine. In the case of this dock, you want to show its personality, its vagaries."

"You mean its flaws, like where it's old and falling apart?"

"Yes, that's exactly right." She touched her face. "If you were to draw me, you'd catch the wrinkles and gray hair to give character and distinctiveness."

Heat flooded Juli's face. "I'm sorry, that's not what I meant. I meant the dock looked like it needed some work. I didn't mean, well, I wasn't talking about—you know, age."

"No harm done. Age is a fact whether it's docks or people." Anna settled back into her lawn chair and stretched her long, narrow bare feet out in front of her. "Folks are funny. They search for beauty. They try to find it, make it if they can't find it, and then try to preserve it to keep it. But perfection is boring." She laid her head back against the metal frame of the chair.

"Look at the Old Masters. Look at paintings that have withstood time and changing tastes. You'll see ideas of beauty, but you won't see perfection of features."

Juli shifted the sketchbook on her knees and stared at the dock.

Anna waved in that direction. "Look at the individual boards. Notice how the nail heads are pounded in at varying angles and how the shape of the shadows around each are different. Forget for the moment that you're sketching the dock and draw one of the boards."

Juli dropped the pad of paper onto the blanket. She walked the few steps to where the dock began and knelt to look at the boards. She touched the weather-smoothed crevices and the worn edges at the cut ends of the planks.

"It's almost a pattern."

"It is definitely a pattern. A unique pattern because each piece of wood will weather according to its grain."

The lawn chair sighed as Juli took her seat again and reclaimed the sketchbook. "This sounds more like a philosophical discussion than an art lesson."

"It's all a part of life, Juli. It's just life."

****

More than a week had passed since she'd asked for Luke's help. He hadn't contacted her and she didn't know what that meant, but then Ben said, "Maia called while you were out. She said you owed her a lunch. She suggested tomorrow, if that works for you."

"I'll call her back."

"No need. Maia said to tell you she'll be there tomorrow anyway and to come at noon if you want to do lunch."

"Do you mind? Would you like to come along?" Juli kept her fingers mentally crossed.

Ben shook his head. "Thanks, but no. I'll let you ladies

have your fun."

She felt like deception was scrawled in lurid letters across her forehead. Ben leaned over and gently planted a kiss right where the letters should have been written.

Maia had called. Had Luke enlisted her help? Was he using Maia as cover? Judging by the way Maia had looked at her when she was leaving the gallery, Juli didn't think she would have called on her own.

Juli took the groceries from the paper bag as Ben climbed the stairs, headed toward a nap.

Ben's naps were more frequent. Sometimes he had *discomfort*—Ben's word. He said it wasn't pain. The doctor had prescribed some pills for him to take as needed. Ben said they made him drowsy.

Juli didn't ask him how he felt because he didn't like the question.

Was she deceiving him? Technically, yes. She wouldn't lie to herself about that, but Ben shouldn't have to worry about her past. Her previous life didn't mesh well with her new one. Juli would stop the mashup before it got messier, she hoped—with a little help from Luke.

****

Maia wasn't at the gallery when Juli arrived. There was a young man with thick black hair behind the counter. His hair looked disordered on purpose, probably plastered with stiff hair gel.

"Is Maia here?"

"Are you Juli?"

He was wearing a dress shirt that was at odds with his frame. Maybe his father's or brother's shirt. Clearly, he hadn't asked his mama or anyone else to iron it for him. It looked clean, though.

"I am."

He held out his hand. "I'm Brendan. I'm new. Maia's at the bank. She'll be back soon."

Juli shook his hand. "I'll hang out here until she gets back."

"Why don't you come in the office and we'll chat 'til Maia returns."

Juli spun around. Luke stood in the office doorway. His voice sounded relaxed, reasonable. For Brendan's benefit, no doubt. Juli walked into the office.

She jumped right into it. "What did he say?"

She was surprised by her breathlessness, her taut nerves. When Luke walked toward her, she nearly jumped.

Luke went to the office door and closed it. The latch clicked softly. He walked back to his desk. "He said he'll stay away."

"And?"

Luke stood in front of his desk with his arms crossed. "And what?"

Maddening. He wanted to punish her—whether for marrying Ben or for asking him to help her resolve the problem with Frankie. Juli resisted the urge to meet him stance for stance, stare for stare. She pretended there was no need, that no electricity was passing between them, snapping and twisting like a loose livewire, threatening to burn.

"I'd like to know what you said to him and what he said back to you. I'll probably have to deal with him sooner or later."

"You'd do better to avoid people like him."

"*People like him?* I should find a better quality of friends, is that right?" Was it hypocritical of her to resent him for saying what she'd already been thinking?

Luke walked to the window. "I told him exactly what you suggested."

"That you'd call the police about the theft at the Hammond's house?"

"He wasn't happy about it, but he seemed to believe me. I'm not confident we can trust him to stay away."

"Why wouldn't he? It's not like he had any solid reason to think he could benefit from my relationship with Ben."

Luke turned back to face her. "I think there *was* something more on his mind. I didn't probe. He looked like the type who'd consider any uncertainty an opening."

Juli nodded. Frankie would stay away, at least for a while. She hoped he'd move on to something else and forget her entirely.

"Thank you, Luke."

"I did it for Ben."

"I didn't think otherwise." Dignity was a handy mask for humiliation. Juli reminded herself that Luke's opinion did not define her and stood straighter. They reached the door at the same time, their hands and bodies in close contact. Juli's capacity for masking her emotion had reached its limit.

Luke was helping Ben, not her. He despised her, and she, him.

Whoever said it was a thin line between love and hate was right. In a flash of insight, Juli realized that despite whatever else she felt, she was attracted to Luke.

She was disgusted with herself for not being a better person. She had money and comfort and a husband, if in name only, who respected and cared about her. Luke was nothing more than an annoyance—a bully who constantly put her down. She would remember that; it should be easy.

Juli slipped past him as he opened the door. Brendan was speaking with a customer and Maia was waiting by the counter. Juli hesitated. Was the lunch invitation real? Brendan might wonder about her closeted meeting with Luke, especially if the lunch plans evaporated.

Maia stepped out from behind the counter. "Are you ready to go?"

"I am." She crossed her arms to hide her shaking hands.

"I hope you don't mind staying on Front Street. Something close and quick?" Maia lowered her voice as they exited the gallery. "I don't want to leave Brendan for too long. Luke will be able to help him, but I want him to learn the job the way I like it done."

Juli used the walk down Front Street to pull herself together. They stopped at the restaurant where she and Ben had brunched on that first morning. The memory was sweet and helped banish other thoughts.

The waitress led them to a corner table near the windows.

Maia said, "You looked a little pale. The short walk did you good. I'm so glad you could make it."

So, Maia hadn't invited her as a cover for Luke.

"I'm glad, too." Juli spoke tentatively.

"I meant to call sooner. It's been so busy. Eileen quit and left me short-handed. That's two in a row. I have to keep Brendan."

"No need to explain."

"When Luke suggested I take a little time away during the day—said, in fact, I was overdue for our rain check, I knew he was right. You know how it is. You get so focused on the work it's easy to lose sight of enjoying life."

So Luke *did* suggest it. Juli let it simmer in her brain for a few minutes while the waitress took their orders.

"Their garden salad is great. You'll like it." Maia bubbled on. "And what about the art lessons? Are you enjoying them? Anna's amazing, isn't she?"

"Yes, to both."

Maia leaned forward and spoke almost in a whisper. "She says you are very talented."

"What? You're exaggerating. I've barely started to learn."

"No, indeed. Her exact words were that you have a lot of natural talent."

"That means my work is amateurish."

"Stop it, Juli. That's not what it means. And, in the end, the fun and the experience is the goal, isn't it? Satisfaction? No one can take that away from you."

Another reminder of her temporary life. It was good to be reminded. It was foolish to forget.

Maia continued, "When you're ready, I want to display some of your art at the gallery."

"What?" It shot through Juli like a cannon blast. "That's crazy."

"Not at all. Everyone starts somewhere don't they? Why not the gallery? We spotlight a lot of local artists."

Juli was grateful to receive her salad and rolls. Never did anyone more attentively butter their bread or inspect their salad. Maia was keeping her off-balance, as if continually yanking at an invisible rug beneath her feet. Juli opened her mouth to speak and was cut off once again.

"How is Ben these days?"

"He's good."

"I'm so glad. He was very sick when he went to the doctor. It was coincidental and had nothing to do with his current condition, but that's how they found it. He was recovering when you met. It's so romantic—meeting in the moonlit garden at the party."

"I didn't know he'd told you."

"Oh, my, yes. He went on and on about this wonderful girl he'd met. Well, you should know I'm a romantic at heart. Unlucky in love, that's me. I told him not to let love slip through his fingers. Not many chances come along. Oh, my, but Luke was angry."

"I'm sure he was worried—"

"He was. But they were fussing over Ben as if he was already gone. They meant well, but it was their issue, not his, if you know what I mean? They have to deal with their grief and not burden him. Does that make any sense?"

"Yes, but it's understandable."

"Sure it is. I've been half in love with Ben since the day I met him, but he never got over his first true love."

"You *are* a romantic."

Maia laughed. "Isn't that what I said?"

"Would you ladies like dessert?"

"No, thanks. Can we have the check?"

Juli was about to rise from the table when Maia reached over and put her hand on her arm.

"Juli, I know you and Luke aren't getting along. I know you're trying to hide it from Ben, not wanting to catch him up in the middle."

"That's true."

"You're both good people, Juli, and you're doing the right thing by trying to work it out. I'm glad you were willing to speak with him today. It's funny how people can have the same motivation, but still be at odds."

"It's human nature, I guess." A catch-all response. It sparked something reckless within her. She was fed up with using good manners to mask the truth. "It's all Luke's fault, anyway."

Maia sat back, startled. "Luke's fault? What is?"

"That I met Ben. I was serving at the party and Luke— didn't know his name then—looked through me like I wasn't there. It hit me wrong. I don't know how to explain it. I felt anonymous, but not by choice. Nameless. Pointless. I went outside because I needed air and that's where I met Ben."

"That's how you ended up in the garden?"

"Luke's fault, like I said."

Maia beamed. "Fate. I call it fate. You and Ben were meant to be together."

"If that's what it is, then I hope fate will be kind for a change." Juli stood. "I've been kicked in the gut by fate more than a few times and I'm ready to kick back. Hard."

Chapter Thirteen

When she returned home, Ben was sitting in his rocker reading a Devotional. Juli wasn't sure what that was, except that it was a 'topic for the day' sort of thing. She curled up on the rattan sofa to read a novel, but every time the rocker squeaked she looked up at Ben and felt guilty. Devious. Juli couldn't regret not telling him about Frankie, or even about asking Luke for help. She didn't want to interfere in his relationship with Luke and, regarding Frankie, she didn't want Ben looking over his shoulder for the creep whenever they left the house. She didn't want to risk Ben trying to act the hero.

Ben was rational. More likely he would try to reason with Frankie, but when it came to people like Frankie, it was better to play hardball.

"You look pensive," Ben said.

Juli met his eyes, thinking for the umpteenth time that she should tell him and be done with it. It wasn't a big deal anyway. She opened her mouth to tell him, but said, instead, "Maia thinks the world of you."

"Maia is a sweetheart."

"She is. Ben, if you were lonely and you two are such good friends, then why me? Why not Maia?"

"Maia?" He looked bemused.

Juli frowned. "Yes."

"Maia is a friend. More like a sister, I guess. I never thought of her that way."

"But for companionship…"

"Why do you ask?"

No way would she tell him about Maia's feelings. It would be like a betrayal. "No reason."

"Are you still wondering why I pursued you?"

She shrugged. She hadn't been, but now she was interested.

"It's been almost two months and you haven't packed your bags and fled, so I guess I can tell you." He left the rocker and sat next to her on the sofa, close, but not quite touching.

"You, Juli, woke my heart." He reached out and took her hand, examining the rings on her finger. "I hadn't considered remarriage in nearly fifteen years. Never even crossed my mind." He turned her hand over, palm upward, and traced the life line and heart line. "How did you speak to my heart? I know you weren't trying to and I wasn't looking for it. It just happened."

Juli reached over and put her free hand on top of his so that she clasped his hand between hers, but she didn't interrupt.

"When you left that night after driving me home, I couldn't sleep. You know how it is sometimes, when you aren't well? You sleep so much that then you can't sleep at all? I was wakeful and I kept thinking about you. You seemed 'shiny' in my mind. That sounds stupid and I can't explain it better, so leave it as said. We'd barely seen each other. It was dark, remember? I watched you by the light of the dashboard. I enjoyed listening to you, but I was so tired.

"How could I trust my memory? I'd just about talked myself out of thinking of you. Then I remembered you worked at Singer's. I figured I'd go, get another look at you. Seeing you again, facing reality, would show me how foolish I was."

Juli spoke softly. "You shocked me when you walked in that morning. I didn't know what to think. It seemed so...unreasonable that you would track me down."

He added his other hand on top of their clasped ones. "When I saw you, I knew I was right. Reason and logic had nothing to do with it. I don't care if I sound like a fool now. I have no regret. I hope you agree."

Juli put her head on his shoulder. "I told myself you were crazy and that I was crazier, but you're right—I don't regret it."

Over time, given time, they might feel differently, but in the short term, this marriage arrangement had been a wise choice for them both, and short term was all they had. Juli sniffled and touched a hand to her eyes.

"Are you crying?"

He sounded concerned and she almost giggled. She knew his romantic heart was hoping to offer comfort.

"Ben, when I was a child I heard a fable about a bet between the sun and the wind to prove which was stronger. Do you know it?"

"Where they took turns trying to wrest a coat from a man to prove their strength?"

"That's it. The wind blew and blew and the man clutched his coat tighter. The sun beamed and gradually warmed him and the man gladly removed his coat."

"That's how I remember it."

"Well, to me, you are the sun."

That evening, when he went upstairs, Juli wondered how it would be if she went with him. She felt tenderness and something like love. And they were married.

Ben didn't ask for that sort of companionship. Never had. Was it was a physical problem or was he was just sticking to their agreement—expecting no more from her than she wanted to give? Rather than risk hurt or embarrassment, she watched him go upstairs each night, always earlier than she.

And because she couldn't bring herself to ask, he went alone.

****

On Wednesday, Ben said, "I want to fix whatever's wrong between you and Luke. I can't have my two favorite people at odds, practically baring their fangs at each other every time the other is mentioned."

It took Juli a moment to choose which expression to put on her face. "What do you mean?"

"I mean you are both reasonable people. You both think you're hiding how you feel about each other, probably thinking you're protecting me, but you're fooling yourselves. Not that I don't appreciate your effort, but every time I'm talking to one of you I have to be careful about mentioning the other. It's ridiculous."

He walked over to where she sat, studying, and leaned over the back of the chair. "Luke will be very helpful to you when I'm gone."

Juli frowned and closed her book. She was perfectly willing to put the world history textbook aside. Seemed like it went from one war to another. It got old.

"Why do you talk like that? I'll take care of myself. I always have." She tried again.

"When I'm on my own again, I'll go back to my life. Luke won't figure into it. You're the only thing Luke and I have in common." She walked over to the kitchen counter and dropped the book on top of the other two. Grammar and math. Ugh.

Ben followed. "Then do it for me. When I bring you two together, try to be open with each other. I know you both. You are wonderful people."

Juli swallowed her pride and faced Ben with a smile on her face. "When do you plan to hold this peace treaty discussion?"

He ignored her sarcasm. "What time is it?"

She looked at the kitchen clock. "Nearly one o'clock."

"How about now? He's bringing lunch."

Luke knocked on the door. He and the pizza boxes were visible through the glass. Juli shrugged. If lunch didn't go well, it wouldn't be her fault. Luke had helped her with Frankie and she owed him. She owed Ben, too.

Ben opened the door and said, "Come on in."

Luke saw Juli and paused in the doorway.

"Come in. Pizza's getting cold." He moved aside as Luke entered. "We're going to share lunch today."

"Is this why you wanted me to bring pizza over? Two pizzas?" Luke set the boxes on the kitchen counter.

Despite her best intentions, Juli deflated. She went to the cupboards to get plates and to hide her expression.

Ben intercepted her. "No, no. I'll take care of this. You two sit down."

Luke asked, still standing, "What's the problem, Ben?"

"You two are the problem. My problem. I care about you both. Sit down. We'll share lunch and get to know each other better."

Luke pressed his lips together. No words were going to make it past that blockage. Juli tried to fill the gap.

"Is that pepperoni?" Oh, so fascinating, pepperoni.

Luke responded, "With mushrooms. Ben likes mushrooms."

"I know. Did you get it at that place about a mile down the road?"

Luke answered like it mattered. "Yes."

An inept attempt at a congenial conversation.

Ben said, "Juli's taking art lessons."

"With Anna. I know. Anna told me." Luke replied.

Ben looked at her. It was her turn, but Juli didn't want to discuss her artistic efforts with Luke over pizza in this artificially staged atmosphere.

Luke stepped in. "Anna's had some very nice sales recently. One of our gallery customers attended a show she held with some of her students at a hotel in Nags Head and was impressed. Asked to see some of the work privately through the gallery."

"Juli, you should consider participating in one of Anna's shows," Ben said.

"Please." Now it was her turn to purse her lips. A sigh. She softened her response.

"Maybe after more training and practice."

When lunch was done—a civil lunch with Luke and Juli subdued by a shared guilt because they'd dealt with Frankie behind Ben's back—Luke excused himself, saying he had business to tend to. Ben kissed Juli's cheek and went to take a nap.

Juli walked out to the porch. There was a change in the air, perhaps only in barometric pressure, but it tingled her skin. The last time she'd felt a change coming was when she'd driven Ben home that night back in April.

The footsteps coming up the outside stairs to the porch were Luke's. Juli knew it before she saw him. When he reached the top of the stairs, he stopped and looked up, above her head.

"His sliding door is closed. Is he napping?"

Luke was speaking in soft tones. Juli did the same.

"Yes, he is. You didn't go far."

"I want to declare a truce."

"A truce?"

"Let's give each other the benefit of the doubt?"

Juli crossed her arms. She felt a stab of sadness. "For the time being, you mean?"

"Yes."

"For Ben's sake?"

"For Ben's sake."

For whatever stupid reason, Juli felt moisture gathering in her eyes. Had there been some purpose in their antagonism? It certainly hadn't been pleasant, and yet, surely over time they could have found some sort of acceptance—might even come to appreciate each other. Now, it would never happen.

She extended her hand and Luke grasped it. His grip was strong. Reassuring. And more?

He continued holding her hand as if time had stilled. She looked into his eyes and saw the amber lights.

Abruptly, they broke their handclasp.

He started down the steps, but looked back and Juli couldn't help herself.

"Luke," she called out.

"Yes?"

"You don't have to worry. I'll take good care of Ben—for both of us."

Chapter Fourteen

For their first month anniversary, Ben had surprised Juli with a card and flowers, but she wasn't going to get caught on the short end of gift giving today, their second anniversary. She'd purchased a beautiful card with lots of hearts and flowers, guaranteed to charm a romantic like Ben. Choosing a gift had been more difficult. Juli hadn't wanted to go overboard, in case Ben didn't celebrate second month anniversaries.

She got up early and put the card and gift box at his place on the kitchen table. A second gift box was under the table. Not perfectly hidden, but good enough. She took the egg carton and butter from the refrigerator and lined up the breakfast food, ready to cook as soon as he made his appearance. The floor above her creaked. Juli was excited—silly excited—almost giggling. She was about to trump Ben, the champion gift-giver of all time.

He came down the stairs and spied the table, already set and with a present waiting. The small box had a big, shiny blue bow. He paused on the stairs and smiled, then continued down into the kitchen and kissed her cheek.

"Happy second anniversary," he said.

"And to you. Now, have a seat. Breakfast will be ready shortly."

"First, I have to get something. I'll be back in a minute."

He went to the study with a big grin on his face. His happiness warmed her from the inside out, making her very glad she'd gotten the presents for him. Her instincts had been right.

She was cracking the eggs over the edge of the frying pan when she heard him returning. Juli tossed the shell fragments into the trash, then turned around and saw a large box on her chair.

"What have you done?"

"You'll have to see for yourself. Are the eggs burning?"

"Oh!" Juli swung back to face the stove and started flipping the eggs with the spatula.

"Ben, Ben, Ben." She came close to swearing. Instead, she settled for laughing.

"What's so funny?"

She pointed the spatula toward him. "You are too much."

His face glowed, lit like a beacon. She shook her head, amazed, slipped the eggs onto the plates, and grabbed the toast.

"Here you go," she said.

Ben asked, "Aren't you going to open your present?"

"After we eat. Food first." Juli couldn't resist doing the teasing for a change.

He said a blessing over the food, but when he was done, he still looked disappointed.

She relented. "On the other hand..."

"What?"

"You could go ahead and look at your card, and maybe the gift. If you'd like to."

Ben picked up the card and opened the flap. He read each word, then blinked his eyes and rubbed his nose.

"Nice." He cleared his throat. "What's this?" He picked up the box and shook it gently. "Not breakable, is it?"

"No. I hope you'll like it. I didn't know if you would, so I have a second gift for you, too. Actually it's for both of us."

"Two gifts?"

"For two months."

Carefully, he worked the blue ribbon off of the package, then unwrapped the paper. He lifted the lid from the box and drew out the chain.

Had she guessed right? Ben was a gentleman. He would pretend he liked it, regardless of his true feelings.

He held the chain, dangling from one hand, the dog tag swinging at the end. He didn't say anything, so she jumped into the void.

"It says FAITH on the back. On the front, there's a cross with the verse noted. The man who makes them said the tiny thing at the bottom is a mustard seed. It has to do with the verse. You're supposed to wear it like a dog tag, but you don't have to. You could attach it to your key ring or whatever."

He examined both sides of the tag. "Matthew 17:20. My name is engraved on it below the verse."

"It was special order. I can't send it back, so I hope you like it."

"I love it." He put it around his neck, but kept one hand wrapped around the dog-tag type pendant. "How did you choose that verse?"

"I read all of the verses on the website. This one says that if you have faith, nothing is impossible. You are the most optimistic, believing person I know. You believed in us, didn't you?"

His eyes looked misty. Maybe he truly did like it, but now she was ready for something more cheerful. She reached below the table and brought out a shirt box.

"This is the second gift?" He held it, looking at the paper with little pictures of wedding cakes and bells.

"Yes, but please, for me, tear the paper off this time? Just rip it."

"Here goes." He started at one end, slipping a finger below to slit the tape, but then gave it a great, ripping tear from end to end. "How's that?"

She stopped him, placing her hands on top of the box. "This is for our evening walks."

"Whatever you say." He lifted the top and pulled the first shirt out. It was navy blue with white letters. He read aloud, "Juli's husband." Then he pulled the second shirt out, "Ben's wife."

It was red, but also with white letters.

"Kind of corny, huh?" Doubt again.

"Only in the most wonderful way. But there's one

problem."

"What?"

"Now that I have these, I have everything I could want. What on earth will you give me for future anniversaries?"

"Hah. Funny. Now, my turn." Juli set the box on the chair next to her. She eased off the bow delicately, carefully, then demolished the paper with abandon.

The contents of the box were wrapped in white packing paper. She picked up the topmost one. It was long and thin and the paper rustled as she unwound it.

Juli stared at the bundle of paint brushes. They were brushes for oil paints. She put them on the table and selected another paper-wrapped item. This was a set of colored pencils. And the next, and the next—they were the physical manifestation of Anna's art supplies list. With each unwrapped item, Ben's smile grew wider. She worked her way through the box, checking out the brushes, paints, and pencils, tablets of specialty papers—on and on. Ben had missed nothing. Juli opened her mouth, but found herself speechless.

"Now, come with me." He grabbed her hand and led her into the study. "I couldn't fit this into the box." He opened the closet door, pushed the coats aside and pulled out an easel. "For my artist wife."

****

In mid-July, Juli told Anna she was ready to join a group. Anna switched her to a class that met late on Thursday afternoons. "You'll love them," Anna said. "They are sweet, incredible people."

Juli arrived on Thursday afternoon. Anna's house was known territory now, but still she was anxious.

A couple of women, an older man and a teenager all looked up from their easels, most calling out greetings. The teenager didn't actually speak, but waved his brush in her direction before he disappeared back behind his canvas.

The white-haired man was a former naval officer. "Call me, Dodge," he said. "I'm retired now."

Juli envied his posture. He stood as if at attention. The teenager was being homeschooled and sent to Anna for art class. When Anna introduced him, he blushed.

"This is Billy Wooten. Billy, this is Mrs. Bradshaw."

"If it's all the same, I'd rather he called me Juli."

"I'm Laura and that's Donna." The darker haired woman pointed her paintbrush at the shorter woman. "We're friends. Donna talked me into this. Oops, sorry Anna. We love you and we love this class." She giggled.

There was no type for her to fit into, or not to fit into. Juli found that comforting. She chose an easel next to the kid. Looked to be a little less chatter at that end of the room.

So far, so good.

Juli opened her art box and laid out her tubes and brushes. From the corner of her eye she caught a glimpse of Billy's work. Seemed to be heavy lines in black and white with splashes of color. While she was peeking, Billy was also looking out of the corner of his eye and when their gazes met, Billy blushed all over again.

She opened the jar of turpentine and using the burnt umber, did a wash in varying degrees of light and dark as a roadmap for the painting to come.

****

Juli was gradually accumulating what Anna called a portfolio. Much too grand a word for what she was bringing home, but she could see modest improvement.

Juli stored her artwork in the topmost room of the *Glory*. The crow's nest. Sometimes, when standing on the balcony with the wind streaming through her hair and the waves crashing below, she imagined she was standing on the prow of a Spanish galleon or on the parapet of a castle that perched on the edge of ocean cliffs. Anywhere, but where she used to be.

Not her old self or old places, but instead, someone with dreams living in a place of infinite promise.

****

For their third anniversary, Ben and Juli agreed to forego

the presents and have dinner out. Ben said they were going to a restaurant over by the sound.

"Do I know it?" she asked.

"It's a small place, but special."

Juli frowned. There was something he wasn't saying. She recognized his tone of voice, the lilt that suggested there were words unsaid.

She was driving at Ben's suggestion. He said he felt fine, but he'd kept his hand on his mid-section for most of the day. It was an unconscious gesture, but Juli figured he was in some pain. He sat with his head back against the headrest, pale, but appearing relaxed as he listened to the radio. There was talk about a hot spot off the west coast of Africa spinning up a bunch of storms. A few of the tropical weather systems had made it across the Atlantic and dropped a ton of water on the islands in the Caribbean, but the storms had dwindled to tropical depressions, or to nothing at all, by the time they neared the US mainland.

Ben switched the radio off.

"Are you worried?" she asked.

"About storms? No. We're prepared."

"Hurricanes move slowly, that's good."

"They can be unpredictable, but there's plenty of time to evacuate if you don't wait until the last minute and we won't."

As they approached where the causeway met Atlantic Avenue, Ben sat up straighter and tapped his index finger against the console. She gave him a quick look.

"There," he said. "See where that huge rack of boats is? Just past that, turn left."

She turned, as instructed, into the parking lot of a marina.

"Did you guess?" he asked. "Park over there."

There were a bunch of boat slips and nice-looking docks. A number of boats were tied up, but Ben wouldn't have had her dress up for anything less than that big shiny, two-story boat at the end of the dock.

"Ben?"

Several men were standing inside. One was dressed in chef's whites.

"It's ours for the evening. It's called a party boat. A friend of mine is loaning it to us for our anniversary dinner and the chef is a friend, too. Have you ever dined on the ocean at sunset?"

****

Sunset on the dock, sunset on the beach, even sunset from their front porch was beautiful—made beautiful because the particulates in the atmosphere scattered the waning rays of sunlight, painting the sky in hues of red and gold.

Lulled into peaceful wonder, Juli sat on the cushioned seat at the side rail of the boat, gently rocked by the movement of the ocean, feeling the touch of a breeze that had traveled from some exotic land far away. She watched the growing splash of vivid color skipping across the shifting surface of the Atlantic Ocean. It was like living in the midst of a poem.

Ben touched her arm. "Amazing, isn't it?"

"I don't know words big enough to describe it. Awesome, inspiring—I can't do it justice with words. Or with paint."

Juli held up her empty hands. Powerless. "Anna said people look for perfection and when they think they've found it, they try to hold onto it forever."

"This is a sunset, Juli. It's beautiful and it will come again. The next will be different and may be more awesome. For me, *joy* is the word I feel."

"Joy?"

"Joy at creation." He threaded his fingers through hers. "The heavens declare the glory of God; the skies proclaim the work of his hands."

"Now, that's beautiful."

"It's Psalm 19. Verse 1."

"The sunset's fading." She leaned toward him. The slump of his shoulders betrayed his fatigue. Juli tightened her fingers around his and was disturbed. They felt bony and the knuckles were large in contrast.

He put his lips against her hair and whispered, "There will be more. Guaranteed."

Chapter Fifteen

The Spagnoli family arrived on a Sunday afternoon in the beginning of August for a two week rental. Juli happened to look out the front window and saw a fair-haired toddler racing down the crossover toward the ocean, his progress revealed between the side rails as he ran along. Without thought, Juli dashed past Ben and out the door.

The toddler, chunky legs churning and diapered butt jouncing, nearly beat her to the end of the crossover. She snagged his t-shirt as a woman yelled, "Charlie!"

"Oh, my, oh, my. He nearly got away this time." The woman was quickly there, arms outstretched to receive her squirming Charlie who was still intent on escape.

Juli passed him to her while noting the skinny, dark-haired pre-teen girl who hung back.

"I'm Victoria. We just got here, unpacking and all that. This one," she moved him over to straddle her hip, "is a very busy boy who loves water. He doesn't know enough to be afraid of it yet, so he gives me gray hair." She motioned the girl forward. "This is Violet, my daughter."

Violet had straight dark hair and knobby knees. She didn't speak, only stared.

"He got away from Violet. I'm grateful you were there and caught him. Thanks so much."

"Glad I could help."

"Are you next door?"

"Yes. I'm Juli. Just me and my husband, Ben."

"Thanks again."

"Well, no harm done. All's well."

She held her free hand over her chest. "No harm, except to

my heart. It's still racing."

"There's a little gate with a latch at the entrance to your porch. That might slow him down next time."

Little Charlie wasn't impressed by his mother's distress. He protested and kicked his legs.

With a rueful grin, Victoria said, "I'd better get back to unpacking. We'll see you around."

Juli followed them back up the crossover. As she entered through the open gate on her side of the porch, Ben reached out and pulled her into his arms.

"That was amazing."

"What was amazing?" She was truly puzzled.

"Your response. You didn't wait to see if someone else was coming after him. You just went."

"What's so unusual about that? There wasn't any danger. Not to me."

"You were wonderful in action. Most people hang back, not wanting to get involved or give offense. You went."

She let him hug her again, glad he was pleased, but not understanding why. After all, little Charlie's parents could've been out there, out of her sight, but still in control. They could have been offended. She could've caused a big headache for Ben.

Dealing with other people was often a crap shoot. Ultimately, you had to do what you had to do—what your conscience could live with.

****

Ron Spagnoli favored early morning jogs. Juli usually walked. They passed each other day after day. They exchanged waves, rarely stopping to chat. It was a very long beach. Twelve miles were specifically tagged as Emerald Isle, but it was only one of the beaches fringing the twenty-one-mile long island of Bogue Banks.

Ron jogged to the pier and back, or so he said.

Given his muscled appearance, Juli believed him. She liked his open face. He seemed a nice guy, calm and quiet in contrast to his wife and the imp, Charlie.

****

Donna spread liberal amounts of red pigment on the canvas. "It's a poppy," she said.

Juli said, "A large poppy. Very red. Lots of energy."

"Red is my favorite color. My husband wants me to hang it in the guestroom when it's done."

Laura spoke up. "It will look gorgeous." She stepped back to admire her own close-up flower painting. "Do you think the color's strong enough? I want the yellow to stand out." She brushed in a dark line of umber along the edge of a petal, then paused to view it. "I wish I could go to the cookout. You're going, aren't you? Donna is. Billy, too. It's super. Anna holds it every year."

"Seems like half the island shows up." Donna wiped her brush on a rag to clear the excess paint.

Anna walked over to them. "I expect you and Ben to be there."

"Ben told me your cookout is practically an island institution. We'll be there. What should I bring? Chips or paper plates or something?"

"No need to bring anything, but if you like, bring a dish to share. So many people will be there I never keep a list of who'll bring what. As long as you and Ben bring yourselves, that's all I ask."

Anna's cookout wouldn't be all that different from pot-luck holiday lunches she'd participated in at Singer's, so she settled for bringing her standard contribution, brownies. Who didn't like a chewy, chocolate brownie?

On the day of the cookout Ben said, "Dress lightly. Even by the water and under the shade of Anna's trees, it will be hot. It's the height of summer. The best you can hope for is moderate humidity."

The aroma of brownies filled the air. They had cooled and were already sliced into portions. Ben was loitering in the kitchen.

Juli took the plastic wrap from the drawer, saying, "The breeze is supposed to be onshore. That'll be good." The salt air blowing in from the ocean helped cut the humidity. "Even in Morehead City, the ocean breeze makes a difference."

"Hah. Well, that's the same salty, drying breeze that corrodes almost everything."

"Take the good with the bad, right?"

He was back in the kitchen door, leaning against the lintel, so she walked past him to the counter. She tugged the plastic wrap so it tore against the metal rib on the box, then floated it carefully over the brownies before wrapping the edges under the plate.

"Seems like one is missing. Is that a good idea?"

Ben smiled. "Didn't want to risk not getting one."

Juli went upstairs to change while Ben did the same. It was too hot to leave her hair down. It would be sticking to her neck, driving her crazy. She clipped it up, but the fine strands were slipping out even before she left her room.

Ben's door was open. She stuck her head in. "Ben?" No answer, but he'd left his slacks folded on the bed.

He was downstairs seated in the rattan rocker with his eyes closed and his head back. Had he fallen asleep? It was past his usual naptime, but he hadn't looked sleepy when they separated to change for the cookout.

Juli walked softly to where he sat. He was wearing shorts. When had his legs gotten so thin? He'd been wearing slacks more often, so she hadn't noticed.

"Are you asleep?"

He shook his head and opened his eyes. "No, not asleep. I shouldn't have eaten that brownie, after all. It isn't sitting well. Please, don't take offense."

"No offense. It was too rich for you." They had been modifying his diet over time, reducing the rich and spicy to bland and tolerable. "Forget the cookout. You lie down and when you get up we'll do something quiet. We'll watch a movie or something."

"You're all ready to go, and Anna is expecting us. Go, and give her my apology."

"I don't want to leave you."

"I can rest whether you're here to watch me or not. I don't need a babysitter." He leaned forward, an arm extended.

"Here." She pushed the footstool within reach and propped his feet on it. His tone was different. He hadn't talked that way before—about babysitting. Petulant.

"If you're sure, I'll go, but I won't stay long."

"Stay for the whole thing. Go have some fun."

"No, Ben. You don't get to have your way about everything just because you're feeling sick. You say 'go,' then I'll go, but I'm not staying for the whole cookout. No matter how much fun it is, I'm coming back home to you. So, there." Juli knelt by his side and stroked her hand through his hair. It was soft, the strands falling between her fingers like silk.

"Can I get you something before I leave?"

He reached up, grasped her hand and pressed both of his hands around hers "A glass of ice water, if you don't mind. And I'll hold you to that."

"To what?"

"Come back to me."

"I'll keep my cell on loud. Call or text if you need me. If you need anything at all."

Cars of every description lined Anna's driveway, the street, and even the neighbors' driveways seemed full. She looked at the passenger seat and the plate of brownies. It seemed a puny offering. Maybe it was better to arrive empty-handed. And then what? Take them back home with her?

Juli pulled into an open space at the end of the block. With this many people roaming her back yard, would Anna notice if she never showed?

When she got out of the car, she tugged her shorts back into place over her thighs, then tucked the escaped hair strands behind her ears. Distant sounds came to her around the houses and trees, distorted so that it was hard to pin down the location.

Barbecue, hickory and charcoal smells filled the air. If Juli hadn't been familiar with Anna's house she might have had to check out some extra back yards to find the picnic. She put her purse in the trunk, made sure the keys were in hand, then slammed the lid. Her phone went into her short's pocket.

"Hey, you're forgetting the brownies, aren't you? I see 'em on the car seat."

"Dodge. Hey, yourself." She reached back into the car and snagged the plate.

He was wearing crisply pressed slacks and a plaid cotton shirt, all tucked in and properly belted. "Can I carry those for you?"

"Yes. Thanks." Good. Everyone would think Dodge had brought the paltry plate of brownies. Not so bad, after all. And she was parked conveniently away from the action. She could sneak away after a few minutes, hike back up the road to her car with no witnesses to see her driving off.

They walked down the street, moist heat baking up from the asphalt.

"Where's your husband? I was looking forward to meeting him. Is he already at the cookout?"

"No. He was coming, but felt under the weather."

"I'm sorry."

She should've refused to leave Ben. Juli almost turned around to go back home. "I didn't want to leave him. He insisted."

"I'm glad you came. Maybe next time."

"Maybe. I can't stay long. I need to get back home."

Maia surprised her in the driveway. Her sundress was brightly colored with tropical flowers. A butterfly hair pin was fastened behind her ear. "Hi, glad you made it." She looked past Juli. "Where's Ben?"

Here we go again. "He was planning to come, but felt a little ill and decided to stay home."

"Ill? Anything I can do?"

"No, it's nothing serious, or, rather, well, you know what

I mean." Juli rubbed her face and tucked the hair behind her ears again. "He wanted to rest."

Maia nodded, then said, "Dodge, look at you. Brownies. I'm impressed."

"No, ma'am. I'm the bearer. Juli's the baker."

Thanks, Dodge.

"They look delicious."

Together, they rounded the end of the house, walking down the slope to the back yard, following the aroma of fired-up grills and hickory.

"What's that heavenly smell?"

Dodge answered, "Gal, I know you recognize the aroma of Carolina barbecue. Don't even hint otherwise."

"What about the neighbors? How do they feel about the cars and the crowd and the smells?"

He laughed. "Well, I think they're all here at the party."

Juli clutched Maia's arm surprising them both. "Look at all the people."

"They're all nice. Relax and be yourself."

Dodge said, "Anna's got the food in the studio—uh, the converted porch, that is. Shall I take her the brownies?"

Anna was visible through the long wall of windows, moving.

"I'll take them to her. I need to speak with her. Thanks for your help."

"Pleased to be of service, ma'am." He tipped an imaginary cap. "I'm going to check out that barbecue. Make sure they get it done right." He walked off toward a stand of oaks and the large black trailer roaster.

"Can you excuse me, Juli?" Maia was looking at a group over by the horseshoe pits. She touched her hair and smoothed her sundress.

Juli couldn't tell which man interested Maia. "Go."

She climbed the few steps to the porch. When the chill of the air conditioning hit her, she shivered almost missing the heat outside.

"Is it too cold in here? I wanted to have somewhere cool for Ben to relax if the heat bothered him. It's better for keeping the food, too."

"I'm sorry, Anna. Ben didn't come. He wasn't feeling well."

Anna paused in taping the white paper to the table. "I'm sorry about that, too, but I'm glad you're here."

"Ben insisted. He really did want to be here. I felt strange leaving him."

"He knows best about how he feels. Put the brownies with the other desserts on that table."

Most of the two long tables were empty. "The barbecue smells fantastic. Do you need help bringing anything out?"

"The caterers are taking care of that. They own the kitchen this afternoon and I'm about to get out of their way."

Caterers. Caterers. The words repeated in her head. Not likely Sammy or anyone she knew. This was out of their territory. Still, no need for a reunion, just in case. "I'll take a walk outside."

"Good idea. I'll join you shortly."

People had sorted themselves into groups—at the roaster despite the heat emanating from it—at the horseshoe pits— down by the A-frame swing near the water's edge. She knew so few. Was that Billy Wooten down on the dock? Juli headed toward that one familiar face. A wild Frisbee whisked past her head.

A couple of small boats were tied up alongside the dock with rubber bumpers to protect them as they shifted in the water. Another boat was approaching slowly so as not to create a wake.

Juli touched her pockets for reassurance. Keys in one, cell phone in the other. Volume was turned up all the way, plus vibration.

"Billy?"

He looked over his shoulder. "Juli, hi."

She sat down carefully to avoid splinters. As worn and rough as the wood was, the smooth feel and the warmth of it beneath her hands and thighs, surprised her.

"No other teenagers around?"

He shrugged. "A few, but I don't know any of them. I can't stay long anyway, so it doesn't matter. Mom said it was polite to come."

"Is your mom here? I'd like to meet her."

"No, she had to take my sister somewhere. She'll be back soon to pick me up." Wistfully, he looked up the slope toward the house. "I don't think we'll eat before I have to go."

"I'm not going to stay for the food either. I need to get back home to Ben."

"I heard he's sick. I hope you don't mind me saying it." Billy blushed.

Juli reached over and touched his hand. His face flamed up like wildfire.

"It's okay to ask. Ben's a great guy and he's making the best of it. It's not easy. I don't mean to imply that it is."

Billy stared down at his sneakered feet hanging over the water as if he saw nothing good in front of him. Juli struggled. Should she? Asking was almost like baring her own hurts. She pushed it out, "Whatever's on your mind, say it out loud, Billy. I'm listening."

The words fell one by one. "My dad. It's been a couple of years now."

"How?"

"No, he left. It's like he died. My mom said she'd be lost without us kids, but I think sometimes it just makes it harder for her."

"You're wrong, Billy." Juli fought a surge of anger. Her mother and Billy's mom didn't have anything in common. Billy's mom took care of her kids. She didn't run away and leave them to fend for themselves.

He sighed. "Do you have kids?"

"No." She swung her foot over and bumped his. "Your mom would be lonely without you and your sister."

"Think so?" He launched a kick, but a gentler one that

brushed the side of her sneaker. He continued staring down at the water, but now he had a grin trying to grow on his face.

From a distance, a woman's voice called his name.

He looked up toward the house. "Gotta go." He placed his hands against the edge of the dock and brought up his legs. He pushed himself up onto his feet and held out his hand to Juli.

Juli reached up to accept his help.

"I think it's time for me to leave, too." She paused. A boat had caught her eye. It was almost to the dock. She looked away quickly, pretending she hadn't noticed Luke. Billy gave her an odd look, but Juli kept her feet firmly on the dock and waited.

Chapter Sixteen

A woman was sitting on the dock with a teenager. Her legs dangled over the side and he noticed them first—very shapely—then his eyes traveled upward and saw her face and the dark hair cascading from her hair clip. Juli.

Luke cast a quick glance beyond her seeking Ben. Luke hadn't seen him in a couple of weeks. He'd waited patiently for Anna's cookout, knowing Ben would be here unless he was too ill to attend. And if Ben's condition had deteriorated that much, Juli would've called him. So, if Juli was here, then Ben was, too. Somewhere. Maybe in the house or sitting in the deeper shade with the other picnickers.

The teenager stood and extended his hand to Juli. She rose gracefully, all fluid movement. It reminded him of how much younger she was. A decade might not be much for some people, but there were days when those years felt like a huge chasm.

"Hello, Luke." A man called out, heading toward the dock.

"Jake." Luke tossed him the guide rope.

Juli turned as his boat came alongside the dock. She looked apprehensive. He focused his attention on shutting the boat down and making sure Jake had secured the line properly.

"Luke," Jake said, "come on up. Sally wants to say hello and she's got someone she wants you to meet."

"No, Jake." He noticed Juli had moved nearer as if waiting to speak with him. He didn't want Sally and Jake to fix him up with anyone, and he certainly didn't want to talk about it in front of Juli and some pubescent kid.

"She's a keeper, Luke. We can't disappoint the ladies."

He looked at Juli, then back at Jake. "I'll catch up with you in a few."

"Serious, man. We're waiting."

"Promise."

As Jake walked away, Luke turned toward Juli, asking, "Where's Ben?"

Juli put a hand on the boy's arm. "Luke, this is Billy. He's one of Anna's students."

Luke nodded. The boy had actually moved closer to Juli and stopped slightly in front of her, almost between them. Luke held out his hand. "Nice to meet you."

Billy looked like he might refuse to shake. Luke waited and Billy gave in.

Juli said, "Billy, do you mind? I need to speak with Luke."

Luke noted Billy's slight swagger, a bit of posturing. He hid his amusement.

"Mom's waiting, anyway. I'll see you later, Juli?"

"Sure. See you in class." She watched him leave the dock and walk up the slope. "I think he's probably relieved to get away from me. I'm one of the old people now." She laughed.

"I think he had other things on his mind." Luke almost laughed with Juli, but he didn't see happiness reflected in her blue eyes and his own good humor dimmed.

"Where's Ben?"

"At home." Juli crossed her arms.

"Why?"

She tossed her head and pushed loose strands of hair behind her ears. "His stomach was a little upset. He wanted to stay home."

He didn't like the sulky attitude Juli was giving him. "But you're here. You came without him." His inflection left it hanging open like a question.

She dropped her arms and even though she put her hands on her hips, the attitude rolled off her shoulders and evaporated. "He insisted."

"I don't understand."

"Two simple words—he insisted. He ate a brownie and it disagreed with him. He's not supposed to eat stuff like that. I would've stayed home happily, but he, well, he wanted me to come."

"But—"

Juli held out one hand. "No, that's enough. I let you get away with a lot because I know you love him. Don't push it."

Luke's name was bellowed. The loud voice was Jake's. Everyone in the back yard, who knew Luke, looked at him. If Jake had been within reach, Luke would've decked him. Fear for Ben, annoyance with Juli, and aggravation at Jake clouded his face. When he looked at Juli, she gasped and stumbled backward. At first, it was a stumble, but then another step and then something happened because she was falling. There was nowhere for her to go but over the edge of the dock and into the sound. He lunged forward and grabbed for her.

Her arms waved instinctively reacting to the fall. Luke grabbed one arm and her waist before his shoe, too, caught the same uneven board or nail, and added his momentum to hers.

Chapter Seventeen

In this spot, Bogue Sound was too deep for her to avoid a thorough drenching, yet too shallow to miss the mud and general crud that layered the bottom near shore, especially with Luke's weight and force added to her own.

Juli caught her breath and held it instinctively because they were bound for the water. She was mortified even before they went under, still it was a wonder she didn't laugh at the expression of shock on Luke's face as they plunged down and down until her butt dragged bottom.

Under the water and in the mud, feet scrambled and arms flailed, and they were up again within seconds. Juli pushed her hair out of her face and pulled at her clothing, all in the same movement. Luke came up rubbing his face and shaking his head. All of the guests whose eyes had followed the sound of Jake's voice were now converging on the dock. She pulled a long, clinging piece of brown grass from her neck.

Luke asked, "Are you all right?"

Juli looked at him incredulously. She sneezed.

"You were falling," he said.

"Thanks for helping." But she didn't say it nicely.

Luke grinned. Water dripped from his hair onto his cheeks and nose. The water that hit him mid-chest nearly reached her shoulders.

"Miss, give me your hand."

Juli looked up to see a man she didn't know. There were mostly unknown faces in the growing crowd. Jake and Anna were pushing through them.

Luke nodded at her. She held her hands up. The rescuer wrapped his fingers around her wrists and Luke put his hands on her hips to boost her. The sure strength of his hands on her was so unexpected she nearly fell back again. Her rescuer pulled and Luke pushed and Juli found herself back up on the dock, her sneakers squishing. Her wet shorts had worked up around the tops of her thighs and she tugged at them hastily.

She looked back for no good reason and saw Luke watching her. Jake crossed her line of vision and held out his hand to Luke.

"Need help?" Jake asked, openly laughing.

Luke reached up and grasped Jake's hand. With his other hand he braced himself on the edge of the dock, brought up his foot, then pushed backward. Someone screamed as Jake wind milled into the Sound.

Anna wrapped an arm around Juli and led her out of the way as the rescuer, also anxious to be out of the way, was bumped by someone else, and he, too, went in with a splash.

"Men," Anna humphed. "Come with me."

Someone handed Juli a towel as they walked up the slope.

"Are you okay, honey?"

"I'm fine." Juli rubbed her face against the towel and patted her neck.

"Come on in. I'll get you a sundress or something. You're a few inches shorter than me, but it shouldn't matter."

"No, please. Don't go to any trouble. I'll drive home."

Anna made a rude noise. "Like that? I should say not."

Juli pushed off the wet sneakers and left them by the porch door. The porch smelled like heaven. The empty tables were now arrayed with chafing dishes. Juli and Anna dodged caterers as they made their way through the kitchen.

Anna hustled her down a hallway and pointed her to the bathroom. "Go dry off. If you want to shower, go right ahead. I'll be back in a jiffy with something for you to wear."

The extra weight in her pocket caught her attention as she shed her shorts.

"My phone. Oh, no." She stopped in the middle of undressing and tried to dial Ben.

Nothing. No signs of life. She would've pulled her wet shorts back on then and there, but Anna knocked and handed in a sundress, cut full and colorful. Juli pulled the dress on over her soggy undergarments. She only needed to wear them long enough to drive home. She was thankful—so totally thankful—that her keys hadn't fallen out of her pocket and gotten lost in the ooze.

Juli grabbed up her wet, tangled shorts and shirt and barreled out of the bathroom.

Anna rushed after her, "What's wrong?"

Bless Anna. Juli didn't want to be rude or worry her. "I'm sorry, but I have to go home right away." She talked as Anna followed her to the front door.

"Juli? What's wrong?"

"My phone. It isn't working."

"Well, I don't know, but maybe after it dries out…"

Juli wiped at her eyes. It seemed like water was still dripping. "It's Ben. He's supposed to call if he needs me. He can't call now."

"It's okay, Juli. He knows my phone number and I'm sure he's fine. You wait right here while I get my keys. I'll drive you home."

"No need. I'm on my way." Juli swiped at her teary eyes, again. She drew in a deep breath and exhaled slowly. "I'm fine, really. I have to get home to Ben, that's all."

Beyond Anna, Luke was standing in the kitchen doorway where the ceramic tile was safe from water damage. He was staring. Suddenly, Juli was so self-conscious, she couldn't bear it.

"Thanks, Anna. I'm sorry for all the craziness. Maybe you can save us some barbecue?"

She painted a smile on her face and gave a last wave as she went down the steps, then half-ran in her bare feet across the lawns bordering the street, to her car.

The car was an oven and she'd never driven barefoot. It felt odd, as if it should be illegal. Maybe it was. She didn't know. Didn't care.

Back home, Juli stepped out of the car and danced on the burning hot black asphalt drive. Her feet didn't stop moving until she entered the side door at the top of the stairs.

No Ben.

He was probably upstairs. She was being silly. Guilty conscience? Probably. She shouldn't have left him when he was feeling unwell, especially for something as silly as a cookout.

But, no, he wasn't upstairs. Juli saw him through the glass insert in the front door. He was on the porch.

He was leaning against the porch rail, but looking to the east as if in conversation with someone on the other side of the porch privacy divider. She opened the door. Ben gave her a sideways look. The corner of his mouth was quirked up and he was saying, "Is that so?"

Juli moved to stand beside him, leaning against him to look around the end of the divider.

Charlie's grubby hand was pointing down the crossover and his intent was as unmistakable as his words were unintelligible. It sounded like, "Yo yo ganesh, huh."

"Hi, Charlie," she said. "Do you need a translator, Ben?"

"No. I think the universal translation is 'I want to go down to the water.'"

Charlie bumped his bare chest against the wooden gate. The gate bounced. The latch held, but the wood was weathered and rough.

"Careful, big guy. You might pick up some splinters," Ben said.

"Hua."

"Right."

Charlie vanished from view for a second. He was quickly back. With one upraised arm, he flung a green plastic shovel over the gate. It skidded a few feet down the crossover and was closely followed by a red bucket. Then Charlie was back again, hands on the gate, shaking it so forcefully the hardware rattled.

Juli reached around the end of the partition and touched

Charlie's arm. She was planning to call out to get his mom's attention, but Violet was there, sitting in the back corner of the porch. She wore earbuds and was texting, her lips moving ever so slightly as she typed.

Juli called out, "Violet!"

She looked up, mouth gaping.

Charlie had stuck one finger in the corner of his mouth and started bouncing up and down, saying, "Um um um..." It was plain to see, in his chubby-cheeked anticipation, he was sure his big sister was being instructed to get up and convey him to his heart's desire.

"What?" Violet asked.

"Your brother is going to get splinters."

"Oh."

Victoria stuck her head out of the door. "Violet, I'm gonna take that thing away from you. Put it away now. Bring your brother in and get him washed up. It's naptime." She waved at Juli and Ben, then went back inside.

Violet grabbed Charlie around the waist with one arm and swung him up onto her skinny hip. Her precious cell phone was held carefully in her other hand as she carried him toward the house. Her outraged brother howled.

Ben retrieved Charlie's hopeful bucket and shovel. He dropped them back over the small gate onto the porch floor.

"Cute kid," he said.

"Grubby. A slightly runny nose, but a man with a mission. What's not to love?"

"Someday... Do you think that one day you'd like to have children?"

She looked Ben squarely in the eyes. "I'm enjoying today. Today is all I need."

"I don't think so."

"What?"

He grasped her arms gently and looked down. "I think you also need shoes. And where did the dress come from? I'm pretty sure you weren't wearing that when you left. What happened to your hair?"

Juli touched her hair. It was damp and felt clammy. "I went swimming in Bogue Sound."

"Swimming? In the sound?"

"Impromptu."

"You got pushed, didn't you?" Ben grinned. "I hope you weren't too angry. We used to do that all the time. Although, we didn't usually involve *unwilling* females."

"We? You and Luke?"

"Among others. We were young, then."

She pushed his arm playfully. "You actually look a little misty over the memory. Too bad you weren't there. I'm glad to see you looking better."

"How'd it happen?"

For some reason, Juli felt like she had to say it right and keep it airy. It was airy, wasn't it? Not a big deal. "It was unintentional. Luke asked how you were and tripped. We both went sailing...well, not really sailing because we definitely didn't float." She watched Ben covertly, from the corner of her eye, and saw nothing concerning. "So then, someone helped me out, but then Jake—do you know Jake? Jake went to help Luke out and got pulled in. After that, I heard other splashes, but I don't know what happened because I left. Anna loaned me this dress." She held out her cell phone. "This is a casualty."

He took the phone. "There are more of these, but only one of you." He hugged her. "I'm glad you only got wet and not hurt."

Later, when she was sure most of the guests would be gone, Juli drove back over to Anna's to retrieve her sneakers.

All was quiet on the street and in front of the house. The noisy hum from earlier was gone and traces of the smell of hickory and barbecue lingered like a sleepy memory. Juli walked around the outside of the house, not going to the door. As she rounded the corner, she saw some guests remained. A group of maybe twenty or so, sat around in lawn chairs talking low with the occasional louder voice and short laughter.

Juli stood on the outside looking in, but with contentment. Some of the chairs were empty and the scene was so relaxed, that even though she didn't recognize anyone in particular, she was confident if she walked up and took a seat, no one would do or say anything to make her feel like she didn't belong.

After she had returned to her life without Ben, this would be one of the scenes in time she would always remember.

"Hi."

"Luke." He'd come up behind her. "He's fine. Ben's fine."

He nodded. "I took the boat home and cleaned up some. Drove back over. You're alright?"

"Yes. The dunking was an accident. I told Ben and he took a trip down memory lane. Apparently, you guys used to make a habit of unplanned group swims."

"Hah." His eyes seemed to look back into the past, far from the flashing amber lights.

"I came back to get my shoes."

"And the barbecue. Anna put some aside for you."

"I'm sure it was delicious."

"No one can do barbecue like Tarheels."

"No one." Juli took a step back and as she turned away, said, "Thanks, Luke."

"For what?"

She shrugged and smiled. "Just thanks." She waved as she walked away. "And I won't forget the barbecue." Under her breath, she added, "Or the swim."

****

Ben went to church every Sunday morning. Most Sundays he took himself, but this time, after his spell on Saturday, Juli was concerned about him driving unnecessarily. Not that she'd tell him. He'd say he was a grown man who knew enough to pull over if he felt ill. But there was also the matter of the medication he was taking. It was bound to slow his reaction, maybe even impact his judgment in an emergency. It wasn't worth the risk. Not for the sake of determined independence.

Juli tidied up the kitchen waiting for Ben to bring up the

subject. He always did. A couple of times she'd gone with him. Church was fine. Mostly.

"Juli?"

Here came the invite. "Yes?"

"I think I'll head upstairs now."

She waited for him to finish speaking, but apparently he already had. He laid his book on the coffee table and stood. He paused on his way to the stairs to kiss her cheek.

"Ben?"

"Yes?"

"Are you planning to go to church tomorrow?"

"Yes."

"I thought I'd go along with you." Juli wiped at the counter, keeping her eyes focused on what she was doing.

"Well, that will be nice."

She let him get to the foot of the stairs. "Ben?"

He looked back at her with a faint smile on his face. "Yes?"

"Why didn't you ask me to go? You always do."

"I didn't think you'd say yes."

"Well, how can I say yes if you don't ask?"

"Would you go to church with me in the morning?"

She stared at him. "Sure. Be happy to."

****

On Monday, Maia said, "I'm glad you didn't forget. I meant to remind you at the cookout, but you vanished after the, uh, mishap." She put the package she was carrying into the trunk and reached for the one Juli was holding.

"You're trying too hard to kill the dimples and not succeeding. Don't laugh. You aren't the one that got dunked."

Maia giggled anyway as she closed the trunk lid. "I know it's not funny." She put her arm around Juli who was stepping away. "I'm sorry." She covered her face with her hand. When she removed it, she was in control again.

"Seriously, I'm not laughing at you, but I'll never forget the look on Jake's face as he went over the edge." Maia went to the driver's side. "You're comfortable with leaving Ben for the afternoon?"

Juli paused, her fingers gripping the door handle. She looked at her car parked nearby, behind the gallery, then slipped into the car seat. "He was well this morning. I got my phone replaced, so he can call or text me."

"Oh, no. Your phone went into the sound with you?"

"Oh, yes."

"I appreciate you coming with me. I don't usually deliver purchases to clients, but this one is a little different. I've been working with her so closely and she's a great customer. Now that I have Brendan, I can take a little field trip from time to time." A short distance down Front Street they turned onto Liveoak and then to Rt. 70.

"I love the gallery, but sometimes it's nice to see it at the other end, from the client's perspective. It's a beautiful drive and you might enjoy seeing the house. I've only seen photos, but it's something special."

"Honestly, I'm not comfortable leaving Ben, but he was looking forward to Luke coming over." She leaned her head back and rubbed her temples. "They'll enjoy their visit more, you know, as just the guys."

Maia didn't answer, but stared at the road, her hands on the steering wheel at ten and two.

She drew in a ragged breath that sounded perilously close to a sob. Juli sat up and put a hand on the dashboard.

"Relax, Juli. I won't drive us off the road. It hit me for a moment." She sniffled and dabbed at her eyes with her sleeve. "You forget, you know? And then reality smacks you in the face." Maia smiled, but with such sadness it almost brought Juli to tears, too. Maia must have felt it because she tried to recover the mood, "I'm so sorry. You're regretting coming along, now."

"No. Worried or not, it's nice to do something different."

"That's what I said, right?"

The road ran due north and was lined with forest, mostly pines. Somewhere to the east was the river.

"I meant to tell you—guess who else took a dunking?"

"At Anna's? Who?" Was this was a better topic? No matter, Juli was happy to get off the subject of losing Ben.

"Leslie." Maia took her eyes off of the road to catch Juli's expression. "Leslie Bryant. Do you know her? She came with Jake and Sally? I'm sure you saw her. She has red hair. Nice looking woman."

"I don't remember her. Oh, wait. I do recall a tall woman with red hair. Jake said he brought a woman to meet Luke. Was that her?"

"Has to be. It was Sally who wanted to fix them up. Jake will do anything to make Sally happy. That's the kind of guy I'd like to meet." Maia reached down and grabbed her water bottle for a sip. "Well, anyway, Sally and Leslie ran down to the dock with everyone else and saw Jake go in. Sally moved to avoid getting pushed off and Leslie went in, instead."

"She has my sympathy." The memory of the weedy, muddy bottom made her shudder.

"Oh, not at all. I think it suited her fine. She was laughing. Leslie's a good sport."

A good sport. Did that mean she, Juli, hadn't been a good sport? Melancholy swarmed over her from out of nowhere. "Maybe she and Luke will hit it off."

"Maybe." Maia gave Juli an odd look. "Aren't you two getting along better?"

"We are. It's important to Ben. And we both want the same thing—to do what's right for him."

"How's it going with Adela?"

"I wouldn't know. Ben talks to her on the phone when he thinks I'm not around. Adela never calls the house, probably because she might have to hear me say hello."

"I think we're almost there. Amanda said it was the first dirt road past the red barn."

Maia slowed as they approached a road. "It's graveled. Should I try it?"

"It looks fresh. I say go for it. If it isn't the Barlow house, we'll try again."

The tires crunched all the way up to the house. It was rose-colored brick, low and sleek in front with a multi-storied back section that rose above the front of the house and was ringed by windows.

A forty-something woman with perfect makeup and a silky-looking suit met them at the door and ushered them in. She gave Maia a quick hug.

Maia said, "Juli, this is Amanda Barlow. Amanda, this is Juli Bradshaw. She was kind enough to keep me company on the drive out here."

Amanda fixed her baby blues on Juli and asked, "Haven't we met? You look familiar. I never forget a name or face."

This was the woman who'd been clinging to Luke's arm at the party. The woman who said her ring had been stolen. Juli felt the words bubbling up, originating somewhere inside and borne up by the air from her lungs—the explanation of why she seemed familiar.

Maia spoke offhandedly, interrupting her. "She's Ben's wife."

"Ben Bradshaw? I heard he married. Sort of last minute, wasn't it?"

"Practically an elopement," Maia said. "So romantic."

"I see." But Amanda didn't look convinced.

Juli shrugged. She bent over to help Maia remove the brown wrapping paper from the etchings they'd brought.

"Maia, dear, would you place them around the room where you think they'd look best?"

She walked across the room, her heels clicking on the stone tile. "You know, I don't believe I've seen Ben since the party at Marcel and Petra's house, and barely then. He must have left very early." She settled her eyes on Juli again. "Were you already married then? Perhaps I saw you at the party with Ben?"

Juli wanted to say it—*I was the help. You might recognize me more easily if I were wearing my little white cap and black skirt.* She was ready to throw the truth out for Amanda's inspection and be done with it. She had nothing to hide.

"My ring was stolen at that party. It was my mother's and I hate to think I've lost it forever."

Amanda's remark dashed her like ice water. Innocence wasn't enough armor.

"I heard. It's terrible. Perhaps it will turn up yet." Maia stood back and pointed. "What do you think? These two would look good over the console."

"You have a good eye for such things. I trust you absolutely."

Juli watched Maia's apple-cheeked, dimpled smile. Didn't Maia feel deceptive? Less than honest?

Amanda spoke up. "I'll have the contractor hang them. You're a dear to have brought them out to me. I'm sorry to rush, but I have to be at the airport in an hour. The car should be here soon."

Back in Maia's car, Juli said, "We should've told her."

"Told her what? I was hoping for a closer look at the house so I'm kind of disappointed. Amanda's personality kind of grates, doesn't it?"

"We should've told her where she'd seen me, as a server at the Hammonds' party."

"Why? I didn't *not* tell her. I jumped to the next step and told her you were Ben's wife. Nothing else is her business."

They rode in silence for a few minutes, southbound on Rt. 70 until the Barlow house was well behind them.

Maia continued, "Amanda Barlow is a gossip of the highest order. Giving her grist for her gossip mill is the same as encouraging her. You wouldn't give whiskey to an alcoholic, would you? Or drugs to an addict?"

"No."

"Well, then."

"It doesn't feel right." A tiny lie here and there. Little white lies. Who did they hurt?

She'd told a bunch of them herself, so she could hardly fault Maia. "Maia, do you think I had something to do with the loss of her ring? Is that why you spoke up?"

The long pause nearly killed her.

"Juli. Why would you ask me that?" Maia's voice was small.

"Then why—"

"Why did I cut you off when you were about to tell Amanda you were working at the party? Because I didn't want Amanda Barlow speculating about you, the marriage, maybe even about what happened to her ring all over creation to anyone who'd listen. And plenty of ears would be thrilled to listen and pass it along."

"I don't have anything to hide."

Maia groaned. "If I thought you had anything to do with the theft, or any other crime—well, I know you didn't because I know."

"You know because you know."

Maia giggled. "Impeccable logic."

"I didn't."

"I know." She reached over and touched Juli's hand.

"Thanks. Maia, keep your eyes on the road, please?"

****

By the time Juli had stopped at the grocery store and returned home, twilight reigned. Juli stood in the darkened living room, silence close around her.

"Ben?"

The first sharp edge of panic touched her. It was too early for him to have gone upstairs to bed. She dropped the grocery bag and her purse on the floor and headed toward the stairs, then saw a silhouetted shadow on the porch. Juli approached the window, but didn't go outside immediately. His head was held low and his shoulders curved inward. He sat, unmoving, with one hand up to cover his face. The grief in his posture gripped her heart and tears welled in her eyes.

Had Frankie come back despite Luke's warning? Had something else happened?

Ben didn't look up when Juli walked out the door, nor when she stopped in front of him, so she didn't speak, but pulled the empty rocker closer to his. The runners scraped against the porch floor. Ben dropped his hand from his face.

"Juli."

She sat in the rocker, rested her arm on the smooth wooden arm rest and reached her hand across to grasp his. "Ben," she answered. This was an abrupt change from this afternoon. Juli was wary and afraid. "What's up? Didn't Luke come over? Is something wrong?"

Ben stared straight ahead for a few minutes. When he spoke, his voice was low and grave, heavily laden with regret. "Luke drove me to the doctor."

Juli was afraid to ask for more. She couldn't find the words that would ease the heart of his sadness. "To the hospital in Morehead?" Where his oncologist had his offices, but she left that part unspoken.

Ben cleared his throat and nodded, yes. "Early on," he gave a rueful laugh, "he suggested some experimental treatments. Clinical trials. I didn't want to be a guinea pig. I felt well enough. I accepted death. I wasn't in a hurry to die, but I wanted to die well, if that makes any sense. Or, I *thought* I was okay with it. Honestly, I don't think I accepted what he told me, that the end was inevitable and not far away. I felt so good, Juli. Tired, yes, but I was recovering from an illness, so that was understandable. Then I met you and knew I was lonely. I asked you to share these last weeks with me. And now..."

"Go ahead. What?"

"Now, I'm regretting the decision not to seek aggressive treatment. The odds wouldn't have been good even then, but maybe." He drew in a slow, ragged breath. "I made an appointment with him for today thinking it might still be worth a try, even if it only extended..."

He fell silent again. The answer he'd found in his doctor's office seemed obvious given his downcast air. Gently, she squeezed his hand.

"I hope you aren't angry Luke took me. I didn't want to say anything to you about it until after I'd spoken with the doctor. False hope and all that."

"I'm not angry."

"Juli, I haven't really lived in many years. I didn't know it. I had things, people, events, in my life, but no real heart since Deb died. Dr. Lewis said I'd waited too long. For treatment, I mean." He snatched his hand away and placed the heels of both fists against his forehead.

Juli's chest seized and her heart ached. For his regret, she could think of nothing to say except the usual platitudes and that wasn't enough. Before this, her personal relationships had never been close. She mentally rummaged through what experience she did have and came up empty. Words failed her. Her lips felt numb.

It was as if a weight was pressing hard against the back of her eyes, forcing moisture out even as she fought crying. She wanted to support Ben, not bring him down further. Why should she care so much about him? This was a business relationship— or rather he crafted their relationship as a business arrangement because her heart wasn't engaged—because it wouldn't hurt her.

But she didn't know him then, his value, and he didn't know her. They didn't know they would come to care about each other. He cared a great deal, Juli knew. Her chest ached, her throat was tight, and the pressure behind her eyes was relentless.

Juli reached over and reclaimed his hand. Her pain at the thought of his loss must surely communicate itself in the tight grip of her fingers, the almost-controlled trembling and the warmth of her flesh. These sensations must say what she couldn't vocalize. *Oh, Ben, I love you.*

He leaned toward her as she leaned toward him. The awkwardness of the two separate chairs didn't prevent them from reaching each other, their hands enfolding. Their foreheads touched in mute despair. When they stood, Juli rested her face on his shoulder, in the crook of his neck.

"I'm sorry," he said. "I was a fool."

"What?"

"A fool. An arrogant fool to think I was ready to die. Remember how I told you that for me it was almost instant, the feeling that I wanted to be with you? I was a fool to think it was enough to bring you into my life for companionship for a few weeks, that it would be good for both of us. A liar. I lied to us both, but it wasn't intentional. I didn't mean to hurt you."

"I don't understand."

"There are many ways to lie." He pulled her more tightly into his embrace. "You were the breath of life, a stranger who didn't see me as a dying loved one, someone with whom I could pretend I had a future, as if you were a lifesaver I could attach myself to, then leave quietly without regret when the time came. I was a fool. I'm not afraid of death, and I'll go when God says it's time, but I don't want to die now, not yet. I want to be with you."

She felt his breath on her hair as he worked his fingers through it, caressing the back of her head, the nape of her neck. A sigh slipped past her parted lips. He urged her head back, stared into her eyes, then slowly his lips touched hers. Their kiss was something they built together, designed by love and grief.

Finally, offended by the premature tears, Juli broke the spell of the kiss.

"You aren't dead yet. You don't even seem sick. Not very. Just tired."

She wouldn't mention his discomfort, or how thin he'd gotten. He needed to eat more, and treatment might help that.

"We'll go see the doctor together. I'm going with you this time, no argument. If there's nothing to be done, I want to hear it for myself." Stubborn, digging in against fate, was her style. Not bewailing her fate, but instead, fighting it tooth and nail.

The corners of his mouth turned up in a shaky smile. "I love you. I love you for many things, in so many ways. I won't try to list them. I love those things because they are you—all a part of you. When I think of you I see crystal, brilliant with light, and diamonds, strong and beautiful."

She laughed. "More like a junkyard dog."

"Persistent, yes, but glorious in action. Nothing junkyard dog about it."

"Will you call the doctor or should I?"

He ran his hands down her arms. "He was very clear when we spoke."

"I'll call him then."

"You win. I'll call him tomorrow morning. I understand you need to hear it yourself, but please don't go hoping for a miracle."

"Why not? What's wrong with believing in miracles?" Asked the girl who never learned to dream and she shivered.

His mood turned solemn, too, and he brushed his lips against her hair. "Dearest Juli, I believe in miracles. I think, however, we—you and I together—may have already had ours."

****

In the morning, Ben called the doctor's office.

"When's the appointment?" Juli asked.

"Not 'til next week."

"Next week?"

"He's out for the rest of this week. Margie got us on his schedule for the first thing Monday."

"I guess it'll have to do."

He kissed her cheek, his lips cool and dry against her skin, and she hugged him back.

"What's one week?" he said.

Chapter Eighteen

Ben slept late on Friday morning and Juli became anxious. The floorboards squeaked overhead when he rose from bed and walked across the floor. She jogged up the stairs, relieved to hear him stirring. He was groggy as he often was when taking his pain medication.

"Good morning, sleepyhead."

He made a noise that didn't qualify as an actual word.

"I'll start breakfast when I hear the shower stop."

He gave her a look that seemed to challenge her assumption that he would start this day as every other day, but then he gave in and nodded.

When the sound of water stopped, Juli started cooking breakfast. Two fried eggs, over easy. The English muffins sat in the toaster oven, waiting for the button to be pushed. The grape jelly sat on the counter.

"Ben? Breakfast is almost ready." Juli called up the stairs.

The eggs cooled on his plate. Not a big deal, there were more in the fridge. She dumped them into the trash. The English muffins still waited for her to start the toaster. Not a problem, they weren't going anywhere.

Juli put his juice back into the fridge to keep it chilled. She refused to acknowledge that today would be, could be, any different from the preceding days.

Ben came to the breakfast table and Juli cooked up fresh eggs.

"Just toast," Ben said.

"Too late, the eggs are already cooking. Just eat what you can."

She pushed because even two bites were two bites more

than he would've eaten otherwise.

During the meal, he said, "I think you should take your GED exam now. You're ready."

"What? There's so much I don't know." She glanced over at the books stacked on the coffee table. They might be a little dusty.

"You'll never know everything. No one can. You're smart. You cut traditional schooling short, but your learning didn't stop. You soak stuff up like a sponge—wherever you are and whatever you're doing. Go ahead and take care of it. If it doesn't work out, you can try again later, but it will and you won't need to."

His hair was still damp around the edges. Juli touched her cheek to his hair as she placed her hands on his shoulders. "I'll sign up. When I pass the test, we'll celebrate."

Ben pulled her hand down to his lips and kissed the back. "A party. And don't be sensitive about it, Juli. Declare it. Praise God for his guidance and declare your accomplishments to the world. We'll invite Maia and Luke. What about Anna? Who else?"

"Let's not get ahead of ourselves. I'll check to see when the tests are scheduled." She ruffled his hair with the hand he hadn't claimed. He wanted her to succeed now so he could celebrate with her. She wanted it, too.

"Juli, I was thinking it might be a good idea to get a small bed, maybe a cot or something, for the study. Not because I need it, but it would be good to have in case I don't want to climb the stairs."

She beat back the protestations and swallowed hard—gulped. "It might be a good idea. Maybe we should trade in the rattan sofa for a sofa bed. It would be useful if we had guests or something." She blurted out, "Plus, if you do those clinical trials, you may feel extra tired for a while."

Ben started to nod, then looked away abruptly. He got up from the kitchen table and walked slowly over to the table by the window to sit and push puzzle pieces around. Juli stayed at the kitchen sink, hunched over the cooling dishwater, scrubbing the already clean frying pan.

The clean sudsy smell reminded her of the Cox Family Restaurant and the meal that had turned out to be their first date.

Inevitability was closing in around them like the sliding walls in some sci-fi and adventure movie—Juli didn't remember which one. The walls were hard and cold, coming together slowly, inexorably, as the hero and heroine stretch their arms wide to prevent the steel walls from meeting. The walls are mechanical in their intent and impossible to prevent, but the brave heroes try nonetheless, unwilling to accept their fate because what lies ahead is unthinkable.

She crossed her arms, gripping her upper arms with her hands, wishing they were strong enough.

Someone knocked on the door. She saw their neighbor through the glass. "It's Mr. Spagnoli, Stay put. I'll get it."

Ron was tall and broad, built like a wrestler, and with a thick head of hair. "There's a hurricane on the way. I'm an inland kind of guy. Do you know if this is anything we should worry about?"

"I'm no expert either. Ben will know." Juli stepped back. "Come in."

"Thanks." Ron extended his hand. "I'm Ron. You're Ben? I don't think we've met. I see your wife on the beach most mornings."

Ben shook his hand. "I'm a late sleeper. Pleased to meet you. I've had the pleasure of meeting your son. Cute kid."

"Thanks. I'm sorry to sound like a worrier, but I want to keep the family safe. No one's talking evacuation. Juli said you two spend a lot of time at the beach. What do you think?"

Ben said, "They downgraded it to a tropical storm. It's forecasted to stay offshore. The authorities will call for an evacuation if they think it necessary. No one's particularly worried because it's weakening, but it'll take away from the end of your visit. Expect rain, wind and rough water tomorrow night into Saturday morning. No guarantees, of course."

Ron stepped back to stand just outside the door. He touched the casing on the side of the window. "These are hurricane shutters, right?"

"You shouldn't need them for this storm, but if something changes or you're not sure, just knock on the door. These shutters are electronic, easy to use, and I've got a set of keys."

She asked him after Ron left, "Are you sure there's no problem?"

"Don't tell me a little rain and wind has you worried. You didn't live far inland, yourself." He walked over and put his arms around her. "I won't take any chances. I don't take anything for granted, and never you."

"Living a little inland is very different than living on the edge of the ocean. Besides, I didn't grow up in the area, remember? I'm relatively new to the coast." Juli held his hand. "I'm a landlubber. Or used to be. I'm still getting used to this."

Ben turned her around and met her eyes. "You never actually said where you grew up."

"Mostly in the Raleigh area. I moved here a few years ago." Juli tried to say it in an offhand manner. She wasn't looking for pity.

"What brought you here?"

She reached up and brought his face to hers and planted a kiss on his lips. "Simple. There was nothing to keep me there."

They took a short walk and they took it earlier in the afternoon than usual. A number of people were stowing and securing loose items. A few were packing up to leave.

Low, heavy clouds had been pushing in all day cooking up an ominous stew in the atmosphere. The red Beach Patrol vehicles rode up and down the strand with regularity warning the few beachgoers about the rough conditions. Ben showed Juli, yet again, where the storm kit was stowed. He set the storm radio on the counter.

They stayed up later than usual that night keeping a close eye on the weather reports as the tropical storm made its way up the coastline. It was rapidly losing its punch and thanks to beneficial steering currents was moving farther offshore. They were forecasted to have high surf, gusty winds and occasional showers, possibly heavy at times, through the night and the next day.

The evening sky was a strange shade of green, like an omen, and it worried her. Ben put one arm around her and pulled her close as they walked upstairs together.

When they paused in the hallway, instead of turning toward her room, Juli touched his cheek. Her face felt warm and she was suddenly shy. She dropped her eyes and started to pull her hand away, but Ben caught her. He kept her hand as if he'd found treasure and brought her palm to his lips.

His eyes were warm with invitation. "Stay with me tonight?"

The hallway became its own special world—this moment only—no yesterday or tomorrow. A place where decisions were simple and obvious. Juli ran her free hand over Ben's chest and down his arm until she claimed his free hand.

"Tonight."

****

Later, when she awakened in the dark and heard rough, even brutal gusts of wind buffeting the front of the house she reached over and touched Ben's shoulder. His hand reached up to cover hers. She snuggled closer, enjoying the shared comfort.

Saturday's bloody red dawn gave way to swiftly moving clouds and crashing waves that beat violently at the land. The ocean was an adversary today and the wind was its ally. Fitful and gusty, at times assaultive, the wind sand-blasted the few beach walkers who'd been beguiled to venture outside by peeks of blue sky between scudding clouds. Juli, herself, was mesmerized by the quickly changing landscape and light as the storm pushed northward.

Ben stood beside her on the porch, each with their arms around the other, protected from the worst of the wind as long as they stayed near the wall of the house.

"Are you sorry?" he asked.

"Sorry?" She shook her head. "No, I'd say it was a lucky thing we were already married." She laughed.

He tightened his arm around her. He started to speak, but coughed instead, then cleared his throat. After a few minutes of standing together and suffering the sandy blasts, Ben spoke near her ear. "Keep away from the water today. I guess I don't need to tell you, do I?"

"No, you don't. The beach is too breezy for me, never mind the water," Juli added, as a walker's straw hat was whipped away, sailing as high as a kite into the distance. "It's just as well most of the vacationers are too busy packing up to be out here."

She felt the sag in Ben's stance. "Why don't you go on in? I'll join you in a few minutes."

He kissed her on the temple, then released her and went inside.

With Ben gone, she'd lost more than a wind buffer. The ultra-white nearer clouds racing with the dark clouds along the horizon, contrasted with beige sand and the savage ocean and found a wild core inside her. It echoed in her heart, the part of her heart not touched by Ben's need, but by her own troubles. At times nature's elements probed that restlessness, stirring it and drawing it forth. Juli drew her arms closely about herself and shivered.

There was a rap on the window. She turned and saw Ben. He waved at her and she turned to go inside to join him, but before she reached the door, she heard a noise on the other side of the porch divider, a bump and sounds of frustration.

"Are you okay?" She peeked around the divider in time to snag an inflated duck that tried to fly away.

Victoria was fussing with a net bag, fighting to stow beach toys as they tried to blow away.

"Charlie got into them. They were all packed. I should let them blow out to sea. Thanks," she said, taking the ducky. "I've got it now."

"Are you leaving tonight or in the morning?"

"Early in the morning. With kids, you have to get it packed up ahead of time."

"We've enjoyed having y'all as neighbors for these two weeks. Have a safe trip home."

"Thanks. You, too."

Juli went inside to join Ben.

Ben was seated in his usual chair at the table by the front window, working on his puzzle. He never seemed to make much progress.

Juli went to the kitchen just as someone screamed. She was turning toward Ben, to ask if he'd heard something, but he was already up and moving out the door.

"Ben?" She crossed the room and looked out the door. He was running down the crossover.

Running? What on earth? Beyond, down on the beach, she saw figures moving at the water's edge.

As surely as she knew something was wrong, she knew what it was—a drowning.

The door was still swinging wide as Juli flew through chasing Ben. He was moving faster than she would've believed possible. He was in the sand and heading toward the ocean as she reached the steps. Juli saw Victoria and her daughter, drenched, knee-deep in angry waves.

Two yellow water wings bobbed out in the water, staying about a foot apart and riding the waves as they swelled and dropped.

Could she see a child's hand? An arm? Too much spray and too distant.

Victoria was pulling at her tangled hair with one hand and pointing out to sea with the other.

Ben never paused as he ran past the women and splashed into the churning Atlantic Ocean making for the yellow plastic, tiny in the ocean, that might still have little Charlie attached.

Juli's feet hit the rough steps, then the sand, running to the rhythm of her frantic thoughts—thoughts that condemned Victoria for not watching her child and for not going into the waves herself.

Ben was Juli's and precious.

She heard Ron's deep voice yelling in alarm behind her. As she raced past, the distraught mother reached out to her, crying and screaming. Juli ignored her and followed Ben into the ocean.

He dove and swam. He did his best to find little Charlie in the roiling ocean. Adrenalin fueled the strength that drove Ben into the manic waves, but it faltered too soon. He couldn't withstand the ocean's power. Nor could she. As Juli grabbed him, the waves slammed their faces and snatched the ground from beneath their feet.

Juli dug her fingers into his arm, fighting the slippery wetness of his flesh. Through the greenish, translucent water, his face was white. Colorless. His eyes stared at her, then past her.

She lost her grip on him, bested by the pull of the ocean. She couldn't find bottom. Her toes searched for purchase and found only water. The next wave came as she surfaced to breathe. It filled her eyes and mouth with vile salt water and sand. *This is it.*

A hand closed on her upper arm with a viselike grip and pulled. She had no sense of direction, but felt ripped through the water, her arm in agony. Her toes hit sand and then her knees, as she was dragged onto the beach. Ron released her. She huddled, gasping and coughing.

Her lungs burned. Ron knelt beside her. She waved him away, rolling over onto her butt and pushing her hair out of her stinging eyes. Desperately, she scanned the waves and the beach.

"Ben?" Juli tried to yell, but only croaked. Her throat was raw. Ben was nowhere in sight.

Charlie's yellow water wings had vanished, too, claimed by the ocean.

Ron, above her, was saying over and over, "I'm sorry, so sorry."

Juli tried to rise. Her legs failed her. Ron caught and steadied her. She felt otherworldly, disbelieving. She wanted to scream this was a mistake. Ben had been working a stupid, boring puzzle. They had a doctor's appointment in two days.

Victoria was crying. Her words came to Juli through thick tears. "He got away from us. I'm so sorry. We saw his floaties and thought he'd... but they were tied together."

Juli turned to look. Beyond Victoria, Violet stood near the crossover. Beyond Violet was Charlie, oblivious, playing in the deep sand beneath the wooden steps, well-camouflaged by the strips of shadow and light.

Someone dialed 9-1-1 and Juli stayed on the beach. She answered the questions of the emergency workers, as did Ron and Victoria. Seeing the Beach Patrol vehicle took her back one day. Just one day made all the difference in the world. A big *if-only*. So she stayed, not because she had hope, but because the idea of returning to the house while leaving Ben in the ocean was more than she could bear. She waited.

For what? Acceptance? Would that come when her heart stopped shrieking, *no, no, no*?

When tears burned the truth into her denying eyes and shattered her control?

For now, she was paralyzed, trapped in denial. She dropped her head onto her arms. A kind stranger draped a large beach towel around her shoulders.

They'd known from the start he would die, but not today. Not this way. She couldn't accept and hold the reality. It kept slipping away from her like mist through fingers.

How grossly unfair that so much of life could be built upon chance, like a mom who believed her toddler had gone into the ocean alone at the moment Ben was handy to hear her frantic screams.

"Ma'am. Mrs. Bradshaw. You should go to the hospital. You took in a lot of water yourself."

"No. I'll stay here." She waited. Why? Maybe for an ocean of tears or for hysteria. Or maybe for someone to come running up the beach shouting Ben was okay.

Ron walked over to the emergency workers and the beach patrol. They'd already tried to convince her to leave the scene. A police officer detached from the group and came to her.

"Is there someone I can call for you?"

"Yes," she said. "His cousin, Luke Winters. Crescent Street. I don't know the phone number."

Coward. But no, not a coward, it was merely a physical impossibility to speak such words into the phone, to say them aloud, to anyone.

"No problem. I can get it."

At some point, when the remaining emergency personnel grew anxious and her vigil began to feel like a spectacle, she trudged up the steps, back over the crossover and faced Ben's empty house. She pushed through the door, but couldn't manage more than to reach the sofa.

Sandy and salty, still wrapped in the stranger's towel, she fell upon the cushions and curled up into as small a ball as she could manage.

Not long after, she heard someone at the door and Luke asked, "What happened?"

Chapter Nineteen

She pushed herself upright. There he stood, filling the doorway.

"He went into the ocean to save a child." Her throat was made of sandpaper. She hardly recognized her own voice.

Luke stared.

Juli ran her hands over her face and forced her breathing to stay within normal bounds. What more was there to say?

"Did he?"

"Did he what?"

"Save the child?"

She shook her head slowly, afraid of breaking into little pieces. "It was a false alarm."

He didn't say, *so, he died for nothing*. Instead, he said, "I called Adela. She's on her way. I guess there's nothing else to be done tonight." His voice sounded numb. "Do you need anything? Are you okay?"

She was obviously not okay, but there was nothing anyone could do for her tonight. Luke left.

Tomorrow was time enough to think. Tonight should be for grieving, but so far the emotions stayed jagged and painful, bottled within her.

It was an endless night.

Soon after the first rays of dawn had touched the sand and lit the water, Luke knocked on the door. Juli opened it. He stood on the threshold looking as rough and unwashed as she felt.

"They found him."

She gasped. Instantly, her chest hurt and her throat closed. She forced the words out before he could utter the dreadful words. "I don't want to know."

No word pictures. No location. She covered her ears and turned away, forcing the image of Ben, as Ben, into her heart and memory, the way she wanted to remember him.

"I understand."

Juli kept her back turned until he was gone, then ran down to the beach.

She sat and listened to the ocean. The tide came in and went back out. People walked past without stopping. The beach, littered with thick layers of broken shells dredged up by the storm, wasn't inviting to swimmers.

What did she look like? Wretched and disheveled? Had the people strolling by heard of the drowning and wondered? Been curious? She didn't care so long as they didn't bother her with questions or sympathy. The wind tangled her hair and the sand and shells abraded her skin.

Classic shock, she knew. And bludgeoned by grief and regret.

She should have been a better partner for Ben. A better wife. Had she done her best? The worst blow was that she'd be paid because Ben died. That had been the bargain from the beginning.

The day's light waned. She became aware someone was standing behind her.

"I knocked. No one answered. I almost didn't look down here."

She didn't turn around. She pushed the hair out of her face and sat straighter.

"Adela arrived this afternoon. She's making the funeral arrangements. Do you want to be involved? If you have special wishes or anything, you can tell her, or I'll tell her for you, if you prefer."

"Whatever she wants is fine."

"You can't stay out here."

She ignored him.

"You have to pull yourself together. The service is in two days."

Juli looked over her shoulder and saw his bare feet. The hem of his dress slacks hung awkwardly without the shoes and socks. She wanted to appreciate that he'd come out here to make sure her wishes were considered, but the trimmings were meaningless. Dead was dead. The ritual might be comfort for some, but it didn't change a thing.

Juli didn't want comfort. She wanted to know she'd given Ben what he needed despite how their marriage had started out, despite the fact she didn't fall in love with him in the same way he'd come to love her. Still, she loved him. Had it been enough for him? Had he known about her divided heart?

"It's time for you to go inside." Luke shifted his feet. "I have to leave now. Call me if you need anything."

She bit her lip to keep from begging, *tell me I made Ben happy. Tell me.* There was no one to whom to address such a question. Certainly, not to Luke.

The sand whispered beneath his feet as he walked away. Juli waited in the twilight to give him time to depart. When she stood and turned toward the house, he was standing on the porch facing toward her and the ocean. By the time she climbed the stairs to the crossover, he was gone.

****

Strangers filled the funeral home chapel in Morehead City for the service. She glimpsed Ron and Victoria standing at the back of the chapel as she entered, but pretended not to see them.

She walked with the family, stood with the family and sat in the pew with the family, but he felt encased in a plastic bubble. She was front and center at the service because, to the world, she was the widow. To Ben's family, she was a calculating interloper. She stared straight ahead, deliberately blind to the people around her.

The smooth wooden pews were hard beneath her. Hard was good. This was not a day for comfort.

She kept wishing she was back at home on Emerald Isle. But it would be without Ben.

And now, with Ben gone, she'd be out soon, too. Her brain

hit a roadblock there and could go no further. She'd think about that tomorrow or the next day.

Pastor Herrin spoke about Ben. She kept her eyes on him and remembered nothing of his eulogy. Each word passed right out of her head. All of her concentration was bent upon making it through.

There was a program in her hand. Someone had written it up and had it printed. Juli held onto the paper like an anchor, but didn't dare read it. She had to survive the service, then the ride to the cemetery and the graveside service.

She could do this for Ben. For Ben's sake and in his memory, she wanted to avoid causing gossip as much as his family members did. They'd get through this day and then they could all move on with their lives.

Tears welled in her eyes, stinging. She sniffled, but refused to cry.

She rode to Bay View Cemetery with Luke and another relative. They sat in the front seat, she sat in the back. They'd had the good sense to put Adela in a different car. Juli settled back in the corner of the seat as if she might find a hiding place. She saw Luke checking on her via the rearview mirror. She met his eyes, then looked away.

He was one of them. She wasn't.

They walked past the thigh-high red brick walls and then between the graves. She tried not to step on them, yet she was trapped in the front of the crowd making its way to the gravesite.

She dared not stop. A tingly, jittery feeling started in her chest. The air felt thick. Someone moved in beside her and took her arm.

"Juli."

Maia. Juli nodded. She wasn't alone amid strangers and hostile acquaintances.

They seated Juli in the front row of chairs, smack in the middle and directly in front of the casket, as befitted the widow. Maia remained standing near the end of the row of chairs. Luke had seated Adela. He handled her gently, murmuring soft words to her.

Adela said, "–Deb. He's next to her now, at rest. They are finally reunited."

Juli heard her clearly as did everyone within a few feet.

Somewhere deep inside, she felt it rising, sharp and suffocating. Her ears rang and she began to panic. She couldn't run for fresh air here. She was trapped and began to shake. Juli looked up, her eyes bypassing the flower-draped casket. She felt her calves tightening, preparing to stand, to escape. Anna caught her eye. She was standing near Maia who lifted her hand in a slight wave.

Beyond Anna and Maia was a weathered, wrinkled face, topped by a snow white crew cut. Dodge. Next to him were Laura and Donna, their eyes red and swollen. Billy Wooten stood with them, hair combed and dressed in a suit.

The frantic feeling flowed out of Juli. She was in control. She could make it through.

Maia and Anna were Ben's friends, but they were also hers. Some of these people were her friends only. They were here because they liked her enough to show support by spending these hours at a funeral for a man they never knew.

****

"Juli, these are my parents, Matt and Susannah Winters."

She saw two middle-aged strangers who looked remote. Sad? Yes. But around her, people were hugging and commiserating with each other over the loss of their friend. She was trying to figure out what to say when Adela's voice echoed across the open cemetery. "What do you mean I can't sell the house?"

Juli cringed at her strident voice and the words. Fred Lawson, a kind man and Ben's attorney, placed a hand on Adela's shoulder and guided her across the sloping green lawn toward the line of parked cars. He was bending toward her speaking low, soothing her.

When Juli turned back, Mr. and Mrs. Winters were gone.

"Juli?" Pastor Herrin took her hands in his. "Your hands are cold. Are you alright?"

He'd married them, and now had presided over Ben's funeral, all within a span of about four months.

"Thank you, yes. I'll be okay."

"Please call me when you're ready to talk."

She nodded, grateful he'd stopped to speak with her. He'd given the eulogy over the closed casket and made brief remarks at the graveside. Juli couldn't recall a single word, only the calming cadence of his voice.

Luke escorted her to the lead vehicle with a hand placed delicately, but firmly, behind her elbow. He wasn't exactly friendly, but she didn't sense the tension to which she'd grown accustomed. Was he subdued by grief? Or was it, now that Ben was gone, she would vanish from their lives in a matter of days?

Adela had made the funeral arrangements and no gathering was planned at Ben's house. Or anywhere. Food and fellowship following the funeral was customary. Juli suspected Adela wanted to cut her out. If everyone came to their home for food and condolences, it would have been impossible to exclude Juli. It was cruel and petty, but unwittingly, Adela had done Juli a favor. Having to host fellow mourners after surviving this day, would've been the ultimate nightmare.

When they returned to the house, she was surprised to see two cars parked on their side of the driveway. Luke gave the rental car a long look.

"The black sedan is Fred Lawson's."

"Mr. Lawson and who else?"

"Adela, I think."

She couldn't miss the chill in his voice. She said, "No one's in sight. Adela may have a key."

Luke frowned. "We'd better go up."

She knew Luke had planned to drop her off and continue on his way. She tried to decipher what this change in plans signaled. He knew Adela better than she. Perhaps he'd play the intermediary.

Did they think she had designs on Ben's furniture and linens? Maybe they wanted to protect Ben's pots and pans.

Mr. Lawson was seated in the living room. He looked stiff and uncomfortable. He rose as Juli and Luke entered. Adela was not in sight.

"Juli, I apologize for dropping in like this."

She felt warmed by his tone, but any comfort vanished when Adela emerged from Ben's study. Juli bristled, an unexpected territorial instinct rising, but she kept her mouth shut.

"Luke. Juli." Adela nodded in their direction. "Mr. Lawson told me I couldn't put the house on the market yet, but refused to tell me more without you being here. Don't think I'm cold."

Far from cold. If she touched Adela, they'd both combust.

"I have to return home. I need to get on with wrapping up Ben's affairs." Adela walked over to Luke and wrapped her fingers around his arm. "I can't leave all of the tasks to you. It wouldn't be fair."

She turned to Juli. "I don't want to be unfair to you either. The way the real estate market is these days, you should have plenty of time to make other living arrangements."

Luke spoke, "Adela. She's just come from Ben's funeral. Can't we take a moment to breathe?"

Fred Lawson moved into the middle of the room, breaking up the conversation. "Adela. Luke. I'm sorry, I must ask you to leave, or, at least, to step outside, while I speak to Juli."

Adela replied, "Is this about the contract? It's not a secret. Ben shared the terms with us. Luke is his executor and I'm his sister."

"I insist," Mr. Lawson said.

"Let's get it over with, shall we?" Juli was tired of it all. "Then everyone can leave and I can have some peace." She winced at the hard sound of her voice. "I'm sorry. It's been a difficult few days."

"I understand completely," Mr. Lawson said.

"Let them stay and be done with it. As Adela says, Ben

shared the details of our arrangement with them."

Mr. Lawson nodded. "If that's what you'd like."

He drew Juli over to the table, gently, as if she was fragile. His solicitude almost did weaken her, but she steeled herself to get this done. This last task.

The pieces of that blasted jigsaw puzzle still littered the surface, about halfway done. Mr.

Lawson sat at the end and she took a nearby seat. Luke stood by the door and Adela simmered a few feet away.

"Ben asked me to speak to you privately about this after his death. Given the family tension, it may be as well to go over this with Adela and Luke present. Ben came to me a month ago and amended his will. He left all of his estate to you. His sole heir. Luke continues as the executor."

An explosive non-verbal sound came from Adela.

Mr. Lawson turned to her and said, "Ben intended to inform you and Luke of the change in terms. His time came sooner than he expected."

Adela's face suffused into a deep red. Luke's face was carefully controlled. He said not a word, but walked up behind Adela and placed his hands on her shoulders. She erupted.

"We'll contest this. This woman took advantage of him. She's a cheat, a thief."

Juli remembered the Hammond's party and Luke's suspicions. It hurt that he'd spoken of them to Adela, but why not? There was no reason for him not to have spoken to Adela about anything concerning Ben.

Luke said, "Adela, please. Come with me." He tried to lead her away, but she wasn't having it.

She shook his hands off of her arms. "This was a business arrangement. This marriage was for convenience. Platonic. Luke, you told me yourself they were no more than roommates."

"Adela, that's enough." Luke's voice sounded weary.

She persisted, "This wasn't part of the contract."

Mr. Lawson had drawn back from her as if not wanting to

be swept up into her tirade. Now, he said, "No. This is apart from the contract, but tied to the fulfillment of the contract."

"The contract was contingent upon her not breaking the marriage vows, being unfaithful. Adulterous." He frowned. "Do you have reason to believe that the terms of the contract were violated?"

Adela's eyes burned.

Luke moved closer to her. "Don't do or say something you'll regret. This is an emotional time. We're all stressed."

Mr. Lawson shook his head. "Luke is right. This isn't the time, and it's a moot point in any case. It would have been up to Ben to revoke the contract, so unless you have some reason to believe—a very solid reason—that Ben intended to revoke the contract for cause, then there is nothing further to discuss."

Juli forced herself to speak. "I want you all to leave now. You're discussing me and my character, as well as private matters between Ben and me. If Ben had wanted your opinion, he would've asked for it. He didn't ask for mine either, but he has made his wishes plain." Juli stood, gathering her dignity, wishing it were armor. "I need to lie down now." She turned to Mr. Lawson, "I hope it will be okay for us to discuss this later. Perhaps in a day or so?"

"That will be fine. Call my office."

"This isn't over, Juli."

Juli held out her hand. "Adela, I'll take the house key."

Adela looked at Luke and at Fred Lawson, as if demanding they come to her aid. She walked to the end table and fished inside her purse, pulling out a key ring. She twisted a key from the ring, then threw it to the floor.

Luke hustled Adela out the door. Mr. Lawson stooped to retrieve the key. He placed it on the table. "Call me," he said, and left.

On unsteady legs, Juli crossed the room and locked the door, deadbolts and slide bolts included. She leaned there, her face against the cool metal for a minute. Her head was spinning and nausea was threatening in a mild way, but impossible to ignore. She hadn't eaten today.

Juli pushed away from the door, then jiggled the knob on the other door. Locked, too. She was tempted to collapse on the sofa, but instead pulled herself upstairs. She stripped as she went, dropping her clothing wherever it landed, and fell into bed.

She slept heavily until three a.m. Frantic, confusing dreams woke her. She got up to use the bathroom. Lightheaded and shaky, she clung to the bedpost until the room settled down. The vertical blinds at the balcony door had been left open. Moonlight lit the open area of the room and across the hall the same moonlight touched Ben's room. She followed the light into his room. It was almost as neat and impersonal as a motel room—like a weekly rental, like its twin in the duplex on the eastern side of the house—except for the shirt hung over the back of a chair.

Juli put the shirt to her face. Ben's scent was faint. This was his white dress shirt, the one he wore to church. She put it on. It reached partway down her thighs. She buttoned a couple of buttons in the middle and went downstairs, fuzzy-headed, thirsty. It was the pre-dawn hours of Sunday morning. The old renters would be gone soon and the new people would arrive later in the day. It reminded her of their wedding weekend, months earlier.

Drawn by her memories, she walked out the door and down the crossover, barefoot and careful of splinters. The onshore breeze—light tonight—plucked at the shirttail, flipping the hem around her thighs and hips.

She was alone again beneath the stars.

The waves rolled up the packed sand and over her feet. Their roar was no longer a novelty, but a constant presence.

Juli couldn't hate the ocean for taking Ben. The ocean did what the ocean did, as did Ben when he chose to rush to the aid of the child, as he'd admired Juli for doing a few days before.

It was as much her fault as anyone's. No one's.

It was just what it was.

She stood silently, head bent against the wind, hair wrapping across her face, catching in her eyes and mouth. She reached up to pull it away and found her face wet. Tears had come of their own volition, running down her cheeks, into the crease of her neck and wetting Ben's white shirt. She fell to her knees and shared her grief with the ocean.

Chapter Twenty

Morning beach walks began and ended earlier—in the translucent dark between night and day. Sometimes the morning fog cloaked Juli, sometimes the air was clear, but few people were up and about at that hour.

Pelicans skimmed the waves for breakfast before dawn. Sand pipers ran across the wet sand leaving miniature, twiggy footprints. One or two fisherman already had their lines out before the sun rose. No one wanted to chat in the pre-dawn hours. No one looked at her with curiosity—or worse, played and laughed, oblivious to what had so recently occurred. Among the transient population, memories of local events departed with the vacationers. History restarted itself for each new set of arrivals.

Before the light was strong, she was back in the house.

During the hazy days surrounding the funeral, new renters had arrived. She didn't want to know their names. They arrived after Ben's death and had immediately and enthusiastically jumped into their vacation with no regard for the tragedy shaking the world.

Shaking *her* world. The only world she had.

The new tenants were on the porch a lot. Their children constantly pounded up and down the crossover, running and chasing. They shouted and had water battles using the hose intended for washing sandy feet.

Disrespectful.

She stood at the front door, observing them through the glass panel, her hand on the knob, resisting the need to tell them—to instruct them—that this was a house of mourning. Her hand trembled. She stepped back and dropped the blinds, closing the slats. She went all around the main floor, closing blinds. When she was done, she sat in the dim living room with her hands folded in her lap.

The funeral was a blur. There'd been a few friendly faces at the service. She'd met a handful of people, fellow mourners. Most had kept their distance. Even given the natural stress,

Luke's parents—Ben's aunt and uncle—were very cool towards her. Or maybe they were grief stricken. When Luke introduced them, they didn't touch her in any way—not a hug or a handshake—and vanished as soon as her back was turned.

Light twinkled between the blinds where the cords cut through the slats. Ben would be disappointed. He liked light. Opening the blinds was the first thing he did every day. If he had his way they would never be closed.

She went back around, pulling the cords to open the slats.

It must be suppertime. Not that she was hungry.

She'd only ever cooked for one, until Ben. It should've been easy to go back to her old habits, yet how many times would she pull the egg carton out to fix Ben's breakfast before remembering?

Her appetite had been suspended, but she knew it was temporary. The clock said one thirty-two p.m.

Only one thirty-two.

She sat again on the sofa to wait until she came up with something else to do.

Surely, this was an ironic form of hell—trying to live Ben's life without Ben.

****

Juli called Mr. Lawson's office on Monday morning and spoke with his administrative assistant. They scheduled an appointment for Tuesday afternoon.

Juli had a problem. Ben had paid all the bills. He hadn't involved her in his finances.

She'd expected to complete the contract, take the final payment and then go her way, so she never asked questions. Ben kept his bills current, but it wouldn't be long before they were due again.

She could hardly believe Ben had changed his will to make her his sole heir. Someone was going to snatch it back. Maybe they should. This hadn't been part of the bargain, but then, neither had the feelings Ben and she had come to share.

Juli had found an address book in the desk drawer and reviewed the names. Luke and Adela had contacted everyone who should be notified of Ben's death. There were so many at the funeral service they could hardly have missed anyone.

She didn't know most of these names, but recognized the pastor's name. She wanted to thank him again for conducting the service. Ben would like that. Juli added his name to the list she was making.

She was in over her head.

Who might help her? If she dared ask him, Luke would be best. He was the executor and Ben had told her to go to Luke if she needed help.

Juli roamed the house most evenings, unable to settle to anything. Every creak and groan in the walls or the stairs seemed to demand attention, to warn of danger. She turned the TV volume up loud so she wouldn't hear them.

Early one afternoon Anna knocked on the front door. Juli saw her through the glass panel. She'd skipped classes since Ben died and she felt like a truant.

Juli opened the door with a smile on her face, but it crumpled abruptly when she tried to say hello.

"Oh, my dear girl. Cry. It will help." Anna hugged Juli and guided her over to the kitchen chair. "I'll make us some tea, shall I?"

"I'm sorry." She sniffled and drew a tissue from her pocket.

"Cry some more if you need to, it's fine. Get it out of your system and then get to work."

"Work?" Sniff. "Find a job?"

"No, no. Get to your easel. There's nothing like putting paint to canvas to cure whatever ails you. Be it heartbreak, grief, anger—paint it out."

She shook her head. Paint? Impossible.

Or maybe not.

She had the easel Ben had given her. She could set it up here and continue to stay inside the house.

Anna found lemon in the fridge and the sugar bowl on the counter. She carried them over to the table and went back for the kettle. "And get out of this house. Come back to class."

Juli shook her head. "I don't think I'm ready."

"Nonsense. If you don't want the others to ask about Ben or how you're doing, I'll tell them not to. But to stay away? No, you need to come back, at least for a while, so they won't think their presence at the funeral was unappreciated."

"It was appreciated." Juli noted Anna's red-rimmed eyes and remembered Anna had been Ben's friend for many years. Anna felt grief, too. "Thank you for coming over."

"I lost my husband years ago. I remember how it was. It's hard to lose someone dear to you." She reached over and patted Juli's hand. "It takes time to learn new habits, to go from being a couple to being on your own again."

"We weren't married very long."

"You cared about him and he cared about you. You two fell into being a couple as easy as pie."

"It's strange being alone now. Especially at night. Noises and all." How could she be confessing this to anyone? Afraid of noises at night? Next she'd be needing a night light.

"That's normal. Get an alarm system. Or maybe it's fronting on the ocean that's the problem. Between the wind and the water, any house is bound to creak. An oceanfront house needs extra care too, more than you're accustomed to living inland."

"It's a lot of responsibility to manage on my own."

Anna laughed. "Now that does sound scary. Noises, not so much."

"I don't know what to do. I don't even believe this is mine. Not really. What did I do to earn it? We had a business arrangement, a generous business arrangement."

"You feel guilty?"

She nodded. "Yes. No. I do, but I'm also happy about it, and I think that's what I feel guilty about. It sounds stupid to say it out loud."

"It does."

"So, I think I'll stop."

"Excellent." Anna clapped. "And you'll come back to class?"

****

Pastor Herrin knocked on the door. It was the one action she'd taken on her own, calling him and inviting him over. Juli was looking forward to his visit. He was a connection to Ben— a living, breathing piece of her wedding memory.

"Tea or coffee?"

"A glass of water would be welcome."

"Please have a seat."

When she returned she was surprised to see he'd taken Ben's chair at the table by the window. She put the coaster down and set the glass of water on top of it. She hadn't noticed before, but the table and the puzzle pieces were already dusty.

"I want you to know I appreciated your support of Ben when we married and later, too."

"I was concerned about Ben's plan to marry. Knowing what he was going through, it seemed too sudden a decision, but Ben opened his heart to me and I agreed to perform the service. When I met you on your wedding day and saw how you two cared about each other, my worries fell away."

"How we cared about each other? We barely knew each other."

"Appearances can be deceiving, I know, but I saw something special about the two of you. Was I wrong?"

"No, I don't think so...I came to love him. I wasn't *in* love with him." Was that stress in her voice? Guilt? Ben had known. They hadn't pretended with each other.

Pastor Herrin nodded. He had soft blue eyes. Kind eyes.

"People marry for love every day. Love means different things to different people. For many, it becomes confused with passion. If a marriage has a good foundation, and the spouses are honest and committed, the 'in love' often grows into love. Love is too precious not to value however it comes to us. Both you and Ben were two people who entered into a marriage with good will—people of good heart and intention with the capacity to love. And, in this case, it was a very special situation."

Her face was warm and likely bright red. "Pastor, I don't want to seem dishonest. You know this began as a business arrangement, right?"

"Yes, I understood. All the more reason to celebrate two loving hearts who supported each other during a time of great need."

"I'm embarrassed to admit I don't know what you said about Ben during the service. I'm sorry, it didn't stick in my mind."

"Juli, this is a very stressful time. Sometimes it's enough to do our best—to get through our troubles with dignity and charity—with hope for a better day. That's one way to think of faith. We are fortunate to be able to call upon our Savior and Lord for help. This was something dear to Ben's heart. When I gave Ben's eulogy, I spoke from the Books of Matthew and Romans."

He waited, but she stayed silent, so he resumed. "When I think of Ben, I think of faith.

Ben believed that, with faith, all things are possible. When I remember how he loved his church, his family, and his friends, I think of a stone that is dropped into a lake. A small stone, a pebble that sends fluid ripples across the surface. Ripples that repeat and repeat, effortlessly, in a shared unity, until they have touched the whole lake."

The pastor folded his hands on the table. "His faith assured him that his actions and words, even the least of them, would touch other people."

"He had faith, but he died anyway."

189

"He did. Faith also means that we bow to God's will. Juli, Ben never prayed to live. He prayed to live well, and that when it was God's will to take him, that he, in his physical form, would die well and go to his Savior with a glad heart."

"You mean that he was spared pain?" She winced at the snappish sound of her voice. "I overheard people say it at the funeral—*at least he was spared the worst of the pain*."

"I'm glad Ben was spared pain, but that's not what I mean. I mean he died, not looking back upon his life with despair, but looking forward to being with his Savior. I know he wasn't ready to go in the sense that he wanted to leave, but when he could've held back, and no one would have blamed him, he went into the ocean to save a child."

She couldn't resolve it in her mind. The pastor's words sounded good and even rang true in her heart, but the idea of faith was foreign to her.

"Juli. I'd like to ask you something." He reached out and touched the puzzle pieces. When he moved one, it left a faint outline. "Are you working this puzzle?"

She shook her head. "It was Ben's."

"I see. Would you like some help picking it up?"

She pushed the box over to him. He started gathering the pieces and she joined in. A stupid puzzle—why did it feel so good to have it out of the way?

Juli shook his hand warmly as he was leaving.

"It meant a lot to Ben when you attended church with him. You know you're always welcome. I hope you'll come and see us again."

"Thank you. Just now, I don't know what I'll do."

"I understand. You are welcome to think about it under our roof." He laughed softly. "Sometimes I do my best thinking there. If you don't mind, I and our congregation will keep you in our prayers."

After Pastor Herrin left, she called Luke and asked for his help. He didn't answer so she left a message on the voicemail.

"Luke, I'd appreciate it if you'd call me. I need some help

figuring out Ben's finances."

****

Luke showed up at her door on Saturday morning. His hair was slightly ruffled by the wind. He wore a loose, casual shirt that made him look broader through the shoulders, plus khaki shorts and sandals.

"Juli?"

"Come in, please." She stepped aside. "I appreciate your willingness to help. Coffee?"

"No." Not even a hint of a smile lightened his face. He nodded toward the study. "In there? What can I help you with?"

Chapter Twenty-One

One of the first things Luke did was to back up the data on Ben's computer. "Let's not risk losing this. Did Ben show you what he kept where?"

She shook her head. "A few things, that's all. Maybe he planned to do more after he changed the will, but, well, you know."

It was Luke's turn to shake his head. "What was he thinking?"

Her temper flared, but before she lashed out he spoke again, answering his own question.

"Ben thought he had time yet to show you through his records. Did he tell you what to do first?"

"He told me to go to you." How embarrassing. "For help," she added.

Luke stared at the keyboard for a few moments before he spoke. "Let's check his computer and desk drawers and see what Ben left us to work with."

"Okay." She gestured at the desk, inviting him to go through Ben's records, but Luke was looking past her.

"What's that?"

Juli followed his eyes to the far wall where Ben had hung the sketched portrait.

"Nothing much."

"Did you draw it?"

"Yes. It was silly of him to frame it."

"Well, he was that kind of guy. A nice man and a good friend."

Juli wanted to declare Ben had hung it because he liked it and because it was special to him, not because he was a nice guy. She held back. She was emotional these days. Out of sight, below the level of the desk where Luke couldn't see, she twisted her fingers. The feel of Ben's rings upon her fingers reminded her to be patient. She shouldn't be so quick to take offense.

It felt like the battle for Ben, for the protection of Ben, had morphed with his death into a new struggle. She first sensed it after the funeral with Adela. Who had loved him more? Whom had he loved most? Grief and loss drove people to do bizarre things. It had been easier when she had no one for whom she cared deeply.

Easier not to care, but that didn't seem as sensible and desirable as it once had despite the hazards.

Luke had something on his mind, but he didn't share it. Instead, he returned his attention to the notes he was making. He listed Ben's accounts, banking and credit, recurring bills, etc.

"You'll have to change these accounts over to your name, close others. You have a checking account in your name already as part of the agreement, right?"

"Yes, and he added me to his other accounts, too. In case of an emergency, he said."

Luke nodded. "If you like, I'll go with you to the bank to help sort out these others."

It would be easier to deal with the bank with Luke there as the executor. "Thanks."

"Do you want me to contact the life insurance company for you?"

The green kept rolling in, undeserved by her, Ben's temporary wife. "Adela was his heir before, right?"

"Yes, she was."

"Ben talked about a niece and nephew."

"You don't need to concern yourself about them. It was Ben's right, and his choice, to change his will and his beneficiaries. Adela and her family aren't in need."

"He said the kids are in high school, I think?"

"Yes."

"I'd like to split the life insurance policy between them. Maybe in a trust for college funds? Could you help me with that?"

"Think about it. It's a lot of money. I'll help you in any way I can, but be sure it's what you want to do."

Luke looked at his watch. "I have to go. Call me when you're ready to go to the bank."

Juli walked with him out of the study and into the kitchen. "We can take care of it whenever it suits your schedule." Had he heard her? He seemed distracted, fingering his keys absentmindedly. When he stopped abruptly, she tensed. Something was coming.

"At the Hammond's party back in April, I saw you. I didn't look through you. I was looking for Ben."

"Oh." Something small and deep within Juli held still, listening. Luke was stern, growing more so as he continued, yet he was looking at the door rather than at her.

"When I went to the coatroom, it wasn't to check up on the staff. I wanted to know if Ben had gotten his coat because he might have gone outside, or even gone home. I happened to see Frankie, and then you, while I was there."

"Okay."

"Ben had claimed his coat, so I went outside and spoke with the valet."

"Who told you Ben had left." She could imagine what else the valet might have hinted at.

"With a woman, he said. He insinuated Ben was drunk and you were…were doing the driving and…well, I knew Ben wasn't drunk. Not drinking at all, in fact, but I didn't know about you. *Anything* about you."

He was out the door in a flash. For a tall man with such presence, he moved quickly. Juli was left, feeling astonished.

Maia had been talking out of turn. Juli went to the study window and looked down at the parking area. Luke opened his car door and paused. He reached up and pressed one hand against his eyes.

If he was going to shed a tear or two, he didn't want her to see.

She put her hands to the window. If she could reach through and touch him, she would. Without hesitation, she would wrap her arms around him with abandon, victimizing them both and slashing her self-respect into humiliated pieces that could never be glued back into their former state.

And Luke would not thank her for the emotional revelation or her sacrifice.

Fate was heartless. Always.

Chapter Twenty-Two

He was trapped, caught between Ben, Adela, and Juli. They demanded time and energy he couldn't spare. He had his own grief. Had businesses to run. Responsibilities.

Ever since Ben first told him the news, he'd been grieving. Every time he decided what should be done, something happened to shake it all up.

Ben's marriage. Juli as the heir. Adela irate.

He was running an emotional obstacle course.

After the funeral, he'd taken Adela to the airport himself and stood by the exit ropes to ensure she didn't come back. For the time being, she'd been dealt with. Sort of like the Dutch boy putting a finger in the dyke to staunch the flood.

Woefully inadequate.

And Ben.

Ben was gone. He'd do his best to abide by Ben's wishes, including helping Juli. Luke understood why Ben wanted him to be friends with Juli. It was hard, though, to look at her without reliving the pain of Ben's loss.

It wasn't her fault, but... he didn't need to remind himself she was his cousin's widow. Or that she was ten years younger. Or that she had married Ben for his money.

She'd fulfilled the contract. She'd made Ben happy.

The trip back to Beaufort was a blur.

He entered the gallery by the back door. "Maia?"

She answered, "I'm here."

He went directly to his office and flipped open the blinds. He wanted the sunlight. He heard Maia in the doorway and said, "We have the Roundtree showing scheduled for next month."

He said it as if pronouncing doom. Maia clasped her hands

together.

"Yes. Are you re-considering?"

He knew she was afraid he'd say *cancel*, and while he wished there were more hours in the day, and that grief hadn't entered their lives, the fact remained bills had to be paid, plus he had obligations to employees and clients.

Responsibilities.

He stayed at the window, staring out at the narrow passageway and the painted brick wall of the store next door. Not a lot of sunlight, but better than no window at all.

"Luke." Maia's voice was almost a whisper. "We don't have to take care of it now. I know what to do and the contract is already signed."

"Then maybe I should make a run down to Charleston."

He could almost hear her worrying about him the way she'd fretted over Ben. He could've reassured her that he was fine, but he didn't. He wasn't fine. The only acceptable antidote was action.

But first he had to see Juli again.

Chapter Twenty-Three

Juli said, "I appreciate your help."

"No problem." Luke drove up to the street and checked for traffic before pulling out of the driveway.

"I hope it's not too inconvenient." Juli could see he didn't want to discuss it, or anything, with her. "I could go by myself." She tucked her hair behind her ear, then rested a hand on the armrest. Her fingers wanted to tap. She kept them still.

He touched his forehead. Did he have a headache? He could do better than speak two words and nothing more. If he would actually talk to her instead of making her prod and poke, she wouldn't have to drive him crazy by pestering him.

Juli said, "I know you're busy."

He kept his attention on the road as they rode down Atlantic Avenue. He said, "I told you I'm willing to help. Not to mention that as Ben's executor, I have to help."

Have to help? Well, if he was doing this because he was required to, then she'd let him get on with it and be done.

"I could've met you at the bank and saved you some time. It's not too late. You can take me back to the house. I'll drive over myself." Juli stared out of the window because she couldn't fake a smile today.

The turn signal clicked-clicked-clicked as Luke slowed and pulled off to the side of the road.

"What are you doing?" she asked.

Silence, except for the sound of the idling engine.

"What do you want, Juli? To drive yourself? Are you uncomfortable in the car with me?" He hit the steering wheel, but lightly. "If I've offended you, I'm sorry. I'm trying to be helpful."

"Offended?" She stared at the side of his face since he persisted in looking forward. "No. I didn't want to force you to do anything you didn't want to do—whether for Ben's sake or mine. I know you'd rather be anywhere but here with me. You didn't ask for this, it's been forced on you. It wasn't part of what you expected to do as Ben's executor."

"No, it isn't." He rubbed his forehead again, then shook his head. "But in a lot of ways it's easier for me now because I don't have to worry about selling the house and countless other tasks because the estate stays with you. If you want to handle it all yourself, say the word. I'll take you back home."

He was right. This was easier on him and he could walk away. He could say, you've got it now, it's your problem. Then what would she do?

"I'd like your help."

"So, what's wrong?"

Out of nowhere, it felt as though her eyes might explode with tears. She covered her face and breathed deeply—in, out, and over again.

"Are you alright?"

She nodded, took another deep breath and withdrew her hands. "It feels final. I didn't expect it to feel that way."

"Final."

"I know it's stupid. I thought I was ready."

"Do you want to wait for another day?"

She shook her head. "No, it won't be any better." She saw his eyes were red, too. "Somewhere Ben is looking at us and laughing at my foolishness." Some of the threatening flood leaked out of the corner of her eyes. She brushed the wet away and forced a smile.

He didn't smile back, but he looked a little less intense as he signaled and pulled back onto the road.

It was simple at the bank. Shortly before he died, Ben had asked her to sign signature cards in case he needed money in a hurry and was unable to take care of it himself. She'd done it and it hadn't seemed remarkable to her that he trusted her. Had he already made her his heir and was getting everything lined up? Today, the only changes needed were to remove Ben's name and his death certificate was sufficient.

It shouldn't be this easy to tidy up the loose ends of a life.

A concept of responsibility mushroomed in her head, momentarily blocking out everything else. The loose ends were tidied, but not erased. They were transferred to her.

The essence of Ben's life was transferred to Juli.

An inadequate vessel.

There'd been a day when she could've taken the money promised to her and run—but for having known Ben. She couldn't disregard the fact of his existence. *Admit it, Juli. His impact, his legacy, is about more than money.*

It was about her whole life.

Now, he was gone, but the ties weren't more easily cut. In fact, they were impossible for her heart and conscience to sever.

"Would you like to go to lunch?"

An unexpected invitation. She looked at Luke. She didn't want to go straight home. Going to the bank had almost been part of the ritual of passing. Something law demanded. It was a milestone that should be acknowledged.

"I'm sorry, Luke. I don't know what's wrong with me. My head is all jumbled. Yes, I'd like to go to lunch."

"Any preference?"

"None. Anything is good."

He pulled into a shopping center parking lot. "How about Rucker John's?"

"Fine. Ben and I ate there once." She wished she hadn't said that.

"Would you rather go somewhere else?"

"No. This is great."

The hostess seated them and the waitress gave them menus. "What would you like to drink?"

"Water," Luke said. Juli nodded agreement.

They were still examining the menus when she returned with the glasses of ice water, and asked, "Do you need another minute before ordering?"

"Yes, please."

Juli reviewed the menu, then placed it on the table. Luke was staring across the room.

"You look like you have something on your mind," she said.

"I do, but it's none of my business."

She shrugged. "Go ahead and say what you're thinking."

"I've never understood something."

"What?"

He shook out the folded napkin. "I know why he asked, but why did you agree to marry him?"

"Is this genetic or just a family tradition?"

"What?"

She fidgeted with the silverware, tapping the handle of the knife on the table. "This need to interrogate over food."

"I'm sorry. I shouldn't have asked."

Juli released the knife and clasped her hands to keep them still. "No, wait. I'm the one who's sorry. Interrogate is a harsh word, but it's a joke—was a joke—between Ben and me. I don't mind. Really." She ran her fingers down the moisture film on the outside of her glass. "I mean that. You know I'm blunt. If I don't want to answer, I won't. If you ask something you shouldn't, I'll tell you."

He sat up straighter. "I'm listening."

"Why I married Ben...." Deep breath. "It was his eyes." She looked at the nearby fireplace, its embers cold. "It was what I saw in his eyes. Honesty. Openness. No, not really openness. Vulnerability, but with courage. The willingness to risk being hurt or ridiculed."

She straightened the napkin in her lap, almost wishing Luke would interrupt, would pick up the thread of this conversation and take it elsewhere.

"I saw someone who, for reasons that made no sense, wanted me. Wanted my companionship. Wanted me on any terms he could get me. Me. Juli. I looked in his eyes and trusted him."

Luke pushed his chair back. "Excuse me," he said, and walked off toward the restrooms.

The first stab of shock at his abrupt departure passed quickly. No call of nature was that compelling. Maybe he couldn't handle the emotion? He'd asked for it, right? What had he expected her to say? That she'd married Ben for the money?

The waitress returned to take their orders. She looked at the empty chair. "Should I come back?"

Juli nodded. "Yes, thanks."

Luke returned within minutes. "Sorry for the interruption." He sat and placed his napkin back in his lap.

"I wanted to say one more thing. There was also the money."

He choked on his water. He coughed and she rose, thinking she needed to pat him on the back, but he motioned to her to sit.

"I'm okay, really." He laughed and coughed again. "I commend your honesty."

"And practicality."

"That too," he agreed.

"And luck. I never had luck, not a bit of it, not until I met Ben."

Silence stretched between them. Juli placed her hands flat on the table and stood. "I'll be right back."

Luke reached out and took her wrist as she walked past. "Ben was lucky, too."

The ladies' room wasn't empty, but no one was at the sinks. She took a paper towel, dampened it, and held it to her eyes. So much for her eye makeup. She didn't wear a lot anyway, so he'd probably never notice the difference.

A woman came out of a stall and stopped to wash her hands. Juli tossed the towel into the trash and returned to the table.

Luke said, "The waitress came, but I didn't know what you wanted to order. She'll come back."

Poor waitress. *All because of our drama.* Well, she

probably had drama of her own she inflicted on others. When she did return, Juli placed her order.

She folded her hands in her lap and tried to adopt a better attitude. "How are you doing, Luke?"

"Me?"

"I know you're busy. You have the galleries. Maia told me you're managing several in different cities and some other business interests, as well."

"Two galleries. I sold the one in Virginia Beach. Traveling to and from Charleston is enough."

"Can't you hire someone to do some of the work for you?"

"I can, but first I have to find that person."

"Is it so hard?" Silently, she thought, *Or do you not want to replace Ben?* That's what Maia had told her. "It's no good giving up your life to work. I know what I'm talking about, although, don't misunderstand me, I'm not comparing the jobs I worked with the work you do."

He nodded, but didn't speak.

"It's summer. You have a boat. What would you be doing if you had time off?"

She stopped talking while the food was delivered. When the server left, he still hadn't answered.

"Maybe that's none of my business." She said it deliberately, knowing he'd protest.

"It's not a secret. Boat, yes. Take a trip for pleasure, not work. Jog. Swim. Read a book."

She leaned forward. "Then do it. Hire someone and take a break."

"It sounds easier than it is."

"What's the hard part?"

Luke concentrated on chewing his food and drinking his water. Juli gave him peace for a few minutes.

It wasn't until they stood to leave that he said, "I'm leaving for Charleston this evening. I'll be down there for a few days. Maybe I'll put the word out again about the job. There are a couple of people I might consider."

"Sounds like a plan."

They drove to the *Glory* in companionable silence. They were almost back when Luke asked, "What about your plans?"

"Plans, me? I'm staying here for the time being."

"Is that enough for you? You don't seem like someone who'd be content to sit around doing nothing."

"I'm taking art lessons and doing some painting. I'm in no hurry. For now, I'm content."

She opened the car door and the hot air rushed in. "Thank you, Luke. We accomplished a lot today."

She shut the door before he could answer. She was feeling teary again.

Who would have imagined a courteous conversation could be so encouraging? Over time, her feelings would settle down and maybe they could be friends, after all. As for work, she liked being a lady of leisure. Sitting around for a while—not doing *nothing*, but doing only what she wanted—was a wonderful gift and she intended to enjoy it.

Chapter Twenty-Four

Juli dropped by the gallery at the end of September. Maia waved at her when she came through the door.

"Want to get lunch?" Juli asked.

Maia spread her arms as if to encompass all of the displays and said, "I have no help today. None. Brendan doesn't come in until this evening." She stapled a couple of receipts together and stowed them under the counter. "If you don't mind sharing my chicken salad sandwich, we can do lunch in the back room. With the door open, I'll be able to hear the bell."

"I doubt you brought enough for two. I'll go down the block and get some takeout if you can wait?"

"Sounds perfect. Lunch in the back room when you return. I could use a sweet tea with lemon, if you don't mind?"

"Got it. Be back soon."

There was a small table in the back room. The door to the room was adjacent to Luke's office door. His office was open; he wasn't in.

Maia positioned her chair near the door. She could watch the gallery and hear the bell ring if someone entered the front door. She took a sip of tea and unwrapped her sandwich. She stared down at her sandwich, then looked at Juli's. "Is that a cheeseburger and fries?"

Juli nodded, chewing.

"How do you stay so slim eating like that?" Maia patted her hip. "I keep saying I'll work this extra padding off." She sighed.

The bell rang. Maia did a quick chew and swallow of what she'd already bitten off and, wiping her mouth with a napkin, took off to greet the customer.

After a couple of minutes Juli peeked around the corner of the door. Maia was lifting a painting from the wall and a man was standing nearby. As Juli was turning back, the door to the alley opened.

"Luke. Hi."

He smiled, caught by surprise, but it looked genuine and she responded in kind. Briefly, they stayed as they were, sharing the moment, until Juli felt a nibble of fear. This was lovely. But dangerous.

"Is Maia with a customer?" His voice was low. His tone was almost conspiratorial, personal, and it gave her a shiver.

Juli nodded toward the gallery. "Yes."

"I'd like to ask you something. I know it's early, but you might want some time to consider it."

"What?"

"Thanksgiving. It's in a couple of months. I'd like you to share it with my family. My mother cooks a fantastic turkey dinner."

Thanksgiving? Ridiculous. This was still September. More than that, why would anyone think she should share a holiday meal with the Winters? She forced the words out. They sounded harsher than intended. "I met them once. Your parents. At the funeral."

"I know. Please understand they only knew what they were told. About you, I mean. If Ben, if the marriage, had lasted longer, they would've gotten to know you for themselves. They're good people, Juli. Whatever negative things people thought of you—whatever judgments they made—blame those on me."

She stared at the table, at the crumbs littering the white paper in which the grill had wrapped the burger.

"Think about it? I hope you can forgive me for making judgments, for acting on my emotions about Ben to your detriment. I've already told you I believe you were good for Ben and he was lucky to find you. I'm sorry it took me so long to see it and admit it. I hope you'll forgive me and give the rest of the family a chance."

She wanted to say, "Does it matter?" Instead, she closed her lips before the incredulous words could be voiced.

Luke's smile was slight, but sincere as he nodded his head and went into his office.

Juli sniffled and blinked her eyes. She wouldn't cry. This wasn't the place for it.

"I'm back." Maia reclaimed her chair and her sandwich. "A sale and a happy customer."

She frowned. "What's wrong with you?"

"Nothing. I'm fine."

Luke closed his office door and the latch clicked.

Juli leaned forward and whispered, "He mentioned Thanksgiving."

Maia looked confused. She whispered back. "That's two months away. Why are we whispering?"

"Never mind. We'll talk about it another time."

"Whatever you say. Can I stop whispering now?" Her dimples bloomed.

"Yes, please. Now tell me about your sale."

"Never mind the sale. What I need is reliable help." She stopped for a moment, then added, "And a boyfriend, a reliable one." She sipped her tea.

"Luke has a good prospect for a new manager down in Charleston. I don't have to tell you how badly he needs someone there who can handle the larger responsibilities. I was afraid he'd never move forward with it, but he actually talked to the guy on his last trip down there. I'm so relieved." She crumpled her trash. "You know, I should've thought of this before. I wonder if you'd mind helping me out?"

"With what? Finding a reliable boyfriend?"

"No, silly. I need help with the gallery for the Roundtree showing."

"You mean like working at the gallery?" She could think of worse jobs, but she wasn't looking for work just now, and certainly not retail. She'd had her fill of customers, enough to last for a lifetime.

"No, well, sort of, yes. We have a show, an open house for a new local artist. It's coming up in a couple of weeks and, for the most part, we're set, but it's the prep time before. See, we close the gallery early and then have to move a lot of the etcetera stuff out of the way. We need the floor space, plus it should look more elegant than seashells crafted into sea creatures with googley eyes will allow."

"Count me in. I'm happy to help."

She waved her hands at the ceiling. "We have to pack it up and move it upstairs. It's a lot of up and down." She sipped her tea. "It's always a big rush, but we have to be careful, too. Willing hands are a big help."

****

When Maia telephoned in mid-October, she said, "If you can get here around two o'clock, we'll have time to clear the gallery floor, spruce it up, then leave to get ourselves dolled up. Bring your outfit with you—it's fancy dress—and we'll get changed over at my place."

"Maia, I can't." Juli stumbled over the words.

"Oh. Something came up? No problem, I've got a couple of other people I can ask."

"No, wait. You misunderstand. I'll help get the gallery set up for the showing, but I can't attend the festivities."

Maia's voice rose. "What do you mean, you can't attend?"

"Think about it. Ben has been gone two months. How will it look?"

Juli heard a groan through the receiver, then Maia said, "I see your point, but is that your only concern?"

"What do you mean?"

"Not because you're shy or feel…you know."

"Because I won't feel good enough or accepted?"

"Acceptance works both ways, Juli."

"What do you mean by that?" She waved her free hand as if someone could see it. "Never mind. It doesn't matter. Bottom line, Ben's memory deserves better. Didn't you say that once?"

"The situation was a little different. Still, I understand. Two months a widow. We know

Ben would want you to enjoy yourself, but it may provoke others to ask questions about things that are none of their business."

"Don't pout. You'll get wrinkles."

"How do you know I'm pouting? You can't see me. And, anyway, I'm disappointed."

"I'll help get the gallery floor cleared and get the decorations up and then discreetly disappear."

Maia grumbled.

Juli said, "I'm glad it matters to you, but face it, we're both marshmallows. If I'm there, and one curious question is asked about Ben, we'll both sob. Think of what it'll do to our makeup. Not good for business at all."

"Yeah, we'll be soggy, wrinkled marshmallows. Not good on a lot of levels."

****

Juli showed up in her jeans and a lightweight cotton shirt, ready to work. Maia led her to one of the round display tables in the middle of the gallery floor. "Thank goodness, you're here. Brendan cancelled. He's got an upset stomach or something. Do you think it's an excuse? I hope he's telling the truth. He's been very reliable. If he's turning into a slacker, well, I can't deal with it."

"He's probably sick. I thought I was coming down with an upset stomach, too, but it passed. Must be a virus going around." Juli noted boxes with white packing paper were near the display tables. She picked up one of the shell sea-creatures and wiggled his eyes.

"I've got a neighbor coming to help. He'll be here any minute." She pointed to one of the boxes. "Wrap these loosely in paper, then put them in this other, empty box."

"He?"

"He's seventeen."

"Not exactly boyfriend material." Juli handled the seashell

creatures gently. The box, when full, weighed little. She carried it to the foot of the stairs.

"Our helper will carry the boxes up." Maia was wrapping the seashell frames when she heard a knock. She rushed to the door. "George. Hey, welcome."

Tall and lanky, George looked strong and shy.

"Juli, excuse us for a minute. I have to explain to George what I need him to do."

Juli finished up the frames, then moved on to other items. She found it peaceful working in the quiet of the closed gallery. She looked around the room and allowed herself a moment of fantasy, imagining her artwork hung on these walls. Perhaps one day she'd have a showing and people would dress up to attend. She'd be gracious and elegant…and the paintings—

"Juli? Are you here with me? You look far away."

"Daydreaming. Did you say something?"

Maia gave her a closer look and seemed satisfied. "As you empty the display tables, George will disassemble the ones we won't need and carry them up."

George was a quiet and willing worker. Juli continued wrapping items and stowing them in the boxes while George helped Maia swap out some of the paintings and larger items from the walls. Not everything would be the work of the one artist, but the prime space on the main wall would be solely his work.

As George carried the last boxes upstairs, Juli noticed Maia checked her watch again.

She waved at Maia. "Go. I can finish this up and then I'll leave."

"The caterer is a small outfit. They'll be here any minute."

"I can let them in." She didn't care if she knew the caterers. That must be some kind of progress.

"You can, thanks." Maia said. "George?"

"Yes, ma'am?"

"Don't leave Mrs. Bradshaw here alone, please."

"No, ma'am."

"There's a vacuum in the closet, George. Will you run it? When the caterer arrives, you can leave. Make sure they're set, though, before you go? Call me if they forget the food or something."

Julie said, "I'm laughing, right?"

"Keep your fingers crossed and call me if there's a problem."

"I promise." She was tempted to salute, but Maia looked too tense to appreciate a joke.

Maia vanished and soon thereafter the caterers arrived, with the food and with no one she knew. Juli spoke with them to verify they had what they needed, then left them to their work.

She took a last look around the main gallery floor. The featured artist was a fabulous watercolorist. Some of his paintings were hung on the walls, others stood on easels. She found one last bit of litter behind an easel. She paused in the back room to drop it into the trash can.

The door opened and daylight spilled in. Luke entered and shut the door behind him.

"You look very nice," she said. His tux was broad through the shoulders and emphasized his lean looks. She remembered him looking much the same at the party many months ago—the night she'd met Ben.

He tugged at his cuffs. "Thanks. It's very kind of you to help. You're welcome to stay."

"Maia and I discussed it."

"I know. I understand the reasoning, but I don't think your presence would've been a problem."

She shrugged. "I'll slip away now. I hope the showing goes smoothly." She started toward the door where Luke stood. "Oops, I almost forgot my stuff." She turned back to the counter and grabbed her purse and sunglasses.

Luke moved away from the door as a caterer came in asking a question about the set up.

He directed his attention to the white-jacketed woman and

Juli slipped out the back.

It was a beautiful evening and still early. She strolled along the uneven bricks of the sidewalk, smelling the water from the marina across the street, feeling the dry autumn breeze.

She had no plans and no need to rush home. She stopped in front of a restaurant a short distance down from the gallery and decided to step in for supper.

The service was slow, but she didn't mind. She had a decent view of most of the street, though not of the gallery itself since it was on the same side of the street. Through the window, she watched people moving along the walk, some elegantly dressed. They passed by in conversation with each other. No one she knew, but they had to be guests arriving for the showing.

Ben would've enjoyed it. The gallery showing, as well as watching the street show. He had a talent for seeing the best in everyone and enjoying every occasion. Did have a talent. Past tense.

She touched the corner of her eye and dabbed at a tear. They could've attended it together if he was still here. Or would they? Two months might have made a big difference in his condition.

Did Luke have a date? She could've asked Maia.

The waitress delivered her coconut shrimp. Juli settled back to enjoy her meal.

Maia hadn't said when they'd bring everything back down, googley eyes and all. Not tonight. Maybe tomorrow morning.

A streetlamp popped on as the last light waned. A woman paused beneath it. Red hair.

Leslie? Had to be Jake and Sally's friend because she looked familiar. She walked away, tall and sleek in a long, slim midnight blue gown. Arriving alone, apparently. Per Maia, Leslie hadn't minded taking an unplanned swim with Luke. Leslie did appear to be a very good sport.

Juli shook her head. No need to be snarky about Leslie.

The waitress brought the check over and Juli opened her

wallet to get the credit card. It was then she realized her car keys were gone.

She searched in the bottom of her purse and in the side pocket, but knew it was futile.

She'd dropped them on the counter beside her purse while in the back room. She didn't remember seeing them when she picked up her purse and sunglasses to leave. Could George or Maia have moved them? Could they have been knocked off the end of the counter?

What was at the end of the counter? The trash can.

Her heart sped up. Crap. Suppose they'd fallen into the trashcan and someone took out the trash? She didn't have a spare set with her and she wasn't up for dumpster-diving.

Talk about inconvenience. This time of the evening on a Friday—she'd have to find a ride home or—double crap—she didn't even have a spare house key with her.

The waitress returned her card and receipt. Hurriedly, she put the card back in her wallet and slipped away.

It was nearly full dark.

Through the large plate glass gallery windows, the interior lights shone bright and inviting. A sign in a black lacquered iron holder by the front door read "Private Event" in fancy script.

Guests moved about inside. Anna came near to the window, her hair worn long with a shiny ornament holding the graying locks back behind one ear. She looked stately. Juli started to wave, but caught herself. She was here in her jeans and sneakers, incognito.

It was pitch dark in the passageway between the gallery and the building next door. She paused at the entrance. Her heart had been galloping with the fear of losing her keys. Now, facing the blind passage, it did a steep dive.

She could creep through this narrow darkness or go through the much longer back alley which was about as dark. Going boldly through the front door in her sneakers and jeans wasn't an option. She was lucky this was one of the few buildings on this side of Front Street with a passage between.

Suddenly, yellow light spilled through the window near the far end of the passageway.

Luke's office window. No guarantee it would stay on, but if she moved quickly, she could take advantage of it.

She didn't intend to look in the window—never intended to spy on anyone—but it was as natural to turn her head in that direction as it was to put one foot in front of the other.

A redhead in a dark blue dress was leaning against Luke. His arm was around her back and his head was inclined toward her, his profile and hair lit by the desk lamp.

Leslie.

She wanted to be glad for Luke, but it made her sad.

Shame on her. He'd been good to her, more than what his duty to Ben had required. She bent over and moved past while she could benefit from the light.

As she rounded the corner from the passageway to the alley, the back door opened. A white-clad figure stepped out with a trash bag. Perfect timing because the door locked automatically.

She trotted over. "Hey, wait. Can you hold the door open?" She recognized the woman as one of the catering crew who had arrived before she left.

"Lost my keys. Did you see them? Maybe on the counter?"

The woman let her in. "On the counter? I haven't seen any keys."

"Thanks." Juli looked among the napkins and cups now stacked on the end of the counter where her purse had been. She tilted the trash can toward her, shaking it slightly. It was half-filled with paper and foil, with some sort of red sauce splattered over everything.

Half-full. Had it already been emptied? Or not used much? The caterer had gone back into the gallery.

Well, it was messy, but she could deal with it.

She reached in, but then pulled her hand back. There must be something she could use to dig around in there.

There were cabinets on the wall and under the sink counter.

A small closet was at the end of the room. A broom, a dustpan, rolls of cardboard, and other assorted stuff. A yardstick was leaning in the corner near the door.

She backed out of the closet, yardstick in hand. She turned and saw a guest decked out in finery and jewels, standing in the doorway watching her.

"Juli?"

She had a choice and made it in a split second. *Not Mrs. Barlow.* They were on equal footing. "Amanda. Hi."

Amanda came around the table, her hands pressed together. A big, shiny green stone glittered on her finger. "I remember you now. And not only from your visit to my house, isn't that right?" Her eyelids dropped partway as she stared, giving her a hooded look, like a bird of prey. She tapped the side of her glass with a manicured fingernail. "I think you've been less than honest, Juli. Why did you pretend you didn't know where I'd seen you before?"

"I wasn't pretending. I was at your house to deliver artwork. My personal business is my own."

The liquid in Amanda's glass sloshed back and forth. She put a hand on the table as if posing, or perhaps to steady herself.

"You were in my home. Everything in my home is my business. *And* you were at the Hammond's home when my ring was stolen. My ring is my business, too." She moved forward.

"Do you know what happened to my ring?"

"How would I know?"

"It was an expensive piece of jewelry." She lifted her hand from the table and waggled it back and forth allowing the overhead light to catch the facets of the green stone. "I like rings.

Those were your co-workers, your chums, right? My husband checked into Robard's Catering.

The police said there were thefts associated with the parties they catered. The police didn't question you?"

Juli was feeling surrounded. Incipient claustrophobia. Amanda, in her own way, was as predatory as Frankie. Time to take the offense.

"Maybe you stole it yourself to collect insurance."

Amanda hissed as the door swung open. One of the caterers stepped in. Amanda swung around to face her and the woman backed out immediately.

Juli followed up while she had the momentum. "I can't think of one good reason to stand here and listen to your nonsense."

"Is there a problem?" A deep voice cut through the tension.

Luke stood in the doorway, tall and distinguished in his tuxedo, with a quizzical look on his face.

Amanda's posture relaxed immediately. She turned toward him with an air of unconcern.

"Not for me. I needed Maia. I thought I might find her back here." She waved her arm. "But look who I found instead? Good of her to help out the caterers. But then she's experienced, right?"

"Juli helped us prepare for the reception." Luke's response sounded tentative.

"She has many talents, it seems. Delivering artwork. Waitressing." She smiled benevolently. "I wonder if Juli has any insight into the theft of my ring? She was there and knew the people who had access."

Luke's voice was curt. "What's on your mind, Amanda?"

"On my mind?" Her eyebrows arched. "She was working at the party where my ring was stolen. If the police didn't interview her, then they need to remedy their oversight. Someone should've reported her so she could be questioned."

Luke moved between them. As Maia came through the door behind him, he said,

"Amanda, this isn't the place for this discussion and you are misjudging Juli."

"What about your guests tonight? Would they agree? Maybe they need to watch their valuables."

Maia came up behind the unsteady woman and touched her arm. "Amanda, come with me. Please."

"What, Luke? You think because she married your cousin, she's above suspicion? She married him for his money, for heaven's sake."

"Now, Amanda." Maia tugged at her arm. She was petite, but her will was iron. "Now."

"One moment." Juli walked nearer to Amanda. She tried to infuse her voice with calm and kindness, without subservience. "I don't know about any thefts. If I knew, I'd tell you." Or would she still be trying to stay below the radar? She beat back her personal doubts. "I'll be happy to speak with the police if it will put your suspicions to rest."

Amanda stared, but didn't answer. Juli didn't allow herself to nod. She stiffened her neck, determined not to revert to the offensive little bob from her past. Dignity.

Maia maneuvered Amanda out through the door to where the other guests were enjoying themselves. "I'm sorry for all of this to-do at the showing. I'll get my purse and—" She lost her cool and put her hands to her cheeks. "I can't leave. I still don't have my keys."

"Your keys?"

"That's why I came back."

"I found keys on the floor. I didn't recognize them as yours."

"I changed to a different key ring recently."

"It's in my office. Come with me."

She followed him and moved with two quick steps from the back room to his office door.

A low level conversational hum and delicate, lilting music filled the space through which she briefly passed.

Luke switched the desk lamp back on and she pushed the door partway closed.

He retrieved the keys from his desk drawer. "Here you are. Sorry you had to go looking for them. I knew someone would, but I wasn't expecting it to be you."

"Thanks for keeping them safe. And thank you for standing up for me—for telling

Amanda she was mistaken about me. I'm sorry about the scene." She waved his response away.

"No, I'm not excusing her behavior, but I can't totally blame her either."

"Why?"

"When we delivered the etchings to her house, she asked where she knew me. Maia and I kind of blew it off and said I'd married Ben, implying she'd seen me with him." She shook her head. "Even then, I knew she wasn't satisfied. To her, it looked like we were hiding something, and once she figured out where she'd seen me, I can hardly blame her for being suspicious." She examined her keys. "What I'm most sorry about is disturbing your party—the showing."

"No harm done. I should get back to the guests, though."

"Of course." She stepped toward the door, then paused. "By the way, Leslie looks lovely this evening."

"Yes, she does." His sentence hung in the air between them like a question.

"You two make a nice-looking couple." There, it was said.

Luke stepped back and sat on the edge of his desk. "Do you think so? If you have something on your mind, just say it."

She cleared her throat. "Not at all. I was walking up the passageway out there." She pointed to the window. "Trying to avoid the guests, not wanting to disturb the party. I guess I didn't manage so well." She shrugged and crossed her arms. "I wasn't trying to spy or anything, but I saw you two through the window."

Luke glared. Or was it a stare? She didn't know. But her heart jumped and she trembled.

"Sorry. None of my business."

"You've gone this far, don't back off now. You saw me giving Leslie a safety pin. She had a wardrobe issue, as she called it."

"Wardrobe."

"Yes." Luke stood and moved closer, his eyes still glued on her face.

She was transfixed. He looked intent. Angry. Not angry. She took a step backward, forgetting the door, and it slammed shut.

Chapter Twenty-Five

Were her eyes now bluer? Her lips were parted slightly as if in question. Were they redder, softer, more delicately shaped? More intriguing?

So much tension had been between them from the start—negative tension. In an instant it seemed to have flipped, perhaps revealing its true nature. How did he feel? Not lightning struck, but as if someone had opened a curtain.

He'd seen her as a person before. What was new?

He was staring and she, well, she looked scared. Luke took a step forward to reassure her and she moved back, bumping against the door and causing it to slam.

The noise jolted him back to his senses. Before he could speak, Juli fumbled with the door knob, opened the door and left. Fled.

He followed her through the back room and out into the alley.

"Juli. Wait, please. What's wrong?"

"I don't know. You looked, well, I don't know. I've stayed too long and you've got guests and an artist, your guest of honor, in there who need your attention." She shifted feet.

She looked like she was about to break into a sprint. Why had he followed her outside anyway? Because she was about to walk alone to her car in the dark, that's all it was.

"Where are you parked?"

"Across the street in the marina lot. Not far."

"Are you going to walk the alley alone?"

"I'll take the shortcut through the passageway. Is the office light still on?"

"Yes, but—"

"Then I'm off. Thanks, Luke. Do you know when Maia will be setting things back up?"

"Tomorrow morning, I think."

"Please tell her I'll be here to help. If she needs me before eight a.m. she should call."

She pivoted and dashed off into the dark.

"Wait, I'll walk you to your car."

"No need."

By now she was nearly to the road and calling *thanks* back to him. It made no sense to chase after her. He felt compelled to follow, to make sure she was safe.

All the more reason not to—rationality was reasserting itself.

He and Juli were doing fine as they were, gradually becoming friends.

He walked slowly down the passageway by the light of his desk lamp. He stopped near the sidewalk and watched as the overhead light came on in her car, then the headlights. The overhead light was doused and then the soft sound of the engine crossed the distance of the quiet street to reach him. She backed out of the parking space, pulled onto Front Street and was gone.

She'd be back in the morning when it was time to put everything in its place.

So would he.

Chapter Twenty-Six

"Hi, Juli. It's Luke. Call me when you can."

She disconnected from voicemail.

If there were two of her, one would've run scared and the other would've danced around the room. Then doubt chilled her. Maybe it wasn't personal. It might be a problem with the estate or something.

But they'd worked together—well, the group had worked together—to put the gallery back in order after the showing. Luke had been attentive and funny. She hadn't expected him to have such a sweet sense of humor.

No time like the present to find out what he wanted. She called his number.

"Juli?"

"What's up?"

"I was thinking about taking the boat out."

She opened her mouth to say something light, but lost the words when she remembered Ben and their sunset cruise.

"Are you there?"

"Yes." Ben wouldn't be jealous. He'd want her to move on with her life. With Luke?

"It's a beautiful day for a sail," she said.

"Why don't I pick you up this afternoon? It's quiet at the gallery."

"Getting away while you can? Sounds like a good idea."

"Would you prefer to do something else? I'm open."

Could she go through with it?

"I'd love to go sailing with you."

"Great. I'll see you about three? Wear rubber shoes, sneakers or something, because the boat can get slick."

"I'll be ready."

Before three p.m. she found herself in Ben's room with a light jacket in her arms and her sneakers hanging from her fingers. She hadn't planned to stop here. *Ben, I have a date. I hope you don't mind.*

She wiped a tear. Luke would be here any minute and she didn't want red eyes.

The doorbell broke the spell. She laughed at herself and hurried to the door.

****

Luke entered, awkward at first, but only briefly. Juli's smile blew away his doubts, too easily. Odd that he found some reassurance in her slightly red eyes. This wasn't easy for her either.

She held out the windbreaker. He held it while she sat and tugged her sneakers on.

"What are you staring at?"

Luke said, "I was just thinking you need to get out and have fun as much as I do."

She stood and when she extended her hand to him, it was as if they'd done this every day for a thousand years and something hurt in his chest.

In the parking lot, she stopped. "Are you okay?"

He looked at the way her brown hair lit with fire from the sun and the blue eyes that matched the sea. "I'm good."

Juli laughed as she threw her jacket into the car. "Only good? On a beautiful day like this? Sometimes good is enough, but not today."

Chapter Twenty-Seven

It came upon her slowly—a gradual awareness. By the time she understood, she didn't find it surprising.

She stared at her face in the mirror. Did she look any different? Her eyes were bright and her face was flushed.

It was impossible. Frightening. Heat flooded her body.

Her heart raced. It was unbelievable. Exciting.

She couldn't do this by herself. She had no experience.

She wished she'd known in time to tell Ben.

Juli placed her hands on her flat belly. Stress could've interrupted her cycle. The past few months certainly had disrupted everything else in her life and she might have lost track.

That was it. She'd lost track. So much had happened, it was understandable.

But then again, her life had been a series of unexpected, unlikely events since the night at the Hammonds' house. This was just one more.

As frightened and excited as she was, there was no question in her mind of how Ben would react. He might not be here in person, but somewhere, somehow, he knew. "Ben, if this is true, if it's real, this is for you."

What would it mean to her and Luke?

Ben had been gone almost three months. She and Luke had worked in the gallery together. Gone sailing together. As friends. She felt more than friendship, but kept it locked up tight. Luke had mentioned Thanksgiving again. He said she should attend because she was Ben's widow.

The rest of the world wouldn't understand their relationship. Those who believed she'd married Ben for his money would—oh, but it was true, wasn't it? Ben got companionship and Juli got money. What neither of them had counted on was that their hearts would become entangled inextricably in the business arrangement.

Juli had loved Ben. She loved him, even if she hadn't been *in* love with him. Luke had taken that prize, perhaps from the first moment she saw him—not a tender love, but something different.

What about her feelings now? So soon after Ben's death, perhaps she was on a rebound.

Luke was attentive. Any decent person would be kind to her because of her loss. She must not read too much into it.

But he might feel more.

Luke and Juli, as a couple too soon, would condemn her forever as mercenary in everyone's eyes. Now, believing she was expecting Ben's child, the idea of a relationship with Luke was out of the question. She didn't understand why she felt that way, but she did. She dreaded telling him.

By Thanksgiving, she'd be somewhere between three and four months along. She had to tell Luke soon.

****

Luke sat on the porch with her one evening in the golden light of a late October afternoon.

"It's not a good idea to live at the beach year-round. Not for a novice."

"People do."

"They do, but the population thins out dramatically as the weeks wind down toward winter. Winter storms here on the edge of the Atlantic can be dangerous and destructive."

She watched Luke's face as he spoke. His eyes rested on the ocean swells racing into shore with a recurring, hypnotic rhythm beneath the tranquil blue of the sky. There was no renter in the other half of the duplex this week. He was right about the off-season solitude.

"I might want to move elsewhere, but not now. Not for a while."

Luke looked at her, then turned back to the view. "You don't have to decide today."

"It's not good to leave a house vacant anyway and I have no idea where I'd go. Maybe inland, maybe not. I like it here. I doubt I'll leave before spring or summer." She hesitated, wondering if this was the moment for honesty, then moved on. "How is Adela doing?"

"Still touchy. She needs time. Speaking of which, it's time for me to be on my way. I have to go by the gallery and take care of a few things."

"I appreciate the time you've spent helping me."

He cleared his throat. "I'm happy to help."

Luke was trying hard not to look at her. Guys handled emotion differently. Luke might not be able to say the loss of his dear friend had left a still tender wound in his heart, but she read it on his face.

This was clearly not the moment to share her news. *Thank goodness*.

****

"Thanksgiving is three days from now. Would you join the family for turkey? Just my parents and a few cousins. Nothing fancy."

Many times she'd stood in front of the mirror, rehearsing, planning how to tell Luke. She couldn't make it come out right no matter how she arranged the words. There was no happy ending here for her and Luke.

She gestured toward the table and put a cup of coffee at his place. For herself, she had a glass of ice water.

"I'm sorry, I can't. I've been meaning to tell you, but I didn't know how."

Luke shook his head. "I wish you'd reconsider. The family is looking forward to you being there."

"Please let me explain. There's no easy way to say it. I have to say it outright. I'm pregnant."

The color drained from his face. He sat absolutely still. The ticking of a clock somewhere filled the void, like the ticking of her heart, her pulse, and the rhythm of each breath. Into the waiting silence, she added, "Just over three months along."

Luke breathed in deeply, held it, and then slowly exhaled. "Frankie? No. Who…Ben?" He trailed off, lost.

He should've just slapped her.

She froze for one long moment. Would he rush to apologize and try to explain what he'd intended to say? No. She grabbed the edge of the table and, as she stood, she shoved it hard into his mid-section. The coffee cup rocked and rattled, then spilled long runnels of liquid over the side. He gripped the edge of the table and looked shocked. Perhaps as shocked as Juli felt.

"Get out." She breathed the words.

"Wait a minute." Luke stood. "What are you angry about? You and Ben didn't…were platonic. You had separate rooms. I saw them. Ben told me."

"If I'm more than three months pregnant and you think it isn't Ben's child, then you're saying I cheated, that I was unfaithful."

His mouth opened, his lips moved, but no words came out. Several times he tried to speak before he was able to. "Look, I'm not being judgmental. I'm surprised."

"It's still adultery and you think I'm capable of it. And have the nerve to hurt me by saying it." Juli stalked to the door and pulled it open. "It's time for you to leave."

He went and it was for the best. She told herself she was a fool to have allowed herself to enjoy his company so much. To depend on him. It was a lucky escape.

Thank goodness, it had ended now, before anyone's heart could be broken.

Juli stood with her back to the door and felt a couple of lonely tears straggle down her cheeks. Ben was gone. Now, Luke was gone. She'd pushed him out, hadn't she? Why? Because she had a long pregnancy to get through and couldn't deal with anything, or anyone, who would create more emotional confusion.

What had happened to her, the girl who was self-reliant and didn't need anyone? She'd been a widow for about as long as she'd been a wife. If Ben hadn't changed his will, she would already have moved on, settlement in hand, still pregnant and still alone.

The difference was, now she was securely and pleasantly housed and financially secure.

Ben's room was untouched. She'd closed the door after the first few days and left it shut.

She opened it now. The bed was made as it had been that last morning. Juli eased her body slowly down upon the cotton bedspread. She stared at the ceiling. It was time to move on with her life and she had to do it on her own terms.

Juli Cooke knew what it was like to be hardworking and independent. Juli Bradshaw knew how it felt to be loved by a good and worthy man. For the first time in her life, she had experienced deep and abiding grief. But motherhood?

She could learn.

Juli pushed up from the bed and looked at Ben's room. Mostly done in shades of blues and aqua. What she'd come to think of as a typical beach rental. A decent rental, but without distinction. Ben said he'd never gotten around to personalizing the house and, for the most part, it was true, but now a change was due.

Now this would be his child's room.

****

Juli stopped by a rental truck place in Morehead City to buy boxes and then went by Carteret Community College to schedule an appointment to take the GED.

Intent upon continuing her forward progress, she carried the boxes upstairs to Ben's room as soon as she returned home. She jumped right into emptying drawers, but handling Ben's garments was more stressful than expected. She didn't attempt to remove the few photo frames and knick-knacks, but she did flush the contents of the amber prescription bottles she found.

With trembling hands, she leaned against the dresser trying

not to look in the mirror, half-suspecting she would see him reflected behind her.

His brown leather Bible lay on the dresser. She touched it, then picked it up and ran her hand over the pebbly cover. This Book had been dear to Ben. She'd seen him with it often, especially in the early morning or late at night when he was wakeful. The soft cover flexed and she nearly dropped it. Securing her grasp, she felt the edge of something, an envelope, its edge protruding from between the pages. She slid the envelope out and opened the flap.

Photos. They were standing close together on the beach. Ben in a dark suit, she in the borrowed blue dress, both of them barefoot and looking amazingly normal. Maia had snapped this shot on their wedding day.

Their faces were almost cheek to cheek and both were smiling. No one would guess from looking at this photo they had barely known each other.

Juli slid the picture back into the envelope, but she didn't return it to the Bible. She laid it on top. She'd frame it. Maybe she could get the negative from Maia and have it enlarged. This would be important to their child.

She carried a cardboard box packed with Ben's clothing into the back bedroom that faced the road, then she climbed the cramped, steep stairs to the topmost room. The room was carpeted, long and narrow, and the sliding doors overlooking the ocean almost filled the entire front wall.

The sunlight streamed in through the glass doors and bounced off the white walls. There were a few items stored up here, including the easel and art supplies and the growing portfolio.

Her studio. Up here, up top. Only she would know. She'd been idle too long. She would fill her days for the next few months and wouldn't worry over what the future might bring.

Chapter Twenty-Eight

One week after the blow up with Luke, Maia knocked on Juli's door. That was Maia's way. She rarely called, but just came straight over.

Juli opened the door. "I guess Luke told you."

"Told me what? I wish he *would* tell me something. He's stomping around like a thundercloud about to dump torrential rains. The least bit of levity in the showroom and he barks at us. I don't want him driving Brendan away. I've finally got someone who'll work evenings and weekends, reliably. I'm not losing him." Maia swept in, speaking sharply, her usual lighthearted chatter nowhere to be heard. She pulled off her jacket and dropped it on the armchair. She put her hands on her hips. "Something has upset him or angered him. I intend to track it down and I'm starting with you."

Maia deserved the truth.

"Sit down. Please. We have to talk." Juli walked around the counter and into the kitchen. "Would you like water or tea? Or a cup of coffee?"

"I don't want anything to drink."

Juli gave her a warning look. "You will."

She frowned. "Alright. Whatever you're having is fine for me."

Maia settled on one end of the flowered sofa and leaned against the white rattan armrest.

Juli put two glasses of iced tea on the glass-topped table in front of them. She added a small dish of sliced lemons, and then went back to the kitchen again for coasters.

"Stop it, Juli. You're scaring me. Sit down and get it over with."

Juli didn't sit. She stood several feet away, not sure why the distance was needed. "I told Luke I'm pregnant."

Maia frowned again. She pursed her lips. She shook her head. Finally, she raised her hands as if in surrender and said, "Are you?" She clapped her hands to her cheeks. "Of course you are. You wouldn't lie about it."

Juli let her sit and stew for a moment. Maia's eyes traveled down Juli's mid-section and focused on her abdomen. Juli couldn't stop herself from touching her slightly bulging belly. She watched Maia's eyes change as they saw past the camouflage of the loose blouse and the actuality registered with her.

"Please sit down and tell me. I want details."

Juli didn't move at first. "It's Ben's."

"You're at least…" She counted, her fingers moving in alignment with her lips. "You're at least four months, I'd guess. Not much more, right? And Ben's been gone for about three and a half months."

"Bingo. You win the prize."

"Oh, my." Maia leaned forward, elbows on knees, hands on cheeks. "How are you? Are you okay with it?"

Juli walked over and sat on the sofa next to her. "I was surprised at first, but, yes, I'm glad."

Maia picked up her glass. She sipped her iced tea, then added lemon and sipped again.

"So you told Luke."

"Yes."

"And that's why…"

Juli shrugged.

"But… I mean, why would he…? So, you're expecting. He believed you and Ben were just roommates, but I still don't understand why he'd be so upset about you carrying Ben's child."

Juli opened her mouth and shut it again, thinking better of what she'd started to say.

"You'll have to ask him."

"But—"

Juli insisted, "I'm not a mind reader. Ask him."

"If I *dare* ask him, is that right?"

"That's about it."

Maia sat up straighter. "Did Ben know? Did he change his…, no, scratch that. Four months pregnant now, so you couldn't have known at the time he died." She slouched and put her hands back to her face. "I'm sorry. I'm such a klutz. This must be awful for you. A dreadful strain on you and in your condition and here I am reminding you." She reached out and grasped both of Juli's hands in hers. "Tell me what I can do to help. How can I make amends for being so insensitive?"

Juli switched her hands around so that she was now grasping Maia's. "No, you're fine. I've had a couple of months to get used to the idea, but it wasn't something I wanted to run out and tell anyone. It felt so complicated. But then, after I told Luke—actually said the words aloud to another human being—it changed. Now, I see it's very simple."

"Simple? It's not simple at all. Do you have a doctor? What will you do about a nursery? And proper maternity clothing? Can I go with you? I enjoy looking at the baby things and the maternity clothing, but more and more I'm thinking I'll never have a reason to choose my own. Can I help you?"

Juli was speechless. Maia's generous spirit overwhelmed her and Juli suddenly burst into tears. She tried to brush them away.

"Oh, my goodness. Oh, my. I'll get some tissues." Maia ran to the kitchen, found no tissue, then to the bathroom where she grabbed some toilet paper from the roll. She raced back to Juli with the tissue bunched up in her hand. "Here you go."

"I don't know why I'm crying," Juli said between sobs. Maia looked alarmed at the tears and her reaction struck Juli as funny. She started laughing and crying at the same time.

"Calm down, Juli. It'll be okay."

Was she hysterical? Juli tried to rein in her wildly swinging emotions. "I'm fine, really. I'm sorry I scared you."

"Hormones. Must be hormones. I remember how it was when my older sister was expecting." She patted Juli's arm.

"Probably," but she punctuated it with both a sob and a laugh. "Do you feel like a walk?"

"It's chilly out there." Maia shivered and rubbed her arms to emphasize it.

"I've missed walking on the beach. I used to walk in the early morning, but now it's too cold at dawn." The sobs were revving up again. "I need fresh air and exercise."

"At dawn? That's crazy. You need sunshine. I suppose if it's too brisk we can come back in." Maia picked up her own jacket from the chair. "Where's your coat?"

Juli waved her hand. "I'll get it."

Maia hovered nearby as Juli walked to the closet.

"I'm fine, really. I don't know what happened. Hormones? You must be right."

They didn't walk far, but far enough. Juli felt calmer, even with the onshore wind whipping up the sand. Maia looked miserable, so they turned around and walked back at a faster pace.

Inside the house, with her cheeks bright red from the cold, Maia said, "I want to know exactly what you've done to prepare, and what you still need to do. I insist."

****

Two weeks later and it was almost Christmas. Some days were mild, some were wintry.

Not only did the weather change according to season, it was also true of her life. In the past month Juli had made major changes, from getting an obstetrician to earning her GED. She framed the certificate and hung it in the study next to her drawing of Ben. She'd see them both when she sat at the desk. She'd made almost no changes in the study or in the rooms on the main floor.

Maia yelled down from upstairs, "Where's those paper towels? I've got to catch some drips."

Juli grabbed a partial roll from the holder affixed to the

kitchen cabinet. "Coming."

Maia had insisted Juli couldn't paint the nursery in her condition. It seemed extreme to Juli, but she was glad of the companionship and the help, so she didn't argue.

Thank goodness for Maia. She was heaven-sent.

Juli had never asked Maia much about her personal life. She'd been so wrapped up in her own drama, she hadn't noticed how one-sided their relationship was. They were true friends now.

To Maia's dismay, Juli had refused to make a final decision on the baby furniture and limited her purchases to a few pieces of maternity clothing.

"Why not choose the furniture now?"

Juli shook her head. "I'm not superstitious, I'm not. But it's too soon. It's not time to buy the furniture and other things yet."

Juli held firm about the furniture but gave in to Maia about the painting.

She carried the paper towels up to the nursery-to-be. She edged around a night stand Maia had pushed out of the way.

Juli said, "I've arranged for people to come and move this furniture out. I'll have it stored in the street-side bedroom for now. There's plenty of time. No need to rush."

Maia dipped the brush in the paint can and smoothed the excess off on the rim as she withdrew it. She applied the soft yellow, edging carefully around the door trim which would be left white. She stepped back to check her work, then looked at Juli and said, "There's never as much time as you think."

****

Maia urged Juli to celebrate Christmas with her family— her parents, her sister's family, some aunts, uncles and cousins. They lived north of Beaufort. Her dad was a retired marine.

Juli shook her head. "I'm sure they're lovely people, but I'd like to stay here."

"It will be too quiet for you."

"I like quiet."

"You were alone for Thanksgiving. Shame on me for not thinking of you then."

"No, Maia. Anna invited me for turkey dinner, but I passed on it. I was in a solitary mood. I've had a lot to think about."

"I understand, but if you change your mind at the last minute, my parents live less than an hour away. I'll come get you in a heartbeat."

Chapter Twenty-Nine

Christmas morning was overcast with drips of rain and occasional snowflakes. By noon, the sky had cleared. It was a hard, brilliant blue, the way it can only look in winter. Juli put on her coat, scarf and gloves. The coat was cut full and still roomy.

She stepped out onto the porch and saw a box wrapped in cheerful Christmas wrapping paper and topped with a huge red bow.

There was no one else in the duplex. The package—the present—must be intended for her.

Was it from Maia? No, not Maia. They had exchanged gifts the day before Christmas Eve, before Maia left for her parents' home.

Juli stepped to the porch rail and looked up one way and down the other. Not another soul was in sight. The box was about the size of a coat box. She picked it up gingerly. It wasn't heavy. She twisted it this way and that looking for a card. No card.

Juli carried her gift inside.

She removed the bow carefully and then picked at the paper. Paper off, she broke the tape that secured the box top to the box bottom.

Oh.

Her eyes prickled with inevitable tears. She'd produced more tears in the last two weeks than in her whole life.

She touched soft, plush velvety fabric, the color of vanilla ice cream. She ran her fingers lightly under the collar, then lifted the whole thing out. A robe. Had she ever seen a garment this soft and luxurious? Never. She shed her coat, slipped her arms into the robe, and pulled it on right over her clothing.

The other garment was a white cashmere sweater with three pearl buttons on the bodice and gathered full below. She held it in front of her. Seed pearls garnished the upper bodice area and the sleeves were different, a kimono shape. Extravagance was the only word she could summon. She held it to her face and felt the light tickle of the fine filaments.

Was it maternity? No, she didn't think so, but it would work, at least until the last months. Beneath the sweater was a perfectly silly pair of slippers, thick and soft with bunny ears and a pink nose.

Juli pushed the tissue wrapping aside searching for a card. Nothing.

She folded the sweater carefully and put it back in the box. Without the robe, the box looked empty. She took off the robe and folded it, too. She placed the bunny slippers on top. Juli slid the box under the boughs of her Christmas tree. Her tiny tree, courtesy of Maia, was situated on the table by the front window. If the gift box was stood on end, it would be taller than the tree.

Luke? Not likely. Adela. Definitely not. Frankie? She shivered. *No.*

If Ben had still been alive, it would have been his style.

She could pretend. In the absence of knowing, she could pretend the gift had come from her husband and her baby's father. Could pretend he had only stepped out for a while.

If not Ben, then from someone who cared about her? That was almost as good.

She plugged in the little tree and its miniature white lights glowed. She returned her coat to the closet. She had her own little bit of Christmas, after all.

The phone rang. Now, she would have her answer.

"Hello?"

"Hi, Juli. How's your Christmas Day? Not too lonely, I hope. Will you join us for Christmas dinner?"

"No, I'm good. Wonderful, in fact." She threw out a feeler. "Thanks for my lovely gift."

"What? That tiny tree? You should see the one Dad bought this year. It's huge and already dropping needles everywhere. Or did you mean the baby book? I'm glad you like it, but it's not so very special."

Not Maia. "More special than you can know."

"Sure you don't want to join us?"

"Positive. Go enjoy your family."

But when she hung up the phone, she did feel alone. A huge tree dropping needles everywhere might be fun. It would certainly smell Christmassy.

The night before, Juli had flipped through Ben's Bible looking for the Christmas story.

She had a vague memory of it from family number one, but with several children in the family, their house had seemed a whirlwind of activity to little Juli. They'd gone to church and someone had read the verses and the little kids were dressed up in angel wings and such.

Yesterday evening, she had tried to read through the New Testament passages, but so many ancient memories were called up, she found it more distressing than comforting.

The memories of her last Christmas at home, a year before she went to family number one, were even sketchier. She remembered a skinny tree. And being alone and hungry in the dark.

Strangers, the child services people, told her she was going with them. A woman's voice, a neighbor, was talking in the background, telling someone about how she'd called the authorities, going on and on until her strident words faded into the distance.

Little Juli had wondered if mama would come for her. She missed mama, but she liked having a full belly, clean clothes, and other people around. Mama didn't come, and finally, Juli relaxed and settled in.

Mama's name was Frances. That's all Juli remembered and all she wanted to remember.

Today, Christmas Day, with the mini-lights glowing in the

little tree and a scrumptious present under the tree, she felt a promise for better memories to be made.

She might start making those memories in the morning with a visit to Pastor Herrin and his flock.

****

On Sunday morning, Juli sat in her car, waiting, watching the digital clock on the dashboard. A minute before the service was scheduled to begin, she went through the doors. She snagged a bulletin from the usher and slipped quietly, discreetly, into a back pew. A few people looked at her. Some of them might remember her from when she'd come with Ben. She didn't want greetings. She didn't want commiserations.

She stood with a hymnal when the others sang, and bowed her head when they prayed. A stranger was in the pulpit. A guest preacher.

What was she trying to prove? That she could do this?

Juli slipped out during the closing prayer, dashed to her car and left the parking lot before the other worshipers made it out the church doors. She asked herself why? And where would this lead? Where did she want it to lead?

During the week between Christmas and New Year's, Juli focused on her artwork. Her easel was set up in the tower room near the glass doors where the light was best. She tried to paint the ocean, but she couldn't capture the quality of the light, translucent and constantly shifting. The task was ambitious, but she kept at it. Another day she focused on the shades of tan in the sand and dry sea oats. The tower room was too high above the beach to get a close view, so she brought some of both upstairs and laid them out on a plastic tablecloth.

She liked pushing her limits without the pressure of expectations she couldn't meet. She dabbled and played in acrylic, then knelt on the floor beside Ben's goody box and pulled out the oil paints.

****

On New Year's Day, Juli cuddled in her robe until nearly noon, watching TV. Finally, she went upstairs and showered and dressed, thinking Maia might drop by now that the holidays were almost over. She hoped Maia *would* drop by. She'd like some good company.

Her jeans hadn't met across the middle for two months, but her maternity pants were too large. She stood in front of the dresser mirror and held the waistband out in front of her and marveled she would fill it out one day in the not too distant future. She settled on navy leggings and a smocked top.

When she returned downstairs, someone was standing on the crossover. She'd gotten used to seeing almost no one day in and day out, especially since she, herself, rarely went out except to take walks. Luke had warned her to expect it to be lonely and he'd been right. The person was standing at the far end, facing the ocean. When he pushed back and turned toward the house, she recognized Frankie.

Breathe, relax. You don't have to protect Ben any longer.

It was stupid to ever think he needed to be shielded. Ben would've known what to do.

She was smart and resourceful. She should know what to do now, but scraps of ideas and fears chased each other around in her brain. She couldn't pull out anything coherent.

Had she been protecting Ben? If so, this should be simple now because protecting Ben didn't apply anymore. She'd been protecting her own ego.

He couldn't have seen her through the windows from so far away. As he came closer to the house, she backed up onto the first step of the stairs, past the corner and out of sight even if he pressed his face to the glass in the door.

Suppose he forced the door? Would the slide bolt hold?

Foolish girl. Living alone, with the dearest bulge growing daily, she couldn't risk confronting him. Where had her toughness gone?

She had too much to lose now.

After a few minutes, she peeked around the corner. Had he left or just moved out of sight? She fought the urge to run to the windows and close the blinds. If she did, she'd be telegraphing she was here and afraid. It wasn't smart to show fear to people like Frankie. The phone upstairs—she could use it without risk of being seen. Could she call the police? Frankie hadn't actually done anything to her.

Was he still out there? Maybe down below, underneath the house where her car was parked? Or on the stairway below the front porch?

He came from behind the partition on the other side of the porch and leaned against the end of it, looking at her side of the house, her windows and her door. The door was more glass than anything else.

She wouldn't live in fear. Stupid fear. Foolish fear. *Get some backbone, Juli. You used to have more grit than was good for you.*

Forcing herself to breathe evenly and slowly, she took her coat from the closet. It was cut full so it still buttoned in the mid-section. Frankie wouldn't be able to see she was pregnant.

She put the cell phone in her pocket and kept her hand in there with it. She opened the front door, stepped boldly outside and closed the door behind her.

"Jules. Hey, there." Frankie grinned and stood straighter.

"What's up, Frankie?"

He frowned. "You act like I've done something wrong, like you've got something against me, but I haven't. I've always been a friend to you."

Frankie paused, either to intimidate her or to draw her into a conversation. Juli didn't know which, but she kept her mouth shut and didn't give him either.

"Not even when you refused to invite me in, or introduce me to your friend, and my feelings were hurt, you know? You sent that guy to tell me to stay away." He moved slowly toward her. "Did I get angry? Did I try to get even?" He stopped. "No, Jules, I didn't. I was good enough to be your friend when you needed a ride somewhere or wanted some other favor, but not when you're living easy."

It was true enough, although she wouldn't have called him

a friend, but more of a neighbor and sometimes a co-worker.

"I appreciate what you're saying, Frankie. I still don't understand why you're here."

"I heard he died. I felt real bad for you. Wanted to know if you needed anything. Figured I'd drop by and ask."

"How did you know he died?"

"Mrs. White told me. She saw it in the obits. I was gone for a while or I would've been around sooner to see you. Offer sympathy and all that."

"Thanks, Frankie. I appreciate it, but I'm good."

"I'll say. Got yourself a nice place here." He looked around at the house and scenery.

"Thank you."

"You're still not going to invite me in, are you?" He looked disbelieving.

She shook her head *no.*

He tried again. "It's lonely out here. Cold, too." He exaggerated a shiver.

He'd kept his hands shoved in his jacket pockets the entire time. It was cold, but Juli had one hand in her pocket, too, and it wasn't due to cold. They were crossing some sort of invisible barrier where she would say "leave" and he wouldn't. Then what? He could continue to act good-natured and keep telling Juli what a good friend he was the whole time he was buffaloing her back into the house and forcing his way in.

She'd lost her edge and her nerve. She shivered for real.

"Cold out here for you, too. How about one cup of coffee, Jules?" He moved a few steps forward. "A few minutes to shake off the chill and I'll be on my way. Plus, there's a little matter of something that belongs to me."

"Juli, are you up there?" Maia came up the stairs from the parking area below, the stairs leading up the crossover where it met the porch. "Oh, you have a visitor?"

Frankie didn't look so chummy now.

Juli said, "An old neighbor, Frank Bowman. He dropped by to say hello."

"Uh, huh." Maia said. She smiled, but not the usual cheery Maia smile.

Frankie looked sullen. "I'll see you around." He brushed past Maia and went down the stairs.

The oddest thing happened. Her head was so light it felt as if it might float away on its own. Her lips tingled and her shivers had turned to shakes.

"Maia—"

"Are you okay? Oh, my, you're white as a sheet."

Maia grabbed Juli's arm with one hand and put her other arm around Juli's waist. Since she was almost five inches shorter than Juli, it seemed almost slapstick, but neither laughed.

"I need to sit."

She helped Juli onto the sofa.

Juli asked, "Is the door locked?"

Maia tried the door knob. "Yes. Locked and bolted. I'll get you a cool cloth for your face. Lie down and put your feet up."

Juli laid her head back against the sofa.

"I told you to lie down. You have to get your head down and your feet up."

Juli did. "Much better."

"I told you so. Now, you tell me something. Who *was* he?"

"An old neighbor." She closed her eyes enjoying the damp cloth on her forehead.

"I knocked and you didn't answer, so I came around front. I heard you two talking. I didn't like the sound of his voice. It gave me goose bumps. Was I right?"

"Maybe. I don't know. I over-reacted. I've known Frankie for a couple of years, but we're not the kind of friends who keep up with each other, if you know what I mean."

"What now?"

Juli pulled the cloth from her face. "I feel better now. You're a wonderful nurse. I got so caught up, surprised by him being here. I'm spending too much time alone. I'll be glad to get back to Anna's class. She took off two whole weeks over the holidays."

"Selfish woman."

"Yes, no doubt." Juli sat up carefully and pushed her hair back.

"Don't get up yet."

"I'm fine now."

"Probably, but mention it to your doctor. To be on the safe side."

"Okay."

"When do you see him next?"

"Her. In a couple of weeks."

"You're going to think I'm pushy, and I don't want to invade your privacy, but don't you think you should give me a key? Suppose next time you pass out and can't answer the door?"

"I think it's a great idea. Remind me before you leave and I'll give you Ben's—I'll give you the spare."

Maia nodded as if all were now as it should be.

"How was your Christmas? Your family?"

"I met someone." Maia spoke in a small voice. She blushed and her dimples crinkled.

"Tell me."

"He works with my brother-in-law. He's very nice. My sister set us up."

Juli shook her head somberly. "I don't know, Maia."

"Don't know what? What are you troubled about?"

"It would take a very special man to be worthy of you."

Maia's mouth dropped open for a moment and her eyes glistened. "You are so silly."

"I'm serious. You're always there for me, for others. But what about your life? You're spending your days and evenings at work—working retail, no less—having to cater to customers. Believe me, I know how customers can be. And when you're not working? What are you doing? Helping me and everyone else."

"Oh, no, Juli. You're wrong." She leaned forward and took

Juli's hand in her own. "I love my job and I love being a friend. I receive more than I could ever give."

"Please. You can't fool me. I've worked customer service jobs since the first one I took, waitressing after school when I was sixteen. No one does that for fun."

Maia stared into her eyes as if reading something there. "You're wrong about me. It's my choice. I love my job. The gallery, the artwork, helping a customer find the perfect piece... My friends give me so much more than I could ever hope for." She looked down to examine the glass coffee table.

"I would like my own sweetheart, someone special to share my life with. Children, too, if I'm blessed with them." She pressed Juli's hand between her own warm ones. "Is my life perfect? No. But I'm one of the most fortunate people I know. Juli, service—serving other people—is a gift to all if it's done with a glad heart. You'll find your opportunity one day and it will be a choice you make, not something you're forced into."

****

Juli woke early on Sunday, the second day of the New Year.

She left the drapes open at night because she liked to watch the dark horizon. The stars might hang low and bright, or the moon might paint highlights on the restless ocean. In the thin line of the horizon, an anonymous vessel might be seen passing, visible by its red and white lights. It was almost hypnotic.

She was a morning person. She welcomed the early rays of sunshine allowed in by the open drapes. On this winter morning, those rays only hinted at dawn.

She shifted position to move onto her other side, resting one pillow longwise and pushed up against her side to provide some support for her belly. Baby belly. Baby bulge. Everyone had a cutesy name for it. She rested her hand on the side of her tummy, then tugged the coverlet up around her chin, determined to sleep late. But sleep had fled and the bedside clock was staring her straight in the face.

It was seven a.m. Plenty of time if she wanted to give

church another try.

Leaving the draperies open provided less insulation from the winter cold. She could feel the chill air on her cheeks. She was warm and snuggly right where she was.

But her bladder was full.

She groaned, then slowly began making the adjustment, limb by limb, from the cozy land beneath the blankets, into the cold room. Ah, but here was her robe at her fingertips. Luxurious warmth, she wrapped it around her, slipping her arms into the sleeves as she crossed the room.

Business attended to, she was no longer sleepy. Second day of the New Year? It sounded right for a second trip to church. The visit had worked well last week. Sort of.

She said out loud, "I'm tired of having these arguments with myself. I always seem to lose the discussion." Her hand was rubbing her belly. Was she talking to the baby? A little soon for that. Or, maybe not.

As before, she arrived shortly before the service began and went into the foyer, accepted a bulletin from the usher at the door and slipped into the back pew. She flipped open the hymnal to the first song, *Blessed Assurance*, and was pleased to recognize it from the Alan Jackson CD Ben had enjoyed so much. The small print in the hymnal said it was written by a lady named Fanny Cosby. Interesting. Juli had never heard of a songwriter named Fanny Cosby.

She was less on edge during this service than the week before. A few people had given her an extra-long look and she knew Pastor Herrin might have spotted her even though she was seated way in the back. The dark-haired woman in red—Juli was sure she'd met her when she came with Ben, but she couldn't recall her name.

As the closing prayer was spoken, Juli gathered her coat and purse, ready to roll. Yet, when Amen was said, she didn't jump up and scoot. It was silly behavior and made her more conspicuous. She was an adult and could answer for her choices, including choosing to be polite instead of scuttling away like some sort of lower life form.

She waited as Pastor Herrin made his way up the center aisle. He was heading for the foyer where he would shake hands with the congregation as they left. She remembered him doing that when she came with Ben. But this time, when he reached the back pew, he stopped.

He reached out and took her hand.

"Thank you for coming." He continued on.

She'd delayed too long and the crowd was gathering as they passed through the open doors to the foyer. She hesitated to push her way into the knot of people. The dark-haired woman in the red sweater stopped.

"My name's Nancy. You won't remember me from before, but I wanted to say hello. It's good to see you again, Mrs. Bradshaw. Juli?"

"Yes, thank you." She stood and walked into the aisle, into the opening Nancy had created for her by pausing. She felt comfortably anonymous again, and used the crowd as an excuse not to reach the pastor, but to continue on out the door.

A small step, but an accomplishment. She started the car, glad to note she was more relaxed this week.

Not so bad. Not bad at all. Maybe next time she'd be a little friendlier. Maybe she'd bring Ben's Bible and try to follow along with the sermon and spend less time planning her departure.

For one crazy moment—one heart-stopping breath—she turned to her right, to the passenger seat, expecting to see Ben. She was already smiling at him, ready to laugh at her foolishness, but even before the turn of her head was complete, she knew he wasn't there.

She felt him though, even if it was only the warm memory of him still at home in her heart.

Chapter Thirty

The rental management company rep called. "Mrs. Bradshaw? Hi, this is Marisa and I've got good news."

The relationship with the management company, while pleasant, had thus far not led to chummy phone calls, so this must be very good news, at least for the management company.

"I don't think we've spoken before. I talked to your husband many times. He was a great guy. We were sorry to hear about your loss."

"Thank you."

"This time of year can be challenging in terms of rentals, but we got an offer for your duplex, *Sea Green Glory East*, from a woman who wants at least a month's stay."

Neighbors for the month of January?

"Great. I think. Is there a catch? How many are in the family?" A little noise might be fun.

"One woman. She expects her family to visit, so she wants plenty of room. She specifically requested *Sea Green Glory*. Said she knew someone who'd stayed there before, who'd recommended it. A month-long rental in January is very fortunate."

"Well, thanks for giving me the news."

Marisa laughed. "I like to deliver good news."

****

Patricia O'Brien moved in at the beginning of the second week in January. She was petite and dark-haired, but the hair was liberally streaked with gray. Juli guessed she was in her fifties. Pat wore an aura of quiet confidence and competence, wrapped in a compact package.

Juli watched her stroll down the crossover toward the

ocean. It was a chilly day, but there was no wind and the sun was strong.

Pat was a mystery. Juli's instinct told her there was more to the woman's story because something about Pat didn't add up, but she seemed so rational and down-to-earth it was hard to work up any worry about her.

A few days earlier, the day Pat moved in, she had surprised Juli. It was a mild day and Juli was enjoying a rocker on the porch. She hadn't heard Pat arrive because the woman had entered the house using the exterior stairs on her side of the duplex.

The woman peeked around the porch divider. "Hi, I'm Pat."

Juli stopped mid-rock. "I'm Juli. Nice to meet you."

"I'd better get to unpacking. See you around." She popped back behind the divider.

Juli waved, but Pat was already gone.

She'd seen Pat a couple of times since through the window when Pat took walks.

Strangely, she often returned from the opposite direction.

After a week, Juli had gotten used to the idea of Pat next door and even drew comfort from it. Honestly, anyone, including an intruder like Frankie, could move in over there and she'd never hear a sound. With Pat in residence, that couldn't happen.

The other side of the duplex was very much like her side. Twins, but flipped. Her side had the sunset. The east side got the morning sun. Her side had slightly better furnishings, but not by much. Ben hadn't been a 'stuff' person. When he'd moved into the *Glory* full-time he was content with the furnishings already in place.

The baby moved. It wasn't the first time, but it was by far the strongest. She put both hands on her moderate bulge and felt movement again.

"I was thinking about your daddy. Did you know that?" Her eyes went misty but the torrential emotional storms she'd experienced in December seemed to have subsided. She was seeing the obstetrician monthly and the doc was happy with the progress of the pregnancy. Juli wanted to be happy, too. In her heart she was quietly glowing, but she was afraid of wanting this too much and having it snatched away.

"Baby, I'm looking forward to meeting you. I'll do my best for you."

Juli picked up the envelope with their wedding photo. She took it up to the tower, slid the photo out and clipped it to her easel.

****

Art classes resumed in the second week of January. Anna had arranged a still life on a table, draped gracefully with a white cloth. She asked the students to start with pencil or charcoal on paper. From there, with the student's eyes more intimately familiar with curves and lines of the objects and their spatial relationships to each other, each student would move to canvas and choose whether they preferred to paint in oil or acrylic. They'd done this routine before, but this time it came more naturally. She held the vine charcoal and swept the lines, not minding the dark smudges on her hands and clothing.

Billy was attentive and the ladies talked about holding a baby shower.

Classes once a week. Errands here and there. That was about it. Juli knew she'd been inside too much. Hiding from Frankie? Maybe, but it was also the end of January at the beach and not generally inviting. This day was beautiful and much too lovely to stay inside. She took her coat from the closet. The buttons no longer met across the middle.

Juli laughed. She needed a separate coat for her tummy. She put on an oversized sweatshirt and then her coat on top of it, and stepped out. She was partway down the crossover when Pat called out.

"Taking a walk? Mind if I join you?"

"Please do." No reason to be rude and maybe Pat would divulge how she managed to return from the wrong end of the beach on most of her walks. There was no other option but to walk along the road and through people's yards. But why would she do that?

"If you don't mind me asking, when's the baby due?"

"April. It seems a long way away." A gust of ocean breeze blew strands of hair across her face. She tucked them back behind an ear.

"Ah, it'll be here before you know it."

"Do you have children?"

"One. A son. He's married."

"Grandchildren?"

"Not yet."

"I see you out walking a lot, even when it's pretty brisk out here. Do you work? Or are you retired?"

"Semi-retired. Taking a break right now."

"I see." But she didn't. If Juli had taken a break from work, back when she worked, winter at the beach wouldn't have been her first choice. Now, there was nowhere else she wanted to be. And what about all those family members Pat expected to visit—per Marisa?

Juli saw a man standing on the beach ahead, too distant for her to see him clearly. She had a moment of alarm and stutter-stepped.

"Something wrong?" Pat's voice sharpened.

"No, I'm fine. Thought I saw someone I know. False alarm."

"Oh? It sounds like someone you'd rather not see."

"That's it, exactly. He's someone I used to know."

"Is he an old boyfriend? They don't always stay in the past where they belong."

She laughed. "Frankie, a boyfriend? No. Never. Although lots of women think he's cute, I've never understood it."

A gust of ocean wind drove cold, stinging sand across their faces.

Pat shivered. "Ready to turn back?"

"Sure."

They turned around. The wind was kind enough to stay at their backs, prodding them toward the house. Ben's house. Her house. It stood out from the nearby houses, an improbable shade of green she would never have chosen, not in a million years, but she loved it.

"*Sea Green Glory*."

Pat peeked out from her hunched up coat collar. "Yes? What?"

"*Sea Green Glory*. The name of the house. You know that, of course. Marisa said you asked for it specifically."

"Of course."

"I call it the *Glory*. I guess it sounds grandiose. Or silly."

"Not at all. *Sea Green* has a nice beachy feel, but *Glory* gives it flair."

"Flair. I like that." Ben had used that word to describe her drawing. It seemed so long ago. "*Glory* sounds like hope to me. Hope and dreams."

Pat went silent as she watched Juli walk through the little gate onto her side of the porch.

Juli gave her a wave and went inside.

Juli fixed a tall drink of tea, did a quick double-check of the door locks, including the slide bolts, then went up to the tower to resume the portrait.

She took comfort in painting the lines of his face, the planes of his cheeks and jaw, the shadow of a brow over toffee-colored eyes. Medium brown, slightly shaggy hair.

No, it wasn't a Rembrandt, and wasn't ever going to grace the walls of a gallery, but this painting, should she finish it and decide it was good enough to share, would be for their child.

There was another image hiding in the shades of light and dark. A leaner face with sharp cheekbones and a strong jaw.

They were cousins. A resemblance was reasonable.

Juli touched her brush into the wet paint on the canvas to soften the lips.

A resemblance, yes, but never a risk of mistaking one for the other.

Chapter Thirty-One

Luke welcomed the retired nurse into his office. He signaled to Brendan he'd be tied up for a while, then closed the door.

"Mrs. O'Brien. Thank you for coming."

"No problem at all. I needed to come over this way to pick up some things from my house anyway. Please call me Pat."

"Maia is with Juli?"

"Yes, I watched them leave together. Maia is going with her to the OB appointment."

Luke nodded.

"But I'm not altogether happy about leaving the *Glory* unprotected, so to speak. Sorry, Juli has gotten me into the habit of calling it that."

"So, she's talking to you? She seems okay?"

"We've walked the beach together a few times. I've seen a man who fits the description you gave me, but the description is so general I can't be certain."

"I see."

"Would you reconsider calling the police?"

Luke shook his head. "He hasn't done anything threatening, or that would even seem mildly threatening, if reported to the police."

"You could tell them he's suspected of theft. You said you'd threatened to tell the police before and it kept him away for a while. I checked with a friend in the department and he said Frank Bowman spent a few weeks in jail recently for some old tickets and a fresh DUI. He won't want to go back."

Luke stood and stared out of the window. "If I say something about the theft now, after so much time has passed, it will look strange. If the authorities do check into it, he'll implicate Juli." In fact, when Luke had warned him off before, Frankie boasted he and Juli had worked a lot of parties together and had never gotten caught.

"Before, you were shielding your friend, your cousin. Now, you're trying to protect his widow. I think you'll find she's tougher and stronger than you think."

"I can't take the chance. First, she loses Ben. Now, she's dealing with the pregnancy. And alone."

"Not so alone thanks to you."

"I want her kept safe and sound."

Pat's scrutiny made him uncomfortable.

He turned away and spoke to the window. "Can you do that, Pat? Are you still comfortable keeping a watch over her?"

"Yes, but I don't know how well I can protect her. There are two points of entry. One is totally outside my view and the house's soundproofing is good. She could have a party over there and I might not hear a thing, but I'll do what I can."

"She's more at risk living there alone with no one nearby. There would be a limit to what you could do anyway. In no way should you put yourself at risk."

"I know my limitations." Pat shifted in her seat. "What does he want, anyway? Frankie, I mean. I've been around enough criminals to know they usually have a reason for what they do, especially if they're risking exposure."

"She has money now. Maybe he thinks he can benefit from it."

"Or—" She stopped mid-sentence deliberately.

"Go ahead."

"Well, the Hammond party theft was only days before Juli married Ben. Suppose she did have a connection to the theft. Perhaps she has something Frankie wants back."

When Luke had asked around looking for someone to keep an eye on Juli, Pat had come highly recommended. She was a nurse who'd never worked a typical shift in a typical hospital. She'd worked emergency services, corrections facilities, and, as she told it, at one crazy point in her life she joined the army and served a stint in the military police. She retired following a bad event she declined to discuss. Luke liked her style and respected her opinion, but he disagreed with the suggestion Juli could've been involved.

"She has all she needs and more. I don't believe she's done anything dishonest, but if she did have something Frankie wanted and if she believed he would take it and go away, she'd give it to him."

"Luke, I'm not as young as I used to be, but I hope I've gained in experience. I trust my instincts. I don't think Juli would be in any real danger under normal circumstances, but living alone at the beach and very isolated this time of year, combine that with being a pregnant widow and she's very vulnerable. I repeat, I'm not sure I would know something was wrong unless it happened right out front on the crossover in broad daylight."

He said, "She should leave the beach house."

"And go where? She feels closer to the baby's father where she is now. From what you've told me about her, this is the closest thing to a home she's ever had." Pat shook her head. "You talked to that man before and he stayed away. Maybe it's time to talk to him again or talk to the police. Right now you're trying to orchestrate a ring of protection around her. Don't let your feelings for her cloud your judgment."

Chapter Thirty-Two

Luke showed up on her doorstep. He was more subdued than she'd ever seen him. He must have looked a lot like that at Ben's funeral, but she couldn't remember seeing anyone—not *really* seeing anyone—that day, except the pastor on whose face she'd focused like a lifeline.

Luke seemed to carry a heavy weight. His head was slightly bowed and his shoulders slumped.

She stood aside to let him enter. He cast one quick sidelong glance at her five-month belly, then walked past. He moved self-consciously. Juli was almost alarmed. She put a hand to her abdomen.

"Is there a problem?"

"I'm sorry. I didn't mean to worry you. I didn't know how you'd feel about me."

"Pardon?"

"If I'd be welcome here, I mean." He turned to face her. "Have you forgiven me? You must know it was surprise speaking—not doubt about your character."

"I do." She motioned to a chair. "Take off your coat and have a seat. Would you like a cup of coffee?"

He stood for a moment, and then nodded. "That would be good."

"You like one sugar and one cream, right?"

"Good memory. It's been how long?"

"Only a couple of months." She put water on to boil and got the cup and saucer ready. "That question you asked? I put it aside long ago. In fact, I was too quick to flare up. I think I was looking for a way to escape something I wasn't ready for."

"The pregnancy?"

"No," she shook her head, "a new relationship. When you were helping me after Ben died, we were getting too close, too fast. When I found out about the baby...."

He gave her that sidelong look again, then focused on her face as if determined to avoid seeing the bulge, which, Juli acknowledged silently, grew more impressive every day.

She poured herself a glass of fruit juice. She set it on the table and then went back to finish fixing Luke's coffee.

"Here you go."

She was glad to see him sitting there. She'd missed him.

He asked, "You're doing okay here?"

"I'm wonderful."

He looked surprised.

"I mean it. I miss Ben, but he left me so much. I don't mean money and a house. He left me ideas. Dreams. The ability to hope for better and a reasonable chance to achieve them."

Luke's expression softened. "Ben was a special guy. He had a good heart. Are you having any problems? Like being here alone? Or with Frank Bowman?"

Had he heard something? From Maia, maybe? "I'm okay. Really."

"Have you considered talking to the police?"

"About Frankie? He's annoying, but he hasn't done anything. I feel vulnerable now because of the pregnancy; otherwise, I don't think I'd be worried at all."

Luke said, "I've been thinking. I'm not sure of your feelings, of how you feel about me, but in the interest of your safety and well-being, I want to say this. I've given it a lot of—"

She interrupted, "Luke, stop." She wanted to reach out and touch his face, his hair. She wanted to encourage him. But as Ben had been between them before, now Ben's child was there, not only visibly, but emotionally.

"Come stay at my house. There's plenty of room and you'll be safe there."

Her disappointment surprised her. She hadn't wanted him

to propose marriage, but she hadn't considered he might simply invite her to move in with him. A roomie? So much for romance. But she didn't want that, right? And Luke had never expressed an interest in romance. Important to remember.

"I'm fine here." Never mind disappointment. In fact, she was relieved he hadn't made a more personal proposal, and she was glad she hadn't said more, hadn't made herself look foolish.

He started to speak again and she raised her hand.

"Please. I don't want to argue about it. Thank you for your concern. It's kind of you, but I'm good."

"Is it because this was Ben's house? You feel closer to him here?"

A lot of words passed through her head, but she kept her lips together until she found the right ones.

"I'm staying here because this is my home."

He pulled his wallet from his jacket pocket and withdrew a business card. He placed the card on the table. "All of my contact numbers are here. I know you already have them, but I want you to keep them handy. Please call me if you have any trouble. Or about anything."

She shook her head after he left. What was that about? Maybe, like her, he'd felt badly about how their last meeting had ended. Perhaps he wanted closure.

Juli climbed the stairs and stood in the middle of the nursery. The yellow was cheerful, but the room was almost empty. Maybe it was time to choose the new furniture. Maia would be thrilled.

****

The phone rang two weeks later and Luke asked, "Would you go with me to the Chocolate Festival?"

She knew about the Carolina Chocolate Festival. It was an annual event on the Crystal Coast, held conveniently a week or two before Valentine's Day, for local fundraising.

"Go with you?"

"On a date, Juli. I'm asking you out. Will you go with me

tomorrow?"

Juli rubbed her belly. She was more than six months along. Should she go? The baby kicked as if it had six legs—bump, bump, bump around her belly. Enthusiastic was the only way she could interpret the movement.

"What time will you pick me up?"

There was a tiny pause and when Luke spoke, his voice was lighter, more energetic. "The Civic Center in Morehead City opens at nine a.m., but there's no need to be out so early. We could go about noon, then have an early supper after."

****

She couldn't blame anyone for looking at the two of them—Luke, tall, handsome, with a light in his eyes and a lilt in his voice, a protective arm sometimes around her, sometimes entwined in her own arm—no one could blame anyone for thinking they were together and in love. Everyone, and every chocolatier at every booth, looked at them, then looked at her belly, and smiled as if they knew a secret and were happy for them.

The tempting scent of chocolate was everywhere.

They stopped at a chocolate fountain and Luke handed her a chocolate-dipped strawberry on a red plate with a heart-shaped napkin.

Suddenly, she was warm again. She tugged at her scarf, pulling it away from her neck. She'd worn the cashmere sweater. Layered with a shirt, the sweater, and her coat, it was no wonder she was roasting.

"Are you ill?"

His tone was solicitous, even eager. The moment reminded her of Ben. Luke welcomed the chance to be gallant, too. Unlike Ben's gentler gaze, Luke's stare was straightforward and intense.

A lesser woman might have gotten weak-kneed under the intensity of his gaze. Juli wouldn't, but the air in the building was hot and stuffy.

"I need to sit down for a minute. It's warm in here." She

tried to shrug off her coat and he was there instantly, helping her out of it.

His gesture, as ordinary as it was, touched her heart. She looked down, hoping he wouldn't see the truth in her eyes.

The woman behind the booth, wearing a pink frilly hat dotted with candy-shaped objects, was kind. "Come right over here, honey. I've got what you need."

A small table and folding chairs were set up outside the booth, but partly behind the booth drapery, probably intended as a break area for the vendors. Juli found herself seated there with Luke while the chocolatier brought fresh lemonade and more chocolate.

"Chocolate heals all."

Luke waited until they were alone, or as alone as they were going to be on the edge of the crowd at the Civic Center. "Better?"

Juli nodded. "I'm fine now."

He seemed to be staring at her, somewhere in the vicinity of where her red shirt pushed aside the edges of the white sweater. She became self-conscious.

"Is there something on my sweater?" She pretended to brush at it, hoping he'd take the hint and stop staring.

"No. You look beautiful."

No words for that.

"The sweater is perfect for you."

The sweater. Was he the giver? Was she supposed to ask? Maybe he'd intended to include a card and wondered why she was so negligent about thanking him? But if she thanked him, and he wasn't the giver...the flush was rising again, warming her cheeks.

"Would you like to get some fresh air? It's cold outside."

"Thank you. I'm better now. I'll finish the lemonade and we can keep walking." Change the subject. "I never imagined seeing and smelling so much chocolate in one place."

"You live in the area. You've never been here before?"

"No."

He escorted her back onto the main floor. They waved their thanks to the kind woman with the silly hat and marvelous chocolate and continued down the row of booths. Juli stopped to view the delicacies laid out on a table and said, "I've heard just smelling and thinking about chocolate can increase the—" She broke off as Luke tightened his arm around her and pulled her close to his side.

"Careful!" he called out.

Two boys chased past paying no attention.

"That was close," Luke said.

"Kids will be kids. I'm fine."

The baby kicked and Luke jumped. Her belly was pressed up against him and he must've felt the soft thump.

He loosened his hold upon her and stepped back. "Was that—?"

"Who else?"

He held her arm again, but didn't draw her close again. A bit of shininess seemed to have rubbed off of his mood. He was still attentive and considerate, but not quite so cozy.

They went to the Port of Call for an early supper served with a wide view of Bogue Sound. They were well ahead of the supper crowd and the restaurant was peaceful.

"The big party—the Chocolate Festival grand finale—is tonight. I was concerned it might be too much for you right now. I don't have experience with, you know, pregnancy."

"You thought correctly. I can feel my feet swelling."

"Do they hurt? Should we leave?"

He was so anxious. She hid her amusement. "I'm fine. I've enjoyed myself and it was fun to get out. Thank you for asking me."

"I'm glad, I wasn't sure."

Juli reached across the table and took his hand. His skin was warm and her hand on his felt right, but more than that, the feel of him had the power to move her almost beyond good sense. She indulged herself a bit and lingered for a moment before taking her hand away. He didn't seem to mind.

"It's okay, Luke, I understand. This whole pregnancy thing...."

"No, I don't think you do. It's not the pregnancy. Not about Ben either. It's like some kind of battle is going on in my head. Think about it, Juli. You have no husband. No father. Not even a brother or a cousin."

She frowned. "I don't need a man to protect me. I can take care of myself."

"That was true before and will be true again, but right now—and it's not male protectors I'm talking about—right now you're very vulnerable. Both you and the child you're carrying."

"It means I have to be extra careful. I don't want anyone's pity. Be my friend. If I need a bodyguard, I'll hire one."

"Juli—"

"Shh."

"Juli, I don't want to be your friend. No, I *do* want to be your friend, but I want more."

His intensity breached her self-control. Her breathing quickened and the flush felt like it was rushing back. Could he mean—was he trying to say—? No, she reminded herself, he hadn't said anything with the word *love* in it.

"Let's wait and discuss this at the house? This isn't the place."

He met her eyes steadily. "Agreed."

****

Luke gestured toward the kitchen. "Mind if I fix myself a cup of coffee? Would you like something?"

"Water with lemon." She fit perfectly into the swivel rocker. She kicked off her shoes thinking this pair, these instruments of torture, weren't going back on her feet for a long time.

She put her feet up on the ottoman. They were puffy and the red indentations looked awful.

Once upon a time, she would have been more discreet, but this was Luke and she had this six-month-plus belly that somehow made her feel less concerned about pretense.

The emotion laced throughout their dinner conversation had diminished. Juli was grateful. Luke's demeanor had relaxed during the ride home and now he was content to fetch refreshments, so he probably felt the same.

"Here you go." He handed her the glass of water, then sat on the sofa. "Do you feel like talking?"

"If *you* do. Why did you invite me out?" She'd asked the same question of Ben a long time ago. Not so long. Not even a year.

"You know I have feelings for you. How could you not know?" Despite the calm voice, he betrayed his tension in the grip of his hands, the white knuckles.

"When you invited me to move in with you, for my safety, I thought…well, I believed you didn't…you were being kind, closing out the time of our lives when we had Ben in common."

"Ben's gone. We're still here."

"I don't know what that means."

"It means this is about you and me" He stood and paced with agitation across the room and back. "It doesn't make sense. I've lived happily for the last fifteen years, but nothing works right anymore. It hasn't in a long time."

"Is that my fault?" But she wasn't angry. In fact, something fun and bubbly was happening inside her chest. She pressed her lips together wanting to hold the happiness in.

Luke misread her expression. He looked stricken. "I've upset you. That's the last thing I want to do."

Did she dare to believe? Those happy feelings were still bubbling inside.

"What do you want, Luke? Please be sure of what you're saying. I'm not as tough as I used to be." Her eyes were wet. How had that happened?

Luke came toward her.

Her feet were now on the floor and she'd moved to the edge of the seat without thought, like a magnet drawn by Luke's approach.

Chapter Thirty-Three

"I want *you*. Juli, I—" He stopped.

She waited, now enfolded in his arms, her head bowed against his chest, willing him to finish the sentence—with the right words. Her own arms were around him, her hands caressing his back.

"I want you to be safe. Come with me—"

Strength left her arms. She turned her face away. The lesson of not putting so much trust in any individual resurfaced. She'd been schooled again.

Juli pulled the remnants of her dignity up from somewhere. She left Luke standing there, his arms still shaped to hold her, and slowly lowered herself back into the chair.

"What did I say wrong?" His face showed confusion.

If he didn't know, she wouldn't tell him. He had to feel the love in his bones and it needed to be such a big feeling it couldn't be restrained. After her time with Ben, she wouldn't settle for less.

Luke fell to his knees beside her. "I respect your independence. I know how important it is to you." He went silent as if summoning his next words with care. "I know you cared about—loved—Ben and he loved you. You need some time. I respect that."

She waited. Did she need time? Was Luke projecting his own feelings onto her? Juli's disappointment in Luke warmed and mellowed. He didn't choose to be confused.

"You like your independence, too, Luke, and you loved Ben." Did she want to run Luke off? The temptation to settle for what she could get was strong. Love would grow. Ben had said those same words, hadn't he? "Maybe we both need more time."

Discouragement flitted across his face, but was quickly banished.

"I'll go away if you tell me it's what you want, but I won't be happy about it. It won't change how I feel. If you want me to leave things as they are for the time being, you have to promise me something."

When had their hands come together again? She looked at their entwined fingers in wonder. His fingers were longer and tanned. Her own fit were smaller, but fit perfectly with his.

"Promise what?"

"That you won't fall for any other man until I have the chance to change your mind."

There they were again—bubbles tickling inside her chest, trying to make her laugh. She brushed away a tear. He did care, even if he couldn't say it.

He touched her wet cheek. "Why are you crying?"

She shook her head.

Luke gently moved his hand from her cheek to her neck. He trailed his fingers along her skin as he smoothed errant locks of hair back behind her ear. Juli closed her eyes unable to bear the sensations.

"Promise me," he said.

The words refused to be spoken. Her heart wanted to shout her feelings for the whole world to hear, but she couldn't. Maybe it *was* both of them. Both confused. He had leaned forward and her cheek was pressed against his, again she was hiding her face, but she nodded.

He held her close, or as close as he could, and seemed to accept her response as a *yes*.

"Until then I'm here for you—in any way you'll have me. As a friend, if that's what you want."

He still hadn't said the words she wanted to hear, but these were pretty good. She might fit in this comfort zone well enough for the time being.

Luke moved away and took his hands with him. She felt

bereft, as if something dear had been stolen. He leaned back against the sofa with an odd smile.

She asked, "What are you thinking?"

"I'm thinking if anyone had asked me before this moment whether I was a patient man, I would've said yes. I've discovered I'm not."

The smile stayed on his face, though, and Juli liked it very much.

"Let's talk," he said. "Ask me anything."

Contentment. Whether it was pregnancy hormones or happiness because nothing needed to end today, Juli was happy to watch him, the way his lips curved, finely chiseled and with a quirky curl on the right side. His cheeks showed a faint trace of beard, five o'clock shadow. His chin. How had she never noticed how strong his chin was?

"Anything." The warmth of his smile had moved into his eyes.

His eyes were so beautiful she wanted to cry. Juli sniffled.

"Need a tissue?"

"I'm fine. Crying seems to come with the territory."

He walked to the kitchen counter and returned with the box of tissues. He put it on the coffee table, near at hand.

"Anything."

Short of an outright declaration of love, what did she want to hear?

"Will you tell me about your marriage?"

Silence filled the space between them for a minute.

"What do you want to know?"

"Whatever you'll tell me."

Luke spoke. His voice was tight, like a bandage over a wound. "We were married for five years. Her name was Helen. We met in college and married our senior year."

Juli waited.

"One day she said she wanted more, something different. She said there wasn't another man. If there had been, at least I would've had something, or someone, concrete to blame. But no, it was our life. Or me."

"You let her go?"

"Not easily. We tried counseling, but it didn't work. In the end, after we separated, she went back to school and got her Master's." He drummed his fingers on the table in a quick-fire motion, then stopped abruptly. "She could have done that with us together. I never understood why she disagreed, but it doesn't matter now."

"Did she ever remarry?"

He shook his head *no*. "I don't know. I haven't heard from her in a long time." He straightened. "Anything else?"

The baby kicked. It startled her. "Oh." She touched her belly where the kick repeated itself.

"Is it a boy or a girl?"

"I don't know."

"Doesn't everyone find out the sex now?"

"I don't want to know. I want to be surprised."

"I'd like to be surprised with you." His words settled over her, warm but sharp. "I'll be a good father to your child. He rubbed his jaw. "Sorry, patience is hard."

Her voice dropped to a hushed tone. "I know you'd be good to this child. That's not the point." Were they going to have this conversation, after all? She put her feet on the floor and sat straighter. "Let me try to explain what I feel."

He nodded.

"Right or wrong, there's been something between us since the moment we first saw each other at the Hammonds' party. If I hadn't seen you, I wouldn't have gone to the garden and met Ben. Yet, if Ben hadn't been in the garden that night, you and I would never have spoken. We were so different from each other—experience, education, life—we would never have crossed the gulf between us. We wouldn't even have thought to try."

"You know I did my best to make Ben happy. To be the wife he deserved. I hope I...." She shook it off. "And I know you were the best friend to him you could be. He loved us both."

Luke interrupted. "Maybe you're right about that gulf, but we're both here now, reaching out to each other. We belong together. You can't deny it any more than I can hide my feelings. Marry me now, Juli. I'll be here with you. You'll be safe and I'll help you and we'll bring this child into the world together."

She shook her head and tears began to gather. She smiled gently. "I don't just owe Ben, I *want* to owe Ben. I want to be Mrs. Ben Bradshaw when this child is born. This baby will never know his father, but the names on the birth certificate will be Benjamin and Julianne Bradshaw."

She raised her hands. "Stay where you are. If you touch me, I won't be able to say this."

After a slow, calming breath, she continued, "So, what stands between us now? You can say you know what you want, but I think it's not so simple for you, either.

"Luke, I never had a close relationship with anyone until Ben, and one thing I learned from him is that love needs a foundation of friendship. Let's work on the friendship part now. Honestly, Luke. If you were ready to love me, I wouldn't still be waiting to hear you say the right words. The most important words."

The animation left his face. Juli plunged onward. Might as well get it all out now since they were already hurting.

"There's something else, too. It might make a difference to you. When I met Ben he said he was a man of faith. I didn't understand what he meant, but I'm learning. One thing I know, I'm not strong enough to stay the course without support." Juli tried to keep her voice steady.

"Ben told me you'd been very involved in the church before your divorce."

She clasped her hands together. "Luke, please don't hold it against me that I need you to be on the journey with me. I was proud of my self-reliance. I never looked beyond myself and my immediate needs. Now I have dreams and hope, I want to grow them in a positive way, and I want the same for my child.

I don't want to slip back into thinking I can handle everything without His help, nor that I *have* to handle it all myself. Please think about whether this is something you could do with me."

Luke's expression was unreadable.

"Think about it, Luke. We can talk more later. We have time."

He looked down at his hands.

"For now, be my friend." She felt strong. No wise-cracking. No pretending she didn't care. Not giving in to impulse, either, despite temptation, and even though she could still feel the warmth on her flesh where his hands and lips had traveled.

Was she stronger now?

She trusted Luke. But she had to remember to temper that trust, and her expectations, with reality. It was wrong to expect more than he could give—or to hold it against him when he disappointed her. Maybe over time....

She might not control her fate, but she could take responsibility for her choices.

But if all that was true, why did grief wash back over her as if she was about to lose someone dear to her yet again.

Luke stared past her and Juli waited.

Chapter Thirty-Four

Luke wanted to tell her he cared for her so deeply he'd hired Pat to watch over her and the baby. He wanted to get up from the sofa, put his arms around her and tell her she'd be safe with him and could depend upon him.

What was it about that one word? *Love.* He felt it, he could certainly say it. He opened his mouth to speak, then shut it again because now there was this other thing.

This faith thing.

He'd been bitter about the divorce. In his anger he'd drawn away from almost everything in his prior life connected to Helen and his marriage, including the church.

Looking back, what had seemed stoic now felt like a puppy crawling into a dark corner to lick its wounds. But the hurt and bitterness were long gone. In the years since, he'd become accustomed to living a different way. Was it so different? He was still a moral man. With flaws, of course. In his heart, though, there was a hardness that never went away and when he considered returning to church, he felt the urge to dig in his heels. To refuse.

He'd forgiven Helen. Was he still angry at God?

He shook inside. Without a word, he rose to leave. Gently touching Juli's hand was the most he could manage. He felt emotions rising to swamp him and he didn't want to be here when it happened.

****

Maia complained he was being gloomy again. "One look at you and the customers will go elsewhere."

"Fine. Hang these yourself. I'll be in the office." But he didn't go to his office; instead, he went to stand at the plate glass windows. Beyond the window and across the street was the marina and a variety of small boats were pulled into the little harbor. The owners were securing them, if they hadn't already done so, preparing for dark. "It's so quiet in here."

"Next week it's supposed to be warmer. We'll have more folks in town." Maia lined up another painting to hang. "Ms. Harper did a nice job with these. We may want to highlight them. They're bold enough to carry it off."

Luke was silent and staring out into the coming night.

Maia sighed. "I spoke to Hal today. They've done brisk business down in Charleston. Some convention. When are you leaving to go down?"

He kept his back to her. "I'm not. I've decided to put off the trip. I don't want to go out of town right now."

Maia set the painting down carefully. "Why? She's not due for a couple of months and Charleston's not so far away."

"The distance has nothing to do with it."

"Sure." She added the hanging clip to the back of the painting. "Did you tell her about the Christmas present?"

He swung around. Did he see a smirk on her face before she turned away? He said, "It's not a big deal. Don't make it into more than it is. Ben wanted her to have those things. For Christmas? I don't know. But he wouldn't have ordered a robe and sweater and had them delivered here if he didn't intend them as a surprise for her. I carried out Ben's wishes. As his executor and friend."

"Without a card or word of explanation."

Luke walked back to stand beside Maia. He picked up the painting and settled it on the hook. "Your point?"

"Well, a lady likes to know who's giving her gifts."

"What about secret admirers?"

"Is that what you are?"

"Enough. My private life is no longer a topic for conversation. I'll say one last thing. I didn't intend to fool her or play games with her. It seemed wrong not to give Ben's gift to her, but to receive a gift from your deceased husband at

Christmas? It might make her sad. Better to have her wonder who."

Maia sniffed and blinked. "You might be right. You know, in thinking about it, this might be the kind of special story you save and share many years from now, like on your tenth wedding anniversary."

"Subject closed." He walked away.

"If you'd like to attend the baby shower next month, let me know. We'll be happy to have you, but remember, it's a surprise!"

He shut the office door, softly, but firmly. For a change, he welcomed the work that would keep him busy.

****

About a week later, Brendan stuck his head through the open doorway and motioned to get Luke's attention. "Mr. Winters, there's a call for you."

Luke, with the phone receiver already to his ear, shrugged as if to say 'so? I'm already on the phone,' but Brendan persisted, "I think it's important."

"Excuse me, I have to go. I'm very sorry to break off like this. Can I call you back later?" He hung up the phone. "What's up?"

"On the other line."

Luke punched line two. "Hello?"

"Luke? It's Pat."

Pat was a professional. If she was calling, then it could be an emergency.

"What's up?" Luke asked, reaching for his coat.

"Not Frankie. It's a woman. Her name's Adela. Your cousin's sister?"

Luke stopped cold. "Adela?"

"Yes, I intercepted her in the parking area. One minute, ma'am. Please. Luke, she wants to speak with you."

"Where are you now?"

"In the house. Juli's out."

"Okay, put her on." A pause and then he heard her voice

saying his name. He interrupted. "Adela? What are you doing in town? You didn't tell—"

"I don't need anyone's permission to come here."

"Adela, listen carefully. I'm on my way over. Until I get there you stay in the house with Pat O'Brien. Understand?"

"I didn't come to see you. I'm here to see Juli."

"I'm serious, Adela. Unless you want to be responsible for the accident I'll have speeding over to the *Glory*, promise me you'll wait with Pat."

"The *Glory*? What are you talking about? Why should I—"

"I'm serious, Adela. Wait there for me." He hung up, not allowing her to continue fighting him. He was pretty sure, no matter how irrational she could be, since Juli wasn't even home, Adela would wait with Pat until he arrived.

Was she here because he'd called to tell her about Ben's unborn child? He didn't regret telling her. How could she not be told? But he wished he'd managed it with more finesse, had found better words to help her understand without flying off the handle.

Luke stopped at the entrance to Juli's driveway. She must still be out because her car wasn't there. He drove a short distance further and parked on the roadside a couple of houses down, hoping Juli wouldn't spot his vehicle. He jogged down the asphalt, noting Pat's car and a rental that had to be Adela's. He ascended the side stairs, two steps at a time.

Pat opened the door before he knocked. Adela was in his face as he crossed the threshold.

"Why are you protecting her? She took advantage of Ben. She took everything he had and now she's having someone's baby. This is preposterous."

"It's Ben's baby."

"I want a DNA test. If this child isn't Ben's, I'm going to sue her for everything she stole from him. It's too late to protect Ben, but I won't let her get away with this. She can't buy me off with college funds."

"There won't be a DNA test and there won't be a lawsuit."

She paced to the kitchen and back again, swinging her arms. The elegantly tailored suit and pumps were at odds with her demeanor. "You can't tell me what to do. Not this time."

"Think about this, Adela. *Think.* This baby will be the only niece or nephew you'll ever have. The only cousin your children will ever have."

"I *have* considered it, that's why—"

He interrupted her deliberately and rudely, "Then think about what you're going to lose. If you push for a DNA test or even question the paternity, it won't matter whose child this is because you will never have a part in its life. Not you, not your children. Juli will never give you another chance to hurt her. And even if she's willing to risk her feelings with you again, she'll never risk subjecting her child to your kind of loving."

Adela froze. "What's wrong with my kind of loving?"

It nearly broke his heart to see her look so stricken, but at least she was silent and he had her attention.

"Sit down." He took her arm and led her to the couch. She walked stiffly and stayed rigid as they sat. Close beside her, he held her hands tightly in his. "You are ruled by your emotions. You need to listen to your heart. Listen *before* you act."

Adela shook her head. "You sound foolish. You *sound* like Ben. What does the heart know? It's not emotion that drives me. It's reality."

"It's your effort to control reality that drives you, not because you want to hurt anyone, but because you want to avoid scary and painful emotions."

"What do you know about it?" She tried to shake his hands free, but he refused to release her. Finally, she stilled. "I'm sorry. I know you were hurt by Helen and, again, by losing Ben."

Pat had left them. Luke saw her through the front window, standing on the porch. He appreciated her discretion. He spoke softly to Adela. "You can't control people or events even if you mean well in the attempt."

This time she shook off his hands. "What am I supposed to do, then? Sit by and watch my loved ones hurt themselves? Sit back while others hurt them?"

"Yes."

"You've lost your mind."

"Adela, you've got to take the risk. You can't control anything, not even what happens to you. You have to have faith."

"Now, you really do sound like Ben. Faith?"

"Faith that all will be well. Maybe not the way you want it to be, maybe sometimes painful, but in the end, Adela, sometimes in the end it comes out better, or resolves in unexpected ways we can't foresee, but in ways that are a blessing. I apologize for saying it this way. We both know I haven't practiced what I'm about to preach, but you have to give up control and put it into God's hands. That's the kind of faith I'm talking about. Listen to your heart and you'll know what I'm saying is the truth."

The front door hinges squeaked and they both jumped, startled. Pat had opened the door to let Maia inside and entered with her.

Maia said, "Luke, I saw your car parked up on the road. Is something wrong with Juli? I was supposed to meet her here, but she's not in her house."

Chapter Thirty-Five

What had he said? The day when Maia came up the stairs and interrupted Frankie? She'd been so wrapped up in her own distress she hadn't really listened to what Frankie was saying.

Why was she thinking about this now? It had been more than a month since that conversation.

Juli stood in the parking lot of the grocery store holding the paper bag. She'd picked up some salad and rice to go with the fish filet she was cooking for herself and Maia that evening.

But it wasn't cooking or fish that teased her. A few cars drove past as she waited for the memory to resurface.

He'd said something about 'you have something of mine,' but that was ridiculous. She'd never taken or borrowed anything from Frankie, had only asked for rides here and there.

Why was it in her head now?

She paused again beside the car. Another memory stirred. She and Ben had been here before. Many times. Why should it trouble her?

"Are you okay?"

A man and woman had stopped, concerned, on their way past. She smiled to reassure them. "I'm fine. Thanks."

Time to move on. She fumbled the keys and they dropped to the pavement. She set her purse and bag on the trunk so she could retrieve her keys.

"Here, let me get those for you."

This time, it was a teenage boy.

"Thanks a lot." She accepted the keys from him. Pregnancy made life interesting and people certainly tended to be more helpful. They moved on more quickly, too, as if they risked being called upon to assist in the delivery if they lingered.

She picked up her purse and the grocery bag began to slide from the trunk.

The trunk.

Ben had opened the trunk and she'd seen her backpack.

What had she done with the backpack? She remembered taking it into the house and dumping it somewhere. Nothing in there she wanted. Certainly not the broken shoes. What a memory it was—the night she'd met Ben and had seen Luke for the first time. Luke had seen Frankie in the coatroom acting suspiciously, and had seen her, too, when she went to retrieve the backpack.

She tried to shake the reverie. Mooning around in a parking lot must be a side effect of pregnancy. Hormones. Hormones got blamed for everything.

She eased herself into the driver's seat and started the car. She let it idle for a moment longer while she adjusted the seatbelt. Everything took extra effort now. Getting up and getting down. Everything but staying seated.

By the time she returned home, she decided if Frankie believed she had something of his, it would have to be in her backpack. It was the only thing she owned that he could've gotten his hands on. He might've put something in there intending to retrieve it later.

She saw Maia's car in the driveway and she felt the warmth of a flush race up her chest and face. She breathed slowly to contain it.

Juli hated the sneakiness, the need to hide…whatever. She hoped against hope that when she looked in the backpack there'd be nothing but old shoes and a pilled sweater. If there was more, she'd like to resolve it with no one the wiser, including Maia. She had a new life now. She wanted to keep it free of past stain.

Maia would be waiting inside or perhaps on the front porch because the day was mild and sunny.

Instead of tackling the steeper stairs on the side, Juli walked under the house and came out in the front, at the base of the stairs leading up to the crossover. As she ascended the steps she was all set to say hello, but Maia wasn't sitting in the rocker. No Pat either.

Key in hand, Juli checked the knob. Unlocked. Maia tended to overlook the importance of locks. Maia was inside, then, probably in the bathroom or maybe in the nursery admiring her paint job again. Juli entered.

"Maia?"

No answer. She locked the front door, but not the slide bolts. If Maia was outside, she could use her key or ring the doorbell. Juli put her purse and the grocery bag on the counter and went upstairs.

Maia wasn't in the nursery. That was good. She could check the backpack right away.

She went into her bedroom and opened the closet.

The challenge of dropping to her knees was not insurmountable at seven months, but the movement was clumsy and awkward. Holding to the end of the dresser, she lowered herself to the floor.

A sweater had fallen from its hanger and a jumble of shoes littered the closet floor. She reached past, grabbed the backpack and pulled it out with a loud *whew*.

Juli unzipped the largest compartment zipper. It smelled stale inside. She saw the black pumps and the old sweater she carried for chilly nights when she worked late. Beneath the sweater lay the detached heel and the servers cap. Not much there.

She unzipped the front pocket and when she slipped her hand in, she didn't find anything unexpected, but she did feel a weight on the other side of the vinyl interior. It wasn't something she could explain away. She unzipped the small inside pocket and there it was—rather, there they were—a jeweler's case, a watch and a bunch of cash, rolled up and rubber-banded, and some empty baggies.

So this was what Frankie was after, this and anything else he might be able to bully, snag or scam from her. She rubbed her fingers together. Some sort of residue. Powdery? She wiped her hand on her slacks.

Juli rose to her feet, keeping tight hold of the backpack. She needed air. She slid the door open a foot or so and stood there, breathing deeply. The breeze cooled her face and eased her fear. Fear? Yes, fear, but not of Frankie. She had more to lose now than ever before in her life and she was still alone, after all.

"Welcome home, Jules. Look at you, you're gonna be a mama."

He stood in the doorway. His sandy hair was as charmingly tousled as ever and he was grinning. Someday, his skin would wrinkle and that smiling countenance would look freakish, but for now, the 'who me?' face must still be working for him because he moved with confidence.

Indecision held her immobile. One hand rested on the frame of the sliding glass door, her other hand clutched the backpack close to the side of her belly. The baby kicked and moved her to action.

"What do you want, Frankie? Is this it? In here? You stashed your stolen goods in my backpack. Suppose they'd been checking bags? I could've been arrested."

"Not all of it's stolen. The cash was earned—a side business for guests who like a little something extra."

He'd moved a few steps further into the room. There was nowhere for her to go. If Pat had been outside she would've been tempted to call for help. That alone might drive him off. But she'd only get one chance. She had to make it count.

Frankie read her face. "Don't do anything stupid. This isn't hard. I won't hurt you."

Take it and go, she wanted to say. If she let him, would she be an accessory? If he went away, she could go on as if nothing had happened. No one needed to know. Ever. But Maia... Where was she? "How did you get in here?"

"Your friend let me in. Not on purpose. She didn't lock the door when she came in and then she went right on out the front

279

door. How considerate was that? And hey, while we're chatting, I saw your painting upstairs. Not bad. A wedding portrait. Real sweet." He moved a few steps closer.

"Her car's still here. Why would she leave without it?"

"Calm down, Jules. It's you and me here. No need to do anything that might hurt your baby or get upset over. Give me my stuff. I'm in a hard place. I was gone for a while and I need it now. I'll take my goods, walk away and no one will know. You'll never see me again."

"Maia? Where is she?"

"I'm telling you, she never saw me. She was out the door in a hurry. Let's get this done quick, before she comes back."

It was so tempting. These were stolen goods and dirty money, but they weren't stolen from her. They didn't really have anything to do with her. Her fingers itched to throw the backpack at him, to yell at him to disappear from her life.

"Darlin', think about it. It's not like you're an innocent. I did stuff from time to time. You knew it and looked the other way and I appreciated it. One more time, that's all I'm asking, and then I'm gone." He moved to within six feet. "From your life. Forever. If that's what you want."

"You're wrong, Frankie. I'm not a thief and never was."

"Don't get sensitive and righteous on me. I don't care, do you understand? No one's going to believe you, anyway. You've got a good thing going here. Why screw it up?" He held out his hand.

It was time.

Juli fell back against the sliding door, pushing it wider with her shoulder, but her heel caught on the sill and she lost her balance. As she stumbled backward onto the balcony, she gave up trying to catch herself and hefted the backpack into the air. It brushed Frankie's fingers before it sailed clear over the railing. She landed heavily to the wooden floor, bumping her head on the rail post.

He reached for her with his fists, his face maroon with anger.

She yelled, "If you want it, it's down there. Go get it before someone else does."

His foot drew back. She brought her leg up and her arms down to protect her belly. He kicked her in the hip, then left, running to the hall and down the stairs.

Frantic, she got to her hands and knees. She had to get to the other side of the bed where the telephone sat on the nightstand. She'd call the police. She had to do the right thing and if it caused her trouble, she'd live with the consequences. Time to fly above the radar.

She scrambled around toward the end of the bed. There was a crash downstairs and within seconds feet were running, pounding up the stairs. Angry, urgent voices shouted. Frankie was returning too quickly. In her haste to reach the phone, her leg hit the corner of the bed and she fell again, onto her knees.

From the floor, she reached up to the phone and was scrabbling for the handset when he came in the door.

No tousled hair.

Luke.

He dropped to the floor beside her. She reached out to him and he drew her into his arms. His face was in her hair, his lips kissing her temple.

"My darling, my love, are you injured? Did he hurt you?"

Juli delighted in his arms around her, his lips brushing her face and neck. She drew strength from his touch. It steadied her and somehow, things seemed clearer, like the air after a storm.

"You said *love*. Do you love me, Luke? *In love* with me, I mean."

"Loving you has never been a problem. It was other things I had to come to terms with. For the rest, we'll work it out."

"I love you, too." She hugged him tight and her lips were meeting his when she remembered there'd been a crash and shouting voices—*voices*.

"Where did you come from? How did you get here so quickly?"

He continued holding her, but with less frantic energy. "I'll tell you later. And I'll collect that kiss later. Now, I have to go back downstairs."

She grabbed his shirt, not willing to let him go. "Where's Frankie? Did he get away?"

"No. The police will be here any minute. In the meantime, the ladies have him cornered."

"The ladies?" She frowned. "Give me a hand up. I'm going with you."

"You stay here." He rested his hand on her belly before he helped her stand, then pointed to the bed. "Sit and rest. I'll yell when it's safe to come down."

"Not this time, Luke. I'm not hiding."

He measured her resolve by her firm stare. "Okay, but stay behind me. I'm serious. Don't put anyone at risk by trying to be brave."

She clutched the rail expecting to be afraid, but as they descended the stairs only calm filled her. She stood at Luke's side just out of Frankie's sight. Out of everyone's sight, in fact, because their backs were turned. Her viewing angle was narrow, but it was enough to give her a good look at Pat holding a gun on Frankie.

One hand was positioned to brace her gun hand and her stance was no-nonsense. Frankie was crouched on the floor in the far corner of the kitchen. Juli could just see his knee and shoe.

Maia stood outside the kitchen holding the fireplace poker two-handed and swaying slightly as if ready to bat.

"I didn't do anything to anyone. Juli and I are old friends. She double-crossed me."

Luke moved forward and Juli did, too, but she put a hand on his arm to stop him, never taking her eyes from the scene before them. She needed to see this. This was the thing she had feared, wasn't it?

Frankie shifted his weight and his hand moved against the cabinet door. It squeaked.

"Don't move," Pat warned.

An unseen woman spit out, "Shoot him."

The hard voice sent a tremor through Juli. Her fingers dug into Luke's arm as Adela walked into view. She was hugging the backpack and a big webbed runner decorated the back of her leg. Juli thought she moved like a bouncer or a pit bull, but in heels and a suit. Definitely, someone not to be toyed with on any level—apparently a truth Frankie understood because he settled back on his heels.

"Go ahead and shoot him."

"I can't, Adela. Not unless he tries something. Then, I can and will. The police will be here any time now."

"Juli's guilty—guiltier than me. It was all her idea. She planned everything. I do the deed, she sneaks it out in her backpack. No one would ever suspect her of anything." He switched his wide-eyed look from Pat to Adela. "Jules is a smart chick. She's the brains. I did what she told me. You let me go, or she'll be in jail like me. Maybe for longer."

He turned his best pleading, boyish expression on Maia. "I'll slip out the door. I'll disappear. None of you, not even Jules, will ever see me again."

Maia's weapon wavered.

Luke had moved down the last step onto the landing. "Stay where you are."

A swift movement and Frankie's position changed to something like a modified sprinter's stance. He spoke to Luke. "You're running out of time. If you want to help her, protect her, let me go. Her fingerprints are on everything. They'll nail her. She was at every location. It's all about opportunity and finger prints. She'll be having that baby in prison."

Juli stepped into full view as Frankie shifted again and half-rose, but when he looked up and saw her standing there, he dropped to his knees.

"You're not going anywhere," Juli said. "I'll tell the police the truth and take my chances."

Chapter Thirty-Six

"No," Juli told the officer, "I'm fine. I just want to rest." Officials, friends and other people—she didn't know what category Adela fit into—filled the living room. Her attention was focused on Luke as he stood by the side door talking to an officer. She didn't try to hide or disguise her stare.

Luke was hers. Anyone was free to think what they would.

He'd said he loved her. It almost eclipsed the whole mess with Frankie.

Regarding Frankie, she could hardly believe it, but no one no one had given the least indication that she'd done anything wrong despite the lies Frankie was throwing around. The authorities, everyone, was treating her gently, respectfully. Like someone of substance.

And Luke loved her.

How much worse could this have been? A tremble seized her. The pocket of calm she'd felt on the stairs had evaporated soon after she'd begun answering questions. Pat had cleared most of the people away to give her some air.

Juli closed her eyes and sent a special thank you straight from her heart to God. When she opened her eyes again, they fell on Pat.

Pat. What had she said? She'd seen the flying backpack and alerted the others. The others? How could they have been so close? Unconsciously, she placed her hands on her belly.

Petite, gray-haired Pat had stood there with the gun trained on Frankie as if she did that kind of thing every day. Juli shook her head. She had questions of her own.

Pat had seen the backpack airborne. How had Adela come into the picture?

Adela was in the study with an officer now. Speaking her mind. Juli shuddered.

From across the room, Luke turned toward her. His smile muted the what-ifs, even about Adela, at least for the moment.

An officer said, "Ma'am, if you won't go to the hospital, then you should see your doctor right away."

He was a grandfatherly man, a local officer, and she appreciated his concern. She was sore, but the last thing she wanted was to attract more attention. Lying low, literally and figuratively under a feather quilt, had never sounded so good. Her feet were propped on the ottoman where Maia had put them—Maia, who was now return-ing with a pillow.

"No, Maia, I'm not going to lie down on the sofa. Not here among all of these people."

Luke crossed the room to join her. "How do you feel? Which do you prefer? Hospital or doctor? We're doing one or the other."

"I'm staying here."

Adela arrived and shoved Luke aside. "Juli—"

Luke tried to step in front of her. "Don't, Adela."

"Nonsense. Get out of my way."

Adela thrust herself forward. Juli cringed. *No more.* She raised her hands, wanting to cover her face, but then changed her mind. She wasn't up to doing battle with Ben's sister, but she wasn't going to hide from the woman either. Juli rubbed her hip. It ached where Frankie had kicked her. She tried to pivot on the sofa, away from Adela's aggressive glare.

"Luke will drive you to the hospital. You've had a shock."

"I'm fine."

"You have obligations."

"Obligations?"

"To Ben's child. My niece or nephew. You have obligations and you can't take chances with his, or her, well-being. Or your own." Adela moved in more closely. She perched on the edge of the sofa. "What would Ben want you to do?"

Juli looked at her in disbelief. Did Adela intend it as a dig? "What would Ben want?"

"He'd want you and the baby to be safe. No more than what Luke wants." Adela's eyes teared up and in a very small voice, she said, "And me, too."

The room was emptying. A fresh draft of cold sea air spilled in as Pat walked outside with the last officers.

Juli took a deep breath, then said, "You know there may be trouble. I didn't steal. I wasn't involved in it, but Frankie will say otherwise. You heard him. My fingerprints are on the stuff in the backpack because when I found it, I touched it."

"You are not to worry. Clearly, you're innocent. Frank…Frankie? Frankie's record will speak volumes."

"You say that, but—"

"I say you are one of us. One of the family. You aren't alone and we aren't without resources. You're not to worry." Adela took her hand. "I don't mind saying what Luke won't. I insist you go to the hospital. If you call your doctor and he'll see you now, fine. We'll take you there. Otherwise, it's the hospital."

Juli looked at him. "Luke?"

He smiled. "What she said."

Maia gave up with the pillow and tossed it across the room. "Juli, what's the doctor's phone number? Oh, never mind. I know her name. I'll get the phone book."

"I'm outnumbered. Fine. I'll go, but you're forgetting something." She pointed at the front door. The door frame was splintered. "I can't leave the door unsecured. I need to get it fixed."

Adela spoke. "Luke didn't have time to fiddle with a key. I'll call a carpenter and get it taken care of."

Pat came back inside. "They're going now. They got the statement from you, Juli, but they'll want more. They understand they'll get it later. First, you need to be checked out."

"So, I'm told. How did you get involved in this? You were

holding a gun on Frankie."

Pat looked at Luke. Luke looked at his shoes.

"Luke?"

"Get angry if you must. You wouldn't accept my help. I had to keep you safe. I hired Pat to keep an eye out for Frankie and for any other threats that might come your way."

She digested that. She didn't like the idea of people keeping secrets about her, from her.

"Okay. You were conspiring to help me. I can live with it this time. Thank you." She turned to the woman sitting beside her. "What about you, Adela? Where'd you come from? Why the change of heart?"

"I came because Luke told me about the baby." She folded her hands together. "I was upset at first because I didn't understand, but Luke explained something to me."

"What?"

She struggled with the words. "That sometimes you have to trust people. Sometimes you have to—you have to have faith."

"What?"

"If you insist, I'll spell it out. Faith. That things will work out, sometimes in ways we don't understand, if we—if *I* put my faith in God and not try to control everything myself." She looked down, shaking her head. "But, it's hard for me."

Juli reached out and took Adela's hands. "It's very hard, I know. I'm trying to learn that wisdom myself."

Maia said, "Dr. Oehler said you should come into the office now." She put her hands on her hips. "Right now."

Luke knelt next to Juli and took her hand. "We're going to the doctor now, but when we're done, you and I have to finish our talk."

"You remember what I said before…."

"I do. I'll wait if you insist, but after Ben's child is born, I hope you'll marry me and there's no reason we can't agree on that now."

Adela snapped, "Marry?"

"I'd marry her this minute if she'd have me."

"Nonsense."

"I mean it, Adela."

"Nonsense, Luke. It will take at least six months to arrange a proper wedding. Longer would be better."

After a few speechless seconds, Luke said, "Six months is too long to wait."

"Shows how much you know about planning a wedding. Let's do this one right."

Maia pushed in between Adela and Luke. "Wait a minute, both of you. You can fight this out later. Juli, get up. We're going to see your doctor."

"I'm taking her," Luke said, "if she'll go with me."

Juli held out her hands. He clasped them, pulled her to her feet and wrapped one arm around her back.

"I'm with you, Juli, on this journey and any other. You can trust me."

"We've already come a long way. Both of us. I can hardly wait to see what lies ahead, Luke. It's going to be wonderful."

Epilogue

On a Friday morning in late April, Juli knocked on the door of *Sea Green Glory East*. She could have telephoned, but she wanted to deliver the news in person.

Luke opened the door. "Is it time?"

"I think so."

"We should have known it would be today."

She laughed. "You mean the anniversary of the day Ben and I met? And—"

"And of the day we met." He grabbed the keys from the table by the door and the jacket he'd kept nearby for the past two weeks. "We're on our way."

There was no suitcase to carry because it had been packed and in the trunk of her car for the past two weeks. Luke had insisted. He held her arm as they stepped carefully down the front stairs. He got her situated into the passenger seat and then himself, cool and calm.

"Where are my keys?" He started checking his jacket pockets.

"In your pants' pocket."

"Right." He grinned. "On our way."

Atlantic Avenue ran straight and true ahead of them, with little traffic until they neared Atlantic Beach and the bridge to Morehead City. The water below, in Bogue Sound, was calm and the sky was serenely blue.

"Are you nervous? Worried?" Luke asked as he turned the car east on Arendell Street.

"I'm excited. I would be worried, but with you beside me, I'm happy."

Benjamin Daniel Bradshaw was born on April twenty-third, seven pounds and eleven ounces of baby boy and for a moment, as the obstetrician received him, Juli felt Ben nearby and knew he was smiling.

THE END

ABOUT THE AUTHOR

USA Today Bestselling and award-winning author, Grace Greene, writes novels of contemporary romance and inspiration or women's fiction with love, mystery and suspense, wth a strong heroine at the heart of each story.

A Virginia native, Grace has family ties to North Carolina. She writes books set in both locations.

The Emerald Isle books are set in North Carolina where *"It's always a good time for a love story and a trip to the beach."*

Or follow a Virginia Country Road and *"Take a trip to love, mystery and suspense."*

Grace lives in central Virginia. Stay current with Grace's releases and appearances. Contact her at www.gracegreene.com.

You'll also find Grace here:

Twitter: @Grace_Greene
Facebook:
https://www.facebook.com/GraceGreeneBooks
Goodreads:
http://www.goodreads.com/Grace_Greene

Other Books by Grace Greene

BEACH WINDS *(Emerald Isle #2)*

<u>RT Book Reviews</u> – June. 2014 - 4.5 stars TOP PICK

Greene's follow up to Beach Rental is exquisitely written with lots of emotion. Returning to Emerald Isle is like a warm reunion with an old friend. Readers will be inspired by the captivating story where we get to meet new characters and reconnect with a few familiar faces. The author highlights family relationships which many may find similar to their own, and will have you dreaming of strolling along the shore to rediscover yourself.

<u>Brief Description</u>:

Off-season at Emerald Isle ~ In-season for secrets of the heart

Frannie Denman has been waiting for her life to begin. After several false starts, and a couple of broken hearts, she ends up back with her mother until her elderly uncle gets sick and Frannie goes to Emerald Isle to help manage his affairs.

Frannie isn't a 'beach person,' but decides her uncle's home, *Captain's Walk,* in winter is a great place to hide from her troubles. But Frannie doesn't realize that winter is short in Emerald Isle and the beauty of the ocean and seashore can help heal anyone's heart, especially when her uncle's handyman is the handsome Brian Donovan.

Brian has troubles of his own. He sees himself and Frannie as two damaged people who aren't likely to equal a happy 'whole' but he's intrigued by this woman of contradictions.

Frannie wants to move forward with her life. To do that she needs questions answered. With the right information there's a good chance she'll be able to affect not only a change in her life, but also a change of heart.

KINCAID'S HOPE   *(Virginia Country Roads)*

A quiet, backwater town is the setting for intrigue, deception and betrayal in this exceptional sophomore offering. Greene's ability to pull the reader into the story and emotionally invest them in the characters makes this book a great read.

This is a unique modern-day romantic suspense novel, with eerie gothic tones—a well-played combination, expertly woven into the storyline.

Brief Description:

Beth Kincaid left her hot temper and unhappy childhood behind and created a life in the city free from untidy emotionalism, but even a tidy life has danger, especially when it falls apart.

In the midst of her personal disasters, Beth is called back to her hometown of Preston, a small town in southwestern Virginia, to settle her guardian's estate. There, she runs smack into the mess she'd left behind a decade earlier: her alcoholic father, the long-ago sweetheart, Michael, and the poor opinion of almost everyone in town.

As she sorts through her guardian's possessions, Beth discovers that the woman who saved her and raised her had secrets, and the truths revealed begin to chip away at her self-imposed control.

Michael is warmly attentive and Stephen, her ex-fiancé, follows her to Preston to win her back, but it is the man she doesn't know who could forever end Beth's chance to build a better, truer life.

A STRANGER IN WYNNEDOWER

(Virginia Country Roads)

Bookworm Book Reviews – January 2013 - 5 STARS

I loved this book! It is Beauty and the Beast meets mystery novel! The story slowly drew me in and then there were so many questions that needed answering, mysteries that needed solving! …Sit down and relax, because once you start reading this book, you won't be going anywhere for a while! Five stars for a captivating read!

Brief Description:

Love and suspense with a dash of Southern Gothic…

Rachel Sevier, a thirty-two year old inventory specialist, travels to Wynnedower Mansion in Virginia to find her brother who has stopped returning her calls. Instead, she finds Jack Wynne, the mansion's bad-tempered owner. He isn't happy to meet her. When her brother took off without notice, he left Jack in a lurch.

Jack has his own plans. He's tired of being responsible for everyone and everything. He wants to shake those obligations, including the old mansion. The last thing he needs is another complication, but he allows Rachel to stay while she waits for her brother to return.

At Wynnedower, Rachel becomes curious about the house and its owner. If rumors are true, the means to save Wynnedower Mansion from demolition are hidden within its walls, but the other inhabitants of Wynnedower have agendas, too. Not only may Wynnedower's treasure be stolen, but also the life of its arrogant master.

CUB CREEK

(Virginia Country Roads)

<u>Brief Description:</u>

In the heart of Virginia, where the forests hide secrets and the creeks run strong and deep ~

Libbie Havens doesn't need anyone. When she chances upon the secluded house on Cub Creek she buys it. She'll prove to her cousin Liz, and other doubters, that she can rise above her past and live happily and successfully on her own terms.

Libbie has emotional problems born of a troubled childhood. Raised by a grandmother she could never please, Libbie is more comfortable *not* being comfortable with people. She knows she's different from most. She has special gifts, or curses, but are they real? Or are they products of her history and dysfunction?

At Cub Creek Libbie makes friends and attracts the romantic interest of two local men, Dan Wheeler and Jim Mitchell. Relationships with her cousin and other family members improve dramatically and Libbie experiences true happiness—until tragedy occurs.

Having lost the good things gained at Cub Creek, Libbie must find a way to overcome her troubles, to finally rise above them and seize control of her life and future, or risk losing everything, including herself.

Thank you for purchasing

BEACH RENTAL

I hope you enjoyed it!

Please visit me at www.gracegreene.com and sign up for my newsletter. I'd love to be in contact with you.

Other books by Grace Greene

Emerald Isle, NC Stories
Love. Suspense. Inspiration.

BEACH RENTAL

BEACH WINDS

BEACH TOWEL (short story)

BEACH CHRISTMAS (novella)

Virginia Country Roads Novels
Love. Mystery. Suspense.

CUB CREEK

A STRANGER IN WYNNEDOWER

KINCAID'S HOPE

www.GraceGreene.com